A
Delicate
Touch

BOOKS BY STUART WOODS

FICTION

A Delicate Touch[†]

Desperate Measures[†]

Turbulence[†]

Shoot First[†]

Unbound[†]

Quick & Dirty[†]

Indecent Exposure[†]

Fast & Loose[†]

Below the Belt[†]

Sex, Lies & Serious Money[†]

Dishonorable Intentions[†]

Family Jewels[†]

Scandalous Behavior[†]

Foreign Affairs[†]

Naked Greed[†]

Hot Pursuit[†]

Insatiable Appetites[†]

Paris Match[†]

Cut and Thrust[†]

Carnal Curiosity[†]

Standup Guy[†]

Doing Hard Time[†]

Unintended Consequences[†]

Collateral Damage[†]

Severe Clear[†]

Unnatural Acts[†]

D.C. Dead[†]

Son of Stone[†]

Bel-Air Dead[†]

Strategic Moves[†]

Santa Fe Edge[§]

Lucid Intervals[†]

Kisser[†]

Hothouse Orchid[*]

Loitering with Intent[†]

Mounting Fears[‡]

Hot Mahogany[†]

Santa Fe Dead[§]

Beverly Hills Dead

Shoot Him If He Runs[†]

Fresh Disasters[†]

Short Straw[§]

Dark Harbor[†]

Iron Orchid[*]

Two-Dollar Bill[†]

The Prince of Beverly Hills

Reckless Abandon[†]

Capital Crimes[‡]

Dirty Work[†]

Blood Orchid[*]

The Short Forever[†]

Orchid Blues[*]

Cold Paradise[†]

L.A. Dead[†]

The Run[‡]

Worst Fears Realized[†]

Orchid Beach*

Swimming to Catalina[†]

Dead in the Water[†]

Dirt[†]

Choke

Imperfect Strangers

Heat

Dead Eyes

L.A. Times

Santa Fe Rules[§]

New York Dead[†]

Palindrome

Grass Roots[‡]

White Cargo

Deep Lie[‡]

Under the Lake

Run Before the Wind[‡]

Chiefs[‡]

COAUTHORED BOOKS

The Money Shot** *(with Parnell Hall)*

Barely Legal[††] *(with Parnell Hall)*

Smooth Operator** *(with Parnell Hall)*

TRAVEL

A Romantic's Guide to the Country Inns
of Britain and Ireland *(1979)*

MEMOIR

Blue Water, Green Skipper

*A Holly Barker Novel
[†]A Stone Barrington Novel
[‡]A Will Lee Novel
[§]An Ed Eagle Novel
**A Teddy Fay Novel
[††]A Herbie Fisher Novel

STUART WOODS

A Delicate Touch

G. P. Putnam's Sons

NEW YORK

PUTNAM

G. P. Putnam's Sons
Publishers Since 1838
An imprint of Penguin Random House LLC
penguinrandomhouse.com

LIBRARY OF CONGRESS CATALOGING-IN-PUBLICATION DATA

Names: Woods, Stuart, author.
Title: A delicate touch / Stuart Woods.
Description: New York : G. P. Putnam's Sons, 2018. |
Series: A Stone Barrington novel
Identifiers: LCCN 2018041585 | ISBN 9780735219250 (hardcover) |
ISBN 9780735219274 (epub)
Subjects: | GSAFD: Suspense fiction
Classification: LCC PS3573.O642 D45 2018 | DDC 813/.54—dc23
LC record available at https://lccn.loc.gov/2018041585
p.   cm.

Printed in the United States of America
1   3   5   7   9   10   8   6   4   2

Frontispiece: Mikhail Olykainen / Shutterstock.com

A Delicate Touch

1

Stone Barrington, breathing hard, arrived back at his house after a run with his Labrador retriever, Bob, to Central Park and entered through the ground-floor office door, stopping at the desk of his secretary, Joan Robertson. Stone was out of breath. Bob was not.

"Pee-ew!" Joan complained. "The shower is four floors up, in the master suite!"

"All right, all right. Any calls?"

She handed him a pink slip of paper. "Mary Ann Bianchi Bacchetti, whichever," she said. "Her cell number."

Stone went into his office and phoned Dino Bacchetti's ex-wife.

"How are you, Stone?"

"Just fine."

"You sound a little breathless. Maybe you should see a cardiologist."

"I've been running."

"From whom?"

"An early death."

"I hope you don't have a heart attack on the street," she said.

"We share that hope," Stone replied. "How can I help you, Mary Ann?"

"Can you recommend a safecracker?"

Stone's mind raced. Mary Ann, née Anna Maria, was the daughter of his late friend Eduardo Bianchi, a mysteriously powerful man reputed to have been near the top of the Mafia as a young man, but who later went respectable and served on the boards of major financial institutions and major charities and nonprofits, while living in the style of a Renaissance prince in the far reaches of Brooklyn, in a Palladian mansion on considerable acreage. Stone was executor of his estate.

"Dare I ask why you need a safecracker?" Stone asked.

"Why, to crack a safe," she replied. "I've discovered a large old one concealed behind a panel in Papa's library. I don't think anyone else ever knew about it, not even Pietro, his butler, or the rest of the staff."

"But you don't know the combination?"

"How did you guess?"

"Mary Ann, people often conceal the combination of a safe, hidden away in a desk or a drawer somewhere, as a hedge against memory failure. Have you looked around?"

"I have, and I've found nothing. Now, back to my original question: Can you recommend a safecracker?"

"No, but I may know someone who can," Stone replied. "What kind of safe is it?"

"Large and black."

"Does it have a trade name on the door?"

"Oh, yes: 'Excelsior.'"

"I've never heard of that one," Stone said, "but I'll make inquiries."

"Today?" Mary Ann asked.

"Is it urgent?"

"I'm about to turn over ownership of the house to the board of the museum Papa founded to house his collections. I won't own the place after today, so yes, it's urgent."

"I'll call you back."

"Soon, please."

"Of course. Goodbye, Mary Ann." He hung up and called Bob Cantor, his source of tech of all kinds.

"Morning, Stone," Bob said.

"Morning to you," Stone replied. "Bob, I need a safecracker."

"Well, I can open half a dozen different brands," Bob said. "What kind of safe?"

"It says, 'Excelsior,' on the front."

"British Excelsior or German Excelsior?"

"What's the difference?"

"The British Excelsiors are cheap stuff that no one with the need for a fine safe would buy."

"In that case, it's German Excelsior."

"Holy shit," Bob said quietly. "Is it in New York?"

"Brooklyn, way out. Is there something special about an Excelsior?"

"You might say that. The last one was made in 1938, in Berlin. The maker was one Julius Epstein. He was in business for half a century, and his safes were in great demand, but he made them one at a time to order, with an assistant or two. So as you might imagine, there aren't all that many in existence, what with the bombing of Germany during the war. Epstein himself didn't get out of the country in time. He died in one of the camps and took his secrets with him."

"Can you open it?"

"There are only three people alive who can open an Excelsior without the combination," Bob said. "All of them were Epstein's assistants, at one time or another."

"And where are they?"

"Two are in an old folks' home in Germany," Bob said. "They survived the Holocaust."

"And the third?"

"In an old folks' home in Brooklyn. His name is Solomon Fink, and he owned a safe store on the Lower East Side from about 1947 until a couple of years ago. He's pushing a hundred. In fact, he could be pulling from the other side of a hundred."

"Is there any other way to get the thing open?"

"Not without destroying the contents, and maybe the building it's sitting in."

"Is Mr. Fink in a condition to be able to open it?"

"I can find out. You know, Sol once gave me a lesson in how to open an Excelsior, but that was more than twenty years ago, and I never had any call to open another one."

"Can you remember how to do it?"

"Probably not, but let me find out if I can get Sol out of the home for a few hours. I'll call you back."

"Bob, the safe needs to be opened today. Otherwise it will pass into other hands."

"Where, exactly, is it?"

"Do you know the Eduardo Bianchi estate?"

"Sure, I used to bicycle past it all the time when I was a kid, on the way to the beach."

"There. Get back to me as fast as you can."

"Will do."

STONE WAS JUST getting out of the shower when Cantor called back. "Hello?"

"It's Cantor. I've sprung Sol Fink for the afternoon. He has to be back in time for dinner at five o'clock."

"That early?"

"They serve the early-bird special every day at the home. I should be able to pick up Sol and make it to the Bianchi place by one o'clock."

"I'll see you there," Stone said. "I want to witness this."

"Wait a minute, Stone," Bob said. "There's a little more to this, and it would be better if you hear it now instead of later."

"I'm listening," Stone said.

"One of the characteristics of the Excelsior is that, if you attempt to open it and get the combination wrong, you get one more try. But if the combo is wrong again, it locks up and can't be opened except by Julius Epstein himself, or one of his assistants, and Julius is unavailable. When he was alive he charged his clients five thousand Swiss francs, plus travel expenses, in cash, to open a safe. That made people very careful to remember the combination—or to hide it someplace."

"Eduardo's daughter, Mary Ann, is at the house, and she said she's already looked everywhere she can think of for the combination, so don't count on that."

5

"Sol may not have opened an Excelsior for twenty years or more, so let's hope he remembers how."

"Shall I pick you up?"

"I'm working on the Upper East Side. I'll come to you, and we'll drive past the home and snatch Sol off the curb."

"Right."

Both men hung up.

2

Bob Cantor showed up on time, stowed a tool kit in the trunk of Stone's car, and then Fred, Stone's factotum, drove them to Brooklyn, where they stopped in front of a large old house on a leafy street.

"Gimme a couple of minutes," Bob said and got out of the car. Shortly, he emerged with an old gentleman, spiffily dressed in a three-piece pinstriped suit and a homburg, and took hold of his arm to help him down the front steps. The old man snatched his arm away and said something sharp to Bob.

Stone got out of the car to greet them and was introduced. "How do you do, Mr. Fink?" he said, offering his hand. The hand that gripped his was smooth and firm.

"At the home," Fink said, "everybody calls me Sol, and I got used to it."

His voice was strong, and he was ramrod straight in his posture. Stone hadn't expected that.

"Before you ask," Sol said, "I'm a hundred and four years old."

"Congratulations," Stone said.

"It's not my fault," Sol replied, climbing into the rear seat. "I did everything that's supposed to kill you, except smoking, so I should have been dead fifty years ago."

Stone got up front with Fred. "Then from now on, Sol," he said over his shoulder, "I will adopt you as my personal example."

Sol laughed heartily.

It was a sunny day, and the drive to the Bianchi estate was pleasant. They presented themselves at the front door. To Stone's surprise, it was opened by Pietro, who had been Eduardo Bianchi's servant for many decades. Pietro was probably nearly as old as Sol Fink, and had maintained a lifelong reputation for being very good with a knife. He had never liked Stone or, perhaps, anyone else.

"Mary Ann is expecting us, Pietro," Stone said.

Pietro muttered something in Italian and indicated that they should follow him. Progress was slow, but eventually, they entered Eduardo's study and library.

Mary Ann got up from Eduardo's desk to greet them and was introduced to Bob Cantor and Sol Fink.

"Where is the safe?" Stone asked.

"See if you can find it," she said.

Stone and Bob looked around the study and shook their heads.

Sol Fink walked to a corner of the room behind the desk and ran his hand over a row of books. He pressed his finger against a leather-bound volume about six books along, and with a little *click*, the bookcase in the corner sprang open an inch. "There you are," he said, pulling open the bookcase to reveal a large black safe with gilt decoration. EXCELSIOR Berlin was lettered at the top.

"How did you know where to find it, Sol?" Stone asked, astounded.

"It was the only book there that was upside down," Sol said. "And," he said with a twinkle, "I been here before."

"I don't remember you," Mary Ann said.

"You wasn't born yet. I came to service the safe."

"Can you open it?"

"Maybe," Sol replied. He reached into an inside coat pocket and came up with a stethoscope.

"Where did you find a stethoscope?" Bob Cantor asked.

"On a doctor," Sol replied. "Safecracking isn't my only sin. I'm a pickpocket, too." He reached into another pocket, pulled out a wallet, and handed it to Bob. "You dropped this," he said drily.

"Mr. Fink," Mary Ann said, "can you open this safe?"

"Everybody at the home calls me Sol," he replied. "I got used to it."

"Sol," she said sweetly, "can you open this safe?"

"Well, let's see," Sol replied. He hooked the stethoscope around his neck and approached the safe. It was a good six feet tall. He ran his hands along the top of the safe's frame. "Can I have that?" he asked, pointing at a rolling library ladder.

Stone pushed it over to where Sol wanted it and held it steady while Sol climbed a couple of steps, then produced a penlight from a pocket, along with a pair of glasses. He put on the glasses, directed the light at the top frame of the safe, and inspected it carefully. "Number 1001," he said, then climbed down from the ladder, while Bob stood by to catch him if he fell. "This was the last safe that Mr. Epstein built," Sol said. "For a Mr. Bianchi, in New York. The day after he shipped it, he was arrested. The following day a friend drove me into France in the boot of his car, under a lot of stuff, then to Paris. I got a train to Lisbon and flew to New York on the Pan Am Clipper a week later, with my pockets full of dollars and Swiss francs that Mr. Epstein gave me. He knew they would come for him, but he wouldn't leave." He brushed away a tear.

Mary Ann started to speak again, then thought better of it.

Bob patted him on the back. "You want to give it a try, Sol?"

Sol approached the safe and reached for the dial. He turned it to zero, then, surprisingly, to zero again. "With Mr. Epstein's safes, you had to go to zero twice. That was to confound the schmucks." He plugged the stethoscope's eartips into his ears and placed its diaphragm just above the top of the dial, then he began to turn the dial very slowly.

"You need two clicks, not one," Bob said, "as I remember."

Sol nodded and kept turning the dial. He stopped at ten, then reversed directions.

Stone, Mary Ann, and Bob stood, transfixed, as he did his work.

"Almost there," Bob said under his breath.

Sol stopped and mopped his brow with the back of his hand. "I'm sorry, I'm feeling a little faint," he said. "May I sit down?"

They directed him to a comfortable chair, while Mary Ann poured a glass of ice water from a nearby pitcher, then handed it to him.

Sol took a sip of the water and stopped. "Do you think I could have a little whiskey?" he asked. "Any kind. Always brings me around."

Mary Ann went to the bar and came back with an old-fashioned glass and a bottle of a single malt scotch and poured him a finger.

"Little more," Sol said, making upward motions with a hand.

She poured more.

"Little more."

Mary Ann stopped at two fingers and handed him the glass.

Sol took a sip, savored the whisky, then emptied the glass and swallowed. "Ahhhhh," he said finally. "It's been a long time. They don't give you single malt in the home—or anything else worth drinking."

"How are you feeling, Sol?" Bob asked.

"Much better, thank you."

"Want to finish up?"

Sol got to his feet without help, went to the safe, and without using the stethoscope, turned the knob right to ten again. "That should do it," he said. "Miss, you want to do the honors?"

Mary Ann approached and reached for the brass wheel. "This?"

Sol nodded.

She turned the wheel, and the door opened.

"Let me show you something," Sol said, beckoning her to follow. He went to the big desk, sat down, and opened the center drawer. He got out his flashlight, directed it at the bottom of the drawer, then, with a fingernail, dislodged a piece of cellophane tape with a slip of paper attached to it and handed it to Mary Ann. "For next time," he said.

"This is the combination?" she asked. "I looked everywhere but there."

"It's where it was when I serviced the safe all those years ago," Sol replied.

3

Everyone turned their attention to the contents of the safe. It was filled, shelf after shelf, with documents and files, except the top shelf. That was filled with banknotes. Mary Ann took a stack from the shelf and riffled through it. "All hundreds," she said.

Stone took another stack further along the shelf and did his own riffling. "All hundreds," he said. "There must be more than a million dollars here. A rainy-day fund, perhaps?"

"Wait a minute," Mary Ann said. She went to a drawer under the bookcase, came back with an electronic cash counter. She fed a stack of the bills, a couple of inches at a time, into the counter until the total appeared above, then counted the number of stacks. "Closer to three million," Mary Ann said.

"This would seem to be a good time to collect my fee," Sol said.

"What do we owe you, Sol?" she asked.

"Ten thousand will do," he replied.

Mary Ann laughed, let the cash counter do its work, then she found a rubber band in a desk drawer, secured the notes, and handed the money to Sol. "Thank you very much, Sol," she said.

"You got a shopping bag handy?"

"Pietro!" Mary Ann said to the butler loudly enough for him to hear, "Find me a shopping bag." Pietro crept from the room.

"Mary Ann," Stone said, "do you have any mover's boxes handy? It's going to take longer than we have to go through all this stuff."

Mary Ann picked up the phone on the desk, pressed a button, and spoke to someone. "Please put together a dozen of those cardboard boxes in the kitchen and bring them to the study with some packing tape." She hung up and spoke to Stone. "You're still the executor. What do you want done with all of it?"

"I think we should move it to my office and go through it there. You should be present, of course."

"What about the cash?"

"We'll do a complete count, then put it in my safe until I can distribute it as per the will."

"All right, that's good."

"We're going to need a vehicle to move all the boxes," Stone said.

Mary Ann called the movers and asked for a large van to be brought to the house. Then she issued more orders to the staff.

Shortly, cardboard boxes began to appear; Mary Ann put the cash into one of them and sealed and marked it, then she instructed a servant to begin packing the other contents of the safe. Then she beckoned Stone. "Come with me for a moment," she said, leading the way into another room, which turned out to be Eduardo's secretary's office. It was filled with pictures, books, and objects.

"What's all this?" Stone asked.

"These are things that weren't distributed specifically in the

13

will and that neither the museum nor I wanted. Why don't you look around and see if you want to take anything home? I think Papa would want that."

Stone looked around. "These things don't look like junk," he said. "Are you sure you don't want any of them?"

"I'm sure, but make a list as you go, and I'll sign whatever you choose over to you."

"Tell you what, have your people pack them all, and I'll take them home and go through them at my leisure."

"As you wish." She called for more boxes and Bubble Wrap for the pictures, then listed each item as it was packed and signed it all over to Stone.

"What are you going to do with the safe?" Stone asked.

"Leave it, I guess."

"May I take it off your hands?"

"Sure, the movers can haul it away."

Stone went back to the study and asked Bob Cantor to remove the lug bolts that secured the safe to the floor.

SOME HOURS LATER, as they were nearing Sol Fink's dinner hour, the moving van awaited, packed with boxes and the safe, and they were ready to go. Stone decided to let the cash ride in the trunk of his car.

"I don't think we can get much more done today," Mary Ann said. "How about if I come to your house tomorrow morning, and we'll make a start?"

"That's good for me," Stone said, getting into the Bentley.

They drove away with the van following.

Bob and Sol began speaking what sounded to Stone like German, and to his surprise, Fred joined in their conversation.

When they went quiet, Stone said to Fred, "I didn't know you spoke German."

"It's not German," Fred said. "It's Yiddish."

"I had no idea you were Jewish."

"Does it matter?"

"Not in the least. You're full of surprises, Fred. How did you pick up Yiddish?"

"My grandmother, who lived with us, never learned English, so we spoke Yiddish at home."

Stone turned and looked at Sol, who seemed to be enjoying the ride. "How are you doing back there, Sol?"

"I'm very well, thank you. Not looking forward to dinner, though. It's meat loaf night, and I've never liked their meat loaf."

"Then why don't you come to my house and have dinner there? Assuming Bob can get you permission."

"I would enjoy that," Sol said, "and I don't need anybody's permission. I rule that joint. I'm the only resident who writes his own check every month to pay my way, and while I'm able, they'll take their instructions from me."

"I'll let them know," Bob said, getting out his phone.

"I was impressed with the way you opened that safe," Stone said. "You have a delicate touch."

"Thank you," Sol replied. "You're quite right."

"But since you already knew where to find the combination, why did you crack the safe? I mean, if you'd made a mistake, we might not have got it open."

"It was more fun that way," Sol replied. "Besides, Mr. Epstein taught me how to open an Excelsior that had locked itself. Now I'm the only person in the world who can do that."

"Would you mind teaching Bob how to do it? If I'm going to use the safe, somebody will have to know how it's done."

"Before I fall off the perch, you mean?"

They all laughed.

"I'd be glad to."

Back at the house they drove the Bentley and the van into the garage, and Stone instructed the movers to put the boxes from the safe on his office conference table and to put the old safe and the things from Eduardo's secretary's office in the storage room next door.

When the movers had gone, Stone ordered dinner from Helene and specified no meat loaf. While they were waiting for dinner, Bob and Sol spent the time with the old safe. When they emerged for dinner, Sol said, "Bob has a complete grasp of the safe. He's a quick learner."

AFTER DINNER and a cognac, which Solomon Fink particularly enjoyed, Bob Cantor drove him back to the home in Brooklyn. Sol climbed the steps slowly, but steadily, without assistance, and he waved away the nurse who waited at the top of the stairs.

4

The following morning Mary Ann arrived shortly after nine o'clock, and they went into the conference room to address the unpacking of the boxes.

They were marked in sequence, by shelf. "Shall we start at the top?" Stone asked.

"Let's do that," she replied.

Stone removed the contents of the first box and spread them on the table. The first item was a manila envelope, closed with a clasp, but not sealed. He shook out the contents—two passports: one Italian, one Swiss.

"Did you know about these?" he asked Mary Ann.

"I did not," she replied. She picked up the Italian passport and opened it. "It's a Vatican passport," she said, "and it's in his own name." The photograph was recent, Stone thought, within the last year of Eduardo's life.

Stone opened the Swiss passport and leafed through it. The name, signature, and photograph were the same. "Seems Eduardo went to Switzerland two or three times a year, nearly always from Italy. Do you know what business interests he had there?"

"None that I know of." She flipped through the Italian passport. "Two or three times a year," she said, then compared it to the Swiss document. "Often coinciding with the trips to Switzerland. Papa had business interests in Italy: wine, olive oil, and other food products he distributed in the United States through a company based in Little Italy. A very profitable company, he sold it a few weeks before his death."

"Perhaps he had banking arrangements in Switzerland," Stone said. "His last trip there was also a few weeks before his death."

"He never mentioned it."

"Perhaps he had a Swiss bank account."

"But those are of no further use these days," Mary Ann pointed out. "The Swiss banks have told all to the IRS, so you can't hide tax-free money there anymore."

"Those are the big, international banks. I understand there are still smaller, private banks that operate in the old way, taking foreign deposits and investing them."

Mary Ann went through the other files and envelopes on the table and came up with an index card bearing neat handwriting. "A website," she said, "along with a user name and a password."

Stone went to a laptop at the end of the table, got online, and typed in the information. "Aha," he said. "The Berg Bank."

"Never heard of it."

"Neither have I." He tapped more keys. "Here we are. He had a cash account and an investment account." He opened the bank account and scrolled down from the top. "Starting in the 1970s, when he opened the account, he made deposits at fairly regular intervals, which will probably coincide with the dates of entry in his Swiss passport. Would you like to hear the total?"

"Please," she said.

"Exactly 240,000,000 Swiss francs." He found a currency app on his iPhone and entered the figures. "About $238,000,000."

Mary Ann put a hand to her breast. "That's breathtaking."

Stone tapped more keys. "The investment account was liquidated at the time of his last visit, and the proceeds transferred to the cash account. Since that account was opened no withdrawals or transfers were made. In fact, no withdrawals were ever made from the cash account. Why do you think Eduardo would be hoarding cash?"

"The Great Depression had a lasting effect on him," she said. "His family was devastated, and it was up to him from an early age to pull them out of it. I can't think of any other reason."

"Let's see if there are any other foreign accounts," Stone said. An examination of the files revealed an account in Rome, with a balance of a little more than 1,000,000 euros. "That's it, as far as I can tell."

"What are we going to do with all that cash?" Mary Ann asked.

"The proper thing to do would be for me, as executor, to contact the Internal Revenue Service and come to an arrangement with them, then import the funds into the estate's account in New York."

"So we're going to have to pay a bundle in taxes and penalties?"

"I'm afraid so."

"There must be some alternative," she said.

"I have to advise you that there is no *legal* alternative," Stone said, "and I'm obligated under the law to report these funds."

Mary Ann sighed. "Oh, well," she said. "I suppose so."

"Think of it this way," Stone said, "after the taxes and penalties are paid, the estate is going to have many more millions than you expected as recently as yesterday. And you and your son are the beneficiaries, according to his will."

"I feel better already," she said.

Stone picked up another envelope and discovered it was addressed to him. He opened it. "Here's something new," he said, reading the document. "It's a codicil to his will, properly signed and witnessed some weeks after the date of his will. 'There being certain of my funds deposited in the Berg Bank, of Zurich, Switzerland, my executor is ordered to repatriate these funds, paying whatever is due to the Internal Revenue Service, and the remaining funds are to be divided between my grandson, Benito Bacchetti, and his father, my former son-in-law, Dino Bacchetti: eighty percent to Benito and twenty percent to Dino. Any other property or funds not specified in my will are to be distributed and divided to Benito and Dino in the same manner.'"

"Dino gets twenty percent? And I get nothing?" Mary Ann shouted.

"I'm afraid that's so, Mary Ann, but you have already received a very large inheritance from your father, and you were very pleased with it. Please remember that."

Mary Ann stood up and grabbed her purse. "I want nothing further to do with all this," she said, waving a hand at the table full of documents. "When you're done with it, write me a letter as executor, explaining anything financial, then as far as I'm concerned, you can dump everything else into your furnace."

She stormed out, slamming the door behind her.

"Mary Ann," Stone said to the door. "There hasn't been a furnace in the house for years."

Stone went back to work on the pile of files and documents, sending for a sandwich at lunchtime. By late afternoon he was down to a dozen files or so, and most of what he had discovered was fuel for his shredder. He began opening the other files and was surprised to find, in each folder, the criminal history of a man, neatly typed out and accompanied by affidavits swearing to their authenticity, signed by Eduardo Bianchi.

Stone went to his laptop and began googling the names. Each of them was a high-level mob boss, but some had established themselves as upright citizens. "Perfect fodder for blackmail," Stone said aloud to himself, "or perhaps, more likely, to protect Eduardo from being blackmailed by them."

All of the men were dead, except one. Stone blanched when he read that name, and he read the file. Twice.

5

Gianni Tommassini was his name. He was sixty-one years old, and he had murdered his father. And not only his father: Eduardo reckoned he had been present on a half dozen occasions when young Gianni had been ordered to commit murders. The dates, times, and those present were noted in the file; at least three witnesses were still alive, if very old.

Eduardo Bianchi and Gianni's father, Enrico Tommassini, had been contemporaries, both highly placed in the criminal organization, serving as final arbiters for the ruling council of bosses, singly or together. No one, not even the members of the council, knew their names; and they each went on to establish themselves as upright citizens, serving on boards of businesses and public institutions. Enrico Tommassini had anglicized his name to Henry Thomas, and he had founded an investment bank known as H. Thomas & Son, with much of its original funding from the Five Families. According to Eduardo, Henry's son, John Thomas—known to his family and friends as Jack—had joined his father in the banking business, severing all visible ties with his past.

Twenty-odd years ago, Henry Thomas had turned the business over to his son, Jack, who had managed the company brilliantly. It had grown into a dominant firm on Wall Street. Jack had a son, Henry II, called Hank, who was now a popular United States congressman from New York, being spoken of as an eventual candidate for the presidency.

Stone locked the file in the Excelsior safe, the combination of which he had memorized and saved in an encrypted file on his computer. Then he made two phone calls:

First, to his accountant, Robert Pesce.

"Rob," he said, "I have knowledge of $238,000,000 in a Swiss bank account, belonging to an estate of which I am executor. I want to repatriate the funds, pay all taxes and penalties, and put the proceeds at the disposal of my client's heirs. How must this be done?"

"Stone," Rob said, "that problem is just slightly above my pay grade. I am going to need to consult with my betters, and a negotiation will have to take place."

"Oh, and I have another three million dollars found today in my client's safe. I'm taking the position that income taxes have already been paid, but inheritance taxes are due. Please let me know how much Uncle Sam is going to demand from the Swiss funds, and those in the safe," Stone said.

"When was the Swiss account opened?"

"In 1976."

"Good, before the law changed. I will certainly let you know— soon, I hope."

"And please note that the estate will compensate you and your firm at your hourly rate," he said drily. "There is no commission involved."

"I will disappoint my people," Rob said, just as drily, and hung up.

Next, Stone called his friend Dino Bacchetti, who had been his partner when they were both NYPD detectives. Dino was now the police commissioner of New York City.

"Bacchetti," Dino said, answering his private line.

"It's Stone. Dinner tonight?"

"Okay."

"Seven-thirty at Patroon?"

"Right."

"I'm going to have some good news and some bad news."

"I can't wait," Dino replied.

They both hung up. A moment later, Mary Ann Bacchetti called. "Stone, I want to apologize for storming out this morning," she said.

"It's all right, Mary Ann."

"Did you find anything else of interest in the safe?"

"Yes, I did." He told her about the Thomas file.

"Holy shit," she said.

"That accurately reflects my reaction to the discovery."

"What are we going to do about this?"

"That's my problem, so all you have to do is forget I told you."

"My lips are zipped," she said.

"My accountant and the management of his firm will deal with the matter of taxes and penalties owing on the Swiss account money. Don't tell Ben about his unexpected inheritance until we have a number."

"Lips still zipped," she replied. They said goodbye and hung up. Stone went into Joan's office.

"What have you been doing in the conference room all day?" she asked.

"Sorting out the contents of Eduardo Bianchi's safe," he said.

"What was in it?"

"None of your business. There's also a large old safe in the storage room, to which you will not have the combination."

"You don't trust me anymore, huh?"

"About as far as I can throw you, and you've gained weight."

"I have not!"

"I just wanted to see if you were paying attention. Do you have a shopping bag and some tissue paper?"

"Is a Tiffany bag all right?"

"Perfect." Stone took the bag and tissue paper into his conference room and cut open the box containing Eduardo's three million dollars and placed it on the table, making quite a pile. Guessing what the estate taxes would be he calculated that Dino's share would probably be in the neighborhood of four hundred thousand dollars. He cut that out of the pile, which was in bundles of one hundred thousand dollars, wrapped it in the tissue paper, and placed it in the Tiffany shopping bag. He opened the Excelsior safe and placed the remaining cash inside, then closed and locked it.

Not wanting to be separated from that much cash, he took the shopping bag upstairs with him and set it on the bed while he showered, shaved, and dressed. Once done, he peeked into the bag to be sure the money was still there.

Since it was a nice evening he thought of walking to the restaurant, but the idea of being on the street with that much cash did not appeal, so he called for Fred and the car.

"Yes, sir," Fred said.

"And, Fred, come armed."

"I always do, sir," Fred replied.

By the time Stone got downstairs the Bentley was idling at the curb.

"Good evening, Fred," Stone said, getting into the rear seat.

"Good evening, sir," Fred replied. "May I ask why armed resistance might be required this evening?"

"I'm traveling with something very valuable," Stone replied, holding up the shopping bag.

Fred eyed it in the rearview mirror. "A new lady, sir?"

"No, it's for Dino."

A long silence ensued. "I see, sir," Fred said.

6

Stone entered the restaurant to find Dino already in their usual booth, and almost as soon as he sat down a Knob Creek on the rocks was set before him. "Good evening," he said.

"What's in there?" Dino asked, nodding at the Tiffany shopping bag.

"I mentioned that I would have good news and bad news," Stone said. "Which would you like first?"

"Is the good news in the bag?" Dino asked.

"It is."

"Well, then. I'm not going to sit here and stare at it, and think about it, while you give me the bad news. So let's have the good news."

"A wise choice," Stone said, placing the bag before Dino.

Dino stared at the bag but did not touch it. "What's in it?" he asked.

"You have only to look inside," Stone replied.

"This is weird," Dino said.

"Why?"

"You've never given me a gift—at least, not one in a Tiffany bag."

"This is not a gift from me, and it has nothing to do with Tiffany's. It's just a bag."

Dino looked warily inside. "Is it going to explode?"

"It is not."

"Why is it wrapped in tissue paper?"

"Dino, open the thing, or I'll take it away and keep it myself."

Dino reached into the bag and grasped the package inside with both hands, then set it on the table and gazed at it for a moment. Finally, he carefully pried the tape loose, as if he were saving the tissue paper, then he opened the tissue and looked inside. He immediately closed it and put it back in the bag. "Are you nuts?" he asked.

"What are you talking about?"

"There's a lot of cash in that bag. Is this a bribe?"

"Certainly not."

"You can't go into a public place and put a pile of cash in front of a public servant. People might get the wrong idea."

"I apologize. I didn't take that into account. I just wanted to see the look on your face when you opened it."

"And what was the look on my face?"

"Appalled," Stone said.

"Good call. How much money is in there?"

"Four hundred thousand dollars."

"Holy shit."

"Well, yes."

"Where did it come from?"

"From Eduardo Bianchi's safe, which was opened yesterday afternoon."

"And why are you giving it to me?"

"Because also in the safe was a codicil to Eduardo's will, specifying that any funds not specifically bequeathed in his will would be divided between Ben and you, eighty/twenty. There was three million dollars in the safe, and that's your twenty percent, less the estimated inheritance taxes." Stone took a couple of sheets of paper from his inside pocket and handed one of them to Dino. "This is the codicil—signed, witnessed, and legal. I think Eduardo must have drawn it up himself."

Dino set the shopping bag on the seat between them, then peeked at the contents again. "Four hundred grand?"

"Four packets of one hundred thousand dollars each, in hundred-dollar bills."

"What am I supposed to do with it?"

"Spend it, give it away, whatever you like."

"Do I have to tell my wife about it?"

"No, but you would be a fool to hide it from Viv."

"She's arriving at Teterboro in a few minutes," Dino said. "She'll join us in time for dessert."

Vivian Bacchetti was the chief operating officer of the world's second-largest private security company, Strategic Services, and traveled a lot on business.

"Don't worry, this money isn't going to matter," Stone said. "I have to give you the bad news before I explain that. That way, you'll be in a better mood at the end of the evening."

"All right," Dino said impatiently. "What's the bad news?"

The headwaiter appeared at the table. "Would you like to order, gentlemen?"

"Yes," Dino said. "What's the most expensive thing on the menu?"

"The Beluga caviar," the man replied.

"We'll both have that, with a bottle of the Dom Pérignon. Then the chateaubriand, medium rare, and a bottle of the Opus One cabernet, whatever you think is the best vintage. And the check comes to me."

"Thank you," Stone said when the man had gone.

"Okay, now give me the bad news, and keep it as short as you can. I don't want it to interfere with the caviar."

"All right. Also in Eduardo's safe were some very thorough dossiers on a dozen men whose names you would remember from the past. They are all dead now, except one."

"And who would that be?"

"Enrico Tommassini."

"Never heard of him," Dino said.

"He was a contemporary of Eduardo, and they both served the council of the Five Familes in New York as confidential advisors. Enrico had a son called Gianni, who in his youth was a hit man for the council. Eduardo was a witness to Gianni being instructed to make hits, and there are three other witnesses still alive who can testify to that."

"Okay," Dino said, looking befuddled. "So what's the bad news?"

"Enrico Tommassini anglicized his name to Henry Thomas, as in the firm of H. Thomas & Son, on Wall Street."

Dino's eyes widened.

"Gianni Tommassini became John Thomas, known to all as Jack. His son—Enrico's grandson, Henry, known as Hank—is currently a U.S. congressman from New York and has a slim chance being the next president of the United States."

"You're telling me Jack Thomas is a murderer?"

"Retired now, but still a murderer. Eduardo pins six hits on him."

Dino stared into the middle distance and thought about it. "And Eduardo kept a file on all this?"

"He did, and very meticulously."

"So you're telling me that you're going to turn over that file to the D.A.?"

"I thought I would turn it over to you and let you deal with it," Stone replied. "That way, you'll get credit for the collar."

"Thanks so much," Dino said, acidly. "And where is this file?"

"It's still in Eduardo's safe, but the safe is in my office."

Dino put his face in his hands and rubbed vigorously. "Jesus Christ," he said, "what a can of worms!"

"You could destroy the file," Stone said.

"Why haven't you already done that?"

"As an officer of the court, it's my legal obligation to turn the dossier over to the proper authorities. That would be you."

The caviar and champagne arrived. Dino stared at it for a moment, then began to eat. "We're not wasting this," he said, "but watch out, I may throw it up."

7

They finished the caviar in silence, except for a few oohs and aahs, then their dishes were taken away.

"Okay," Dino said. "Now I could use some more good news."

"All right," Stone said, "here goes. Also found in Eduardo's safe were bank records from accounts in Rome and Switzerland. There was about a million euros in the Rome account."

"And I get a chunk of that?"

"After taxes and penalties," Stone said, "about a quarter of a million euros, maybe three hundred thousand dollars."

"So now I'm up to seven hundred thousand dollars in windfall?"

"More than that," Stone said. "You're forgetting the Swiss account."

"How much is in that?"

"Approximately $238,000,000, depending on the value of the Swiss franc."

"Two hundred and thirty-eight *million*?"

"Right. After taxes and penalties and Ben's eighty percent cut, yours comes to about twenty-four million dollars."

"Twenty-four million?"

"That is correct."

"American dollars?" Dino looked under the table. "Do you have another shopping bag or something?"

"It would take a steamer trunk to hold that much," Stone replied.

"Okay, you got me," Dino said. "Dinner is still on me, but what's the joke?"

Stone leaned forward and spoke softly, but with emphasis. "There is no joke, Dino. This is real."

Their chateaubriand arrived, as did their Opus One. Dino tasted it and approved.

"I recommend decanting it," the sommelier said.

"Please do," Dino replied.

He did so, and the staff departed, leaving them to their dinner. Dino got quiet again. Not until he had finished his beef and started a second glass of wine did he speak again. "Assuming you're not completely nuts—and I realize that's a dangerous assumption—when do I receive all this money?"

Stone unfolded the second sheet of paper he had taken from his pocket earlier and handed it to Dino, along with a pen. "Sign this receipt, and the four hundred thousand is yours to take home. I believe you have a police escort waiting."

Dino read the receipt, signed it, and gave Stone his pen back. "I guess I'll have to pay a ton of taxes," he said.

"You pay nothing. The estate pays the inheritance taxes and everything else, so your share is free and clear."

"What am I going to do with twenty-four million dollars?" Dino asked weakly.

"You'll think of something," Stone replied. "In fact, you'll think of lots of things. Don't worry, Viv will help you with that.

You might start by putting the four hundred thousand dollars in your bank, first thing tomorrow morning."

"When does the rest arrive?"

"First I have to hear from my accounting firm that they have made a deal with the IRS; then I have to repatriate the funds into the estate's account and pay the feds, then I can write you and Ben checks for your shares. Depending on how long the negotiations with Uncle Sam take, I'd guess a week or two."

"As quickly as that?"

"Barring complications."

"What sort of complications?"

"Unforeseen complications, and I don't see any of those ahead."

Dino's phone rang. "Hey," he said, then listened. "You go ahead. I'll be home pretty soon." He hung up. "That was Viv. She said she's tired and going straight home from the airport—and I'm not to wake her up when I come in."

"You can give her the good news in the morning, when you're both fresh and rested."

"Are you kidding? I'm not going to sleep a wink. I'll be exhausted in the morning."

"Take a pill. No, take two pills. And don't go to work tomorrow."

"What am I going to do with all this money?"

"Isn't there something you want, that you could never afford?"

"Well, let's see. I could buy a jet airplane, but you've already got one, so I don't need that. I could buy a vacation home, but you've got half a dozen, so I'd rather stay with you, free."

"Anything else?"

"I could give some of it to Ben."

"Well, you shouldn't do that, because Ben's already a lot richer than you are."

"That's true."

"Why don't you wait until the funds are ready to be distributed before you tell him?"

"I don't want to tell him. I want you to tell him. It's more official that way."

"If you like."

"I like. If I told him he might try to have me committed."

"Here's a thought, Dino. You could retire, both of you."

"Retire? From my dream job?"

"Maybe Viv would like to retire."

"And spend all her time with me? She'd go nuts. As it is, she's gone about half the time, and that seems to be just about right for both of us."

"Anything else you want?"

"Yes," Dino said. "I want Eduardo's file on Jack Thomas and his family to not exist anymore."

"Not going to happen," Stone said. "I'm not going to play a part in papering over a bunch of murders and getting Hank Thomas elected president. I couldn't sleep nights. You can have a choice: I'll give you the dossier or I'll give it directly to the D.A."

"All right, give it to the D.A., and tell him I told you to do that. I don't want it to pass through my hands."

"I'll do it tomorrow," Stone said. "You think he'll see me?"

"I'll call him and tell him that some important information is coming from you, and that he should see it before anyone else does."

"That's a good idea," Stone said. "He should be in complete

charge of when and how he handles it, without worrying about leaks to the press from his staff."

"Good. Does anybody else know about this, as we speak?"

"Only Mary Ann."

"'*Only Mary Ann*'?"

"She called and asked me what I found in the safe, and she's sort of my client in this, so I told her."

"Then by this time tomorrow, the entire world will know!"

"What are you talking about, Dino?"

"Mary Ann has the loosest mouth on the planet."

"Well, she kept a lot of secrets about Eduardo's life all these years."

"Only because she knew that, if she said a word, Eduardo would send Pietro to see her some dark night, dagger in hand."

"His own daughter?"

"If she had blabbed about him, Eduardo wouldn't have considered her his daughter anymore, just a liability—and an expendable one, at that."

"Who do you think she'll tell?"

"Who's available? One or more of her girlfriends, certainly. Let's hope that none of them is acquainted with Jack Thomas, or he'll know before breakfast. In which case, you might feel more comfortable in another country, while you think about where to hide for the rest of either your life or his."

"You think Jack Thomas is still connected?"

"He never stopped being connected; I've known that for years, but I could never prove it."

Dino paid the bill in hundreds from his Tiffany bag, and they left the restaurant. On the sidewalk, before they got into their respective cars, Dino said, "I'll call D.A. Ken Burrows tonight and tell him to expect you in his office tomorrow morning. What time do you want to show up?"

"Ten o'clock," Stone said, then they both were driven away.

"Did your friend enjoy his gift?" Fred asked.

"You might say that," Stone replied.

8

Dino got home without using his car's flashing lights, and he went upstairs to his apartment. He checked on Viv and found her snoring softly. He knew it was a bad idea to wake her, so he undressed, got into his pajamas, went into his study, and called the district attorney.

"Ken Burrows," a sleepy voice responded.

"Ken, it's Dino Bacchetti. I'm sorry to call at this hour, but it's important."

There were sounds of the man rearranging himself in bed. "All right, Dino, what is it?" He was fully awake now.

"You're acquainted with my old partner on the NYPD, Stone Barrington?"

"Sure."

"Stone is going to turn up at your office at ten o'clock tomorrow morning with something you should see. Are you going to be available at that time?"

"I've got a staff meeting at ten-thirty, but I can give him a few minutes, if you think I should."

"I think you should. He's told me about a file that has come into his possession that, if it becomes public, might blow the lids off the lives of some important people."

"Who are these people?"

"I haven't seen the file, but I can tell you that you are going to want to hold this information as closely as possible, perhaps even keep it from your staff, and especially from anyone with an Italian name."

"So, we're talking Mafia stuff?"

"Yes, but I believe it goes way beyond that."

"Come on, Dino, tell me all of it."

"I won't, for two reasons. One, you wouldn't get any sleep tonight—God knows, I won't. And two, you should have the file in hand when you learn about this. You may want to keep it entirely to yourself, but that will be up to you."

"All right, Dino, I'll see Barrington, and I'll listen to him and I'll read his file, then I'll call you and talk about how to proceed."

"Ken, you may not want to proceed. If I don't hear from you on the subject, I'll know why, and I'll feel better about it. Good night."

"Good night, Dino." Both men hung up.

STONE GOT READY for bed, then looked at his clock. It wasn't all that late, and it was three hours earlier in L.A. He picked up the phone and called Ben Bacchetti.

"This is Ben."

"Ben, it's Stone. How are you?"

"I'm just terrific, Stone, and you?"

"Very well, thanks. Your father asked me to call you and give you some good news."

"About Granddad's Swiss bank account?"

"Well, yes."

"Mom called me two hours ago about what you found in Granddad's safe," Ben said.

"Ah. Well, congratulations. What are you going to do with your newfound wealth?"

"I've been thinking about that all evening," Ben replied. "I'm going to start buying shares in Centurion Studios and keep on buying until I have the controlling interest. Peter and I, of course. I've already talked to him about it. He's going to call you in the morning and ask if he can use funds from his trust in the effort."

"I'll certainly agree to that," Stone said, "and if you need more, I'd be happy to make a personal investment."

"Thank you for that, Stone. We may well need it. I know we have a good coalition of shareholders, but that can always change: people die or lose interest. I'd like the real authority to rest in mine and Peter's hands."

"So would I," Stone said. "Did your mother talk at all about the other contents of Eduardo's safe?"

"She said there was three million in cash, which sort of blew my mind, and some old papers, that's all."

"I think we can clear up the tax hurdles in the next week or two, then I'll be able to write you a very nice check."

"I'll look forward to that," Ben said.

"I'll wait for Peter's call in the morning."

"Good night, then."

"Good night." Stone hung up and went to bed.

THE FOLLOWING MORNING Stone went down to his office early and opened Eduardo's safe. He took the Tommassini file from the safe, went to the Xerox machine, made six copies, numbered them, bound them, then put the copies in the Excelsior, retaining the original and putting it into his briefcase.

FRED WAS AT THE CURB with the Bentley at nine-thirty. They were halfway downtown when Stone's cell phone rang.

"Hello?"

"Stone, it's Mary Ann."

"Good morning, Mary Ann," Stone replied.

"I'm calling about the files we found in Papa's safe."

"Yes?"

"I want them, especially the one we talked about in some detail."

"Why do you want them, Mary Ann?"

"Because they could cause a lot of trouble, and I want them safe."

"Safe, or destroyed?"

"Never mind, I just want them."

"Mary Ann, I want to be very clear with you. You may not have the files—not at this time, anyway. There are legal ramifications, and I must follow the law in this."

"What 'legal ramifications'?"

"I won't go into that, but as executor of your father's estate, I have to be very careful with how this is handled."

"But . . ."

"Mary Ann, have you told anyone—anyone at all—about the contents of those files?"

"Why, of course not," she sputtered. "Why on earth would you ask me that?"

"You may remember that I directed you not to speak with

anyone about those files. If you've ignored that directive, I need to know it right now."

"Well, I . . . I certainly haven't mentioned it to anyone whose discretion I don't have the utmost confidence in."

"To whom, exactly, have you spoken about this?"

"It would be a breach of confidence for me to tell you that."

"It was a breach of confidence for you to tell that person or persons."

"I just can't tell you."

"Mary Ann, you may have placed yourself in an untenable position by telling someone else about those files. Now the only way I can protect you is to know whom you told and what you told."

Long silence. "Well . . . all right, I told my friend Heather about them."

"Who else?"

"No one else, I swear to God."

"And what is Heather's last name?" Stone asked.

"Stone, please don't make me . . ."

"Answer me, Mary Ann!"

"I'm not accustomed to being spoken to that way," she huffed.

"All right," Stone said gently. "*Please* tell me Heather's last name."

Another long silence. "Thomas," she said finally.

Stone stopped himself from groaning. "Any relation?" he asked.

"She's Jack's ex-wife," Mary Ann said. "Hank's stepmother."

"Please give me her cell phone number," Stone said.

"You're not going to call her!"

"I have to speak to her," Stone said, "for her own safety."

Mary Ann gave him the number. "Please don't be unkind to Heather," she said. "She's a rather delicate person."

"I won't be unkind to her, Mary Ann," Stone said. "I'll speak to you later, after I've spoken to her. For God's sake, and for your own, don't say another word to anybody about this. And please don't call Heather until after I've spoken to her."

"Goodbye," Mary Ann said, then hung up.

Now, Stone thought, I've got to handle a woman I don't know who is "delicate." He was very much afraid that "delicate" meant "unstable."

The car stopped. "We've arrived, sir," Fred said. "Sorry about the traffic."

Stone looked at his watch: five minutes before ten. He'd have to call Heather Thomas later.

9

Stone went through the metal detector at the entrance to the building and allowed his briefcase to be looked through. He took the elevator to the top floor and gave his name to the woman at the reception desk. She made a call, then said, "You may go in."

Stone walked into the district attorney's large, paneled office, and Ken Burrows rose to greet him. "I've got a ten-thirty meeting, Stone," he said, "so sit down, and let's get right to it."

Stone took a seat and set down his briefcase beside him. "Can anyone hear us?" he asked.

"Do you mean, do I have a recording system in this office?"

"Can anyone hear us, any way at all?"

"No," Burrows replied.

"I am the executor of the estate of Eduardo Bianchi," Stone said.

"I knew him," Burrows replied. "He and my father were close."

"A couple of days ago," Stone said, "Eduardo's daughter, Mary Ann—"

"Dino Bacchetti's ex-wife?"

"Correct. Mary Ann called me and told me that she had found a concealed safe in Eduardo's study, but she couldn't find the combination. She asked if I knew someone who knew a safe-cracker."

"And do you know such a person?"

"I know a person who knows a person who worked on the building of this particular safe, which is very hard to open. The two of them and I drove out to the Bianchi estate and looked at the safe. The elderly gentleman we took along was able to open it. Inside we found three million dollars in cash, which will be reported on the final estate tax return. There were some other records that I retained for the estate, and on the bottom shelf we found twelve files, or dossiers. Each outlines the criminal activities of a prominent mafioso, eleven of whom are now dead."

"And the twelfth?"

Stone picked up his briefcase, opened it, and handed Burrows the Tommassini file.

Burrows weighed it in his hands and began to leaf through it. "Who is Enrico Tommassini?" he asked. "I've never heard the name."

"Many years ago, the family name was anglicized to *Thomas*. This file concerns Enrico, now named Henry, and his son, Gianni, now named John and called Jack by everyone."

"Not H. Thomas & Son," Burrows said, frowning.

"Yes. The file contains what amounts to an affidavit from Eduardo Bianchi, who witnessed the son being assigned to commit the assassinations of half a dozen people, who were, in fact, murdered. I have no reason to doubt Eduardo's veracity. There are names and dates."

Burrows closed the file and placed it on his desk. "And what do you expect me to do about this?"

"I have no expectations in that regard," Stone replied. "I have a duty as an officer of the court to report the contents of that file to the proper authorities, and I have just done so. You may do with the file as you wish." He took a receipt from his briefcase and handed it to Burrows, who signed it without comment and returned it to him.

"Ken, you might also find the other eleven files of interest. I haven't read them through, but there could be evidence connecting others to various criminal acts—some of them, no doubt, beyond the statute of limitations. But murder has no statute of limitations. If you'd like to see them, please let me know and I will turn them over." He closed his briefcase and stood. "Now, Ken, if you will excuse me, I'll leave you to your reading."

"Thank you for coming to see me," Burrows said.

As Stone was leaving the office he heard Burrows pick up his phone. "Cancel my ten-thirty meeting and reschedule," he said.

STONE WAS NEARLY HOME when his son, Peter, called. "Good morning, Dad."

"Good morning, Peter. Are you well?"

"Very well. Ben has told me about his inheritance and his intentions of buying up shares in Centurion. As my trustee, would you be amenable to my using funds from my trust to help us buy those shares?"

"I would be happy to do that. And I've told Ben that if he needs further investment I would like to participate."

"That's good news."

They chatted a bit longer, then said goodbye.

. . .

STONE RETURNED to his office and found Heather Thomas's cell number. He tood a deep breath and exhaled, then dialed the number.

"Hello?" a woman said.

"Mrs. Thomas?"

"Speaking."

"My name is Stone Barrington. I am the executor of Eduardo Bianchi's estate and a friend of his daughter, Mary Ann Bacchetti."

"I know who you are, Mr. Barrington, and I think I know why you're calling. You want me to keep my mouth shut about what Mary Ann told me."

"I want more than that, Mrs. Thomas," Stone said. "I want you to forget that Mary Ann ever told you what she did."

"What she did, Mr. Barrington, was give me grounds to re-open my divorce case and to greatly enhance the terms of my settlement."

"I'm very sorry to hear that," Stone said. "Have you consulted your divorce attorney yet?"

"I was about to call him when you called."

"I must tell you that if you reveal the details of what Mary Ann told you, your attorney will be ethically bound to report them to law enforcement. Can you imagine what a chain of events that would set off?"

"I'm not sure what you mean, Mr. Barrington."

"Let me be blunt, Mrs. Thomas. If the information you have passes to another person, then that person's life and yours will be in danger."

47

"Are you suggesting that my former husband would murder me?"

"No. I'm quite sure he would pass that work to another person or persons, and then arrange to be out of town when your body is discovered."

"I cannot believe that he would behave in that fashion."

"Think about it, Mrs. Thomas. You must know your ex-husband well. Do you believe that he would allow anyone to live who learned that he has already commited at least half a dozen murders? Do you think the content of his character includes a forgiving nature?"

"Well . . ."

"And have you considered the effect on your stepson's political career?"

The woman began to sob.

"Mrs. Thomas . . ."

"No, you shut up."

"Please tell me what your intentions are."

She seemed to get control of her emotions. "I would never do anything that might harm Hank's standing in Congress."

"Then you must try to forget that you know what you know," Stone said. "If I can be of any assistance to you in this matter, please do not hesitate to call me. I'm a partner in Woodman & Weld, and you can reach me through the firm."

"Thank you, Mr. Barrington," she said, "but I don't think we'll speak again."

"As you wish. Goodbye."

"Goodbye."

They both hung up and Stone breathed a sigh of relief.

He called Mary Ann.

"Yes, Stone?"

"I've spoken to Heather Thomas, and I believe she now understands the seriousness of the situation. More than anything, she's concerned about her stepson's political standing."

"Would you like me to speak to her again?" she asked.

"I would like you to avoid doing so, unless she contacts you. In that case, let her know that you can't discuss it further."

"All right."

"I'm going to work on the Swiss and Italian bank accounts now. I spoke to Ben last night."

"Thank you, Stone, and goodbye."

He thought that he would hear from Mary Ann again only if it were very, very important.

Shortly after he hung up, Joan buzzed him. "Mary Ann Bacchetti on one."

Stone picked up the phone. "Yes, Mary Ann?"

"I am going to tell you something, and then I'm not going to discuss it further. I'm just going to hang up."

"What?"

"Heather had already told Jack Thomas about the file before you spoke to her, perhaps immediately after my conversation with her. I'm hanging up now." And she did so.

Stone was left staring at the phone in his hand.

10

Stone considered what to do next, but he didn't have a clue. He tried to think of what Jack Thomas would do next and found he didn't want to think about that.

So, he busied himself with details. He googled the Berg Bank and found an e-mail address for the managing director, one Friedrich Hampel, and sent him an introductory note. In it he identified himself, the estate he represented, and the terms of Eduardo's will. He also found an address for the State Bank of Italy and its managing director, Alfredo Dante, and sent him a similar e-mail.

He called Joan in, took her to the Excelsior safe, opened it, and showed her the eleven files on the bottom shelf. "Please copy each of these twice, bind them, and return them to this safe. Pack the original files and have them hand-delivered to the district attorney, Ken Burrows, and get his signature on the delivery receipt." Joan went to work.

By this time, Stone had received a reply from the Swiss bank, though he had not expected one until the following morning because it was much later there. The e-mail read as follows:

Dear Mr. Barrington,

I can neither confirm nor deny that Mr. Eduardo Bianchi owns or has owned accounts at this bank. Before

I can discuss the matter further, you must appear in person in our offices and bring with you the following documents:

1. The birth and death certificates of Mr. Bianchi.

2. A certified copy of his will, naming you as executor, and any codicils.

3. The originals of any passports held by Mr. Bianchi.

4. The most recent of any account statements in Mr. Bianchi's name from this bank.

5. Your professional credentials, including your law license, and a letter from your law firm's managing director confirming your employment there.

6. At least three letters from credible persons attesting to your professional qualifications and good character.

7. Your personal identity documents.

Yours truly,

Friedrich Hampel

Managing Director

Stone responded to the e-mail, saying that he would appear at the bank's offices in two days at ten AM. Then he went to work gathering the documents he needed.

He called Bill Eggers, the managing partner of Woodman & Weld, and explained what he needed from the firm.

"The Swiss are nothing if not meticulous," Eggers said, chuckling. "I'll messenger the letter over to you. You may require local legal advice, as well, so I'm e-mailing the managing director of our associate firm there, Heinrich Kraft, and I'll include his card with your letter."

Stone thanked him, hung up, and called Holly Barker at the State Department and was sent to her voice mail.

"Holly," he said, after the beep, "I need a letter from you attesting to my professional qualifications and my good character, addressed to the Berg Bank of Zurich, Switzerland, and I need it sent by courier to New York." He explained about the Swiss bank's demands, then hung up and called Dino.

"Bacchetti."

"It's Stone. How would you like to be closer to your newfound fortune?"

"I'd like that very much," Dino said.

"Unfortunately, to do that, you will have to fly to Switzerland with me and visit Eduardo's bank."

"When?"

"Tomorrow morning. We should be back the day after tomorrow, late afternoon."

"I'm in," Dino replied.

"You can bring Viv, if you like."

"She's off to Hong Kong, I think."

"Have you told her about your new wealth?"

"Kind of."

"I don't even want to know what that means. Wheels up, Jet Aviation, Teterboro, ten AM tomorrow."

"Gotcha."

Stone hung up and buzzed Joan. "Please call Faith Barnacle and tell her we're flying to Zurich tomorrow morning, wheels up at ten AM. Ask her to make all the flight arrangements, including a copilot for the flight, returning the day after tomorrow. She should book hotel rooms for crew for one night."

"Okeydokey."

"Also, please book a two-bedroom suite for me at the Dolder Grand Hotel, Zurich."

By late afternoon, Stone had assembled the requested documents and placed them in a file, which he put into his briefcase. Joan entered with an envelope from the State Department. "I opened it. It's your references."

Stone stuffed the envelope into the file. "Please type the account number and wiring instructions for the Bianchi estate account on a sheet of paper, and put it into the file." She did so.

THE FOLLOWING MORNING, Stone found an e-mail from the Italian bank in his inbox, requesting pretty much the same documents the Swiss bank had, but not his personal appearance. He asked Joan to copy the Swiss file and e-mail it to the Italian bank.

He was about to leave for the airport when Joan buzzed him.

"The D.A. for you on one."

Stone pressed the button. "Good morning, Ken."

"Good morning, Stone. I received the files yesterday, and I've leafed through them."

"What did you think?"

"I think some of them are dangerous, but none so much as the Tommassini file."

"I can't bring myself to disagree with you. May I ask: What are your intentions?"

"I intend to go into this very thoroughly. But I'm going to appoint two of my best people to examine all the files very carefully before I do anything."

"I think that's wise," Stone replied.

"I don't need to tell you that all of this must be held in the closest confidence," Burrows said. "It would be dangerous if this leaked."

"Ken," Stone said. "I'm sorry to tell you that the existence of the files—or at least the Tommassini file—has already been leaked to Jack Thomas."

There was a long silence at the other end before Burrows spoke. "How is that possible?" he asked.

Stone explained the path through Mary Ann Bianchi and Heather Thomas.

"That is catastrophic news," the D.A. said finally.

"Jack Thomas knows that the file exists and that I have it," Stone said. "There is no reason to believe he knows you have it— unless there's a leak in your office."

"That's good news of a sort," Burrows replied. "I think the best thing for me to do, then, is to place all the files in my vault and keep my mouth shut."

"That's a good plan," Stone said.

"What are you doing to protect yourself?"

"Well, I'm leaving the country today, though not for that purpose."

"When are you returning?"

"The day after tomorrow."

"I would like to know if Jack Thomas or anyone representing him attempts to contact you while you're gone."

"I'll let my secretary know," Stone said.

"Check in with me on your return."

"I'll do that." Stone hung up, grabbed his briefcase, and ran for his car.

11

S tone sat at the end of Runway One at Teterboro, with Faith in the right seat and the hired copilot in the cabin with Dino. Stone set the auto-throttles, then pushed the throttles forward for full power. Twenty minutes later they were at cruising altitude, 45,000 feet, and pointed toward their refueling stop on Santa Maria, in the Azores, a mid-Atlantic Portuguese island group.

FOUR HOURS LATER he set the airplane down on the Santa Maria runway. While they refueled, Faith took their passports and cleared customs and immigration. Less than an hour passed before they were on their way to Zurich, with Faith and the new pilot, a woman named Chrissie, at the controls.

Stone settled into a seat across from Dino.

"So," Dino said. "What are we doing at this Zurich bank?"

"Hopefully, we're wresting from their greedy hands all the funds deposited there by Eduardo over many years."

"And how do they feel about this?"

"They're accustomed to dealing in large sums," Stone said, "but perhaps unaccustomed to paying them out. If I were the bank's CEO, I would certainly resist their departure."

"What if they refuse?"

"Then I'll call my attorney," Stone said.

"You have a lawyer in Zurich?"

"Woodman & Weld knows lawyers everywhere."

THEY ARRIVED in the late evening, cleared the airport, and Stone and Dino were met and driven to their hotel, a grande dame of Zurich.

"What do you know about this Hampel guy?" Dino asked.

"He's the managing director of the Berg Bank, that's it."

Dino unearthed his cell phone and took it into his bedroom, returning after a few minutes.

"Who do you know in Zurich?" Stone asked.

"Why do you think I was calling Zurich?" Dino asked back.

"Oh, never mind."

THE FOLLOWING MORNING, at the crack of ten AM, Stone presented his card to a receptionist, then sat down to wait. Forty minutes later they were ushered into a large office, and a very tall man rose from his desk to greet them—icily, Stone thought.

Friedrich Hampel regarded them calmly from behind his desk. "How may I help you?" he asked.

"Perhaps you recall the e-mail I sent you regarding the estate of Eduardo Bianchi?" Stone said.

"Perhaps," Hampel replied.

Stone handed him a copy of his own response. "This is the list of documents you require," he said. "First of all, my personal credentials." He handed over his passport and Bill Eggers's letter.

Hampel gazed at the passport, then read the letter slowly. "And your legal credentials?"

"Copies of my university and law school diplomas and my law license in the state of New York," Stone replied, handing them over.

Hampel again read slowly. Then he began building a pile of paper before him.

Stone handed him Eduardo's birth and death certificates, then his three passports, the will, and the codicils.

It took Hampel a good twenty minutes to digest the documents. When he looked up, Stone handed him the folder with his character references. It occurred to him that he had not bothered to read them first.

Hampel read what Stone could tell was Dino's letter, then the one from Bill Eggers, then from Holly Barker and then, to Stone's surprise, a fourth one.

Hampel read the fourth letter then looked up at Stone with new interest. "I have never received one of these," he said, handing it to Stone.

Stone read the letter while keeping a straight face. Apparently, Holly had called Katharine Lee for help, and he was reading a fulsome response from the President of the United States. He looked back at Hampel. "Oh?" he asked.

"This is very impressive," Hampel said, "but, of course, we must clear you with the federal police."

Dino produced his badge and NYPD ID. "Will this do?" he asked.

"I'm sorry, no. We will need to speak to the Swiss federal police about this."

"Excuse me," Dino said. He went to the door, opened it, beckoned to someone, and a solidly built man in a police uniform entered the room. "Mr. Hampel," Dino said. "This is Director Schweitzer of the Federal Office of Police," he said. "Will he do?"

Hampel rose and shook the man's hand. "Of course," he muttered.

Schweitzer had an exchange with Hampel in German for a minute or so. The policeman seemed to be annoyed.

The two Swiss men shook hands again, Schweitzer nodded to Dino and then left the room.

"Is there anything else you require?" Stone asked Hampel. "Anything at all?"

"Only the name of your local legal counsel," Hampel said.

"It wasn't on your list," Stone replied, handing him the business card, "but here you are."

Hampel read the card and blinked rapidly.

"Any questions?" Stone asked.

"No," Hampel replied. "This gentleman is my personal attorney."

"Now," Stone said, "shall we get down to business?"

"Of course," Hampel said. "What is it you require?"

"First, I would like to see current statements of any and all accounts of Eduardo Bianchi held by this bank."

Hampel reached into a desk drawer, extracted a single sheet of paper and handed it to Stone. "There is just the one account," he said. "In dollars, at the current exchange rate, the balance is $237,800,000."

Stone handed him a sheet of paper. "These are the wiring

instructions for the account of the Eduardo Bianchi estate," he said. "I would like all the funds from your account wired to the estate account."

Hampel examined the instructions. "When?"

"Immediately," Stone said. "Now."

Hampel sighed, picked up his phone, and pressed some buttons; a young man entered the office. Hampel handed him the instructions and the account statement. "Please wire transfer these funds to this account in New York," he said. "Come back when you are done and bring the confirmation of receipt."

The young man replied in German and departed.

"It will take only a few minutes," Hampel said to Stone.

"We'll wait," Stone replied.

Hampel cleared his throat. "Perhaps we could discuss the possibility of reinvestment of some of the funds," he said. "We have an outstanding track record of return on investment."

"Perhaps later," Stone said.

There was a long silence, then Hampel spoke again. "I hope your accommodations were satisfactory," he said.

"More than satisfactory."

Nothing else was said until the young man returned and handed a sheet of paper to Hampel. The banker read it carefully, then produced a stamp from a desk drawer and applied it. He then signed the document and handed it to Stone. "I hope this is satisfactory?"

Stone read the receipt. "Quite satisfactory," he said, rising and offering his hand.

Hampel shook it, then pressed a button. A woman came in and escorted Stone and Dino from the building.

Once on the sidewalk, Dino mopped his brow. "Whew! You really handled that well, Stone."

"It didn't hurt that you produced the director of the federal police. How the hell did you do that?"

"I know cops everywhere," Dino said.

12

Their return flight was uneventful, though longer because of the prevailing winds that had been so helpful on their prior crossing. They were served a catered meal by the copilot, who then returned to her cockpit duties.

"So," Dino said, over his filet mignon, "when do I get the money?"

"I'll let you know," Stone said.

"You mean you're going to keep me waiting?"

"Did you think you would return from Zurich with a satchelful of money? There are protocols to be followed."

"I would prefer the cash."

"If you had it you would be immediately arrested at Teterboro by customs for carrying in excess of ten thousand dollars without having filed the proper documents. Believe me, the way it's being done is the best way."

"What happens if we crash and burn on this flight?"

"Then the attorney for your estate will contact my office, and they will handle the transfer."

"You are the attorney handling my estate," Dino reminded him.

"Dino, I think I know the reason you're so nervous about this."

"And what would that be?"

"You haven't told Viv about the money, and you're afraid she's going to react badly."

"Define 'badly,'" Dino said.

"First, she's going to berate you for not having told her earlier. What will your answer be?"

"That I wanted to be absolutely certain that this is real before telling her."

"Pretty good. Then you're afraid she's not going to believe you about where the money came from, that she'll think you've done some shady business."

Dino was silent, then came to his own defense. "Viv would never even think such a thing."

"Dino, she's in a business where people are trying all the time to do shady things to her clients."

"Well, you have a point there," Dino said.

"It will be a reflex for her. Don't worry, when she calms down and you show her the bank statement, she'll be very happy."

"I don't have a bank statement to give her."

"Tomorrow morning, call your banker, who will confirm the transfer. Then ask him to e-mail you a copy of your account statement. Believe me, he will be very happy to help you."

STONE WAS IN BED before midnight. The following morning he went down to his office to catch up on mail and messages.

Joan came in. "We've had confirmation this morning of two enormous wire transfers to the Bianchi estate account from the Swiss and Italian banks." She handed him a piece of paper with the numbers.

Stone did some adding and dividing on his calculator, then wrote down two numbers. "Please wire transfer these funds to Dino and Ben Bacchetti. They're expecting them."

Joan nodded. "Don't we get to keep any of it?"

"Just my fee as executor, which we will collect before we're finished."

Joan went back to her desk. A half hour later she buzzed him. "Yes?"

"The funds have hit both accounts."

"Thank you." Stone called Dino.

"Bacchetti."

"It's Stone. The money is in your account. Ben's is, too."

Dino took a deep breath and said, "Whoosh."

"You sound relieved."

"That's the sound of being suddenly rich."

"If you're not very careful with this money, you're not going to be very rich for very long. Want some advice?"

"No, but advise me anyway."

"Don't buy anything that costs more than a million dollars."

"I hadn't planned to."

"Viv is coming home today, isn't she?"

"She is."

"Tell her immediately and you'll stay out of trouble."

"From your lips to God's ear," Dino said, then hung up.

LATE IN THE AFTERNOON Dino went to his bank, completed a transaction, and got a copy of his bank statement. He made another stop for some purchases, then went home to his apartment.

• • •

WHEN VIV ARRIVED HOME, just after six, Dino was sitting in one of a pair of armchairs before a fire. On a table between the chairs was an ice bucket with a bottle of Dom Pérignon chilling in it, a bowl of Beluga caviar was nestling in another bowl of ice, and something on a plate had a napkin over it.

Viv dropped her carry-on at the door, walked over to him, kissed him hello, then viewed the tabletop. "What's all this?" she asked.

"I have some news," Dino replied.

She flopped onto a chair. "Oh, God, this is going to be bad," she said. "You're dying, and you're trying to soften the blow."

"I'm very healthy, thank you," Dino said, pouring her a flute of champagne and removing the glass cover from the caviar. He spooned a heap of the roe onto a blini and handed it to her on a plate. "Eat and drink," he said. "You'll feel better."

"Dino," Viv said. "Tell me what the fuck is going on or I'll throw that champagne bottle at your head."

Dino picked up the napkin-covered plate and placed it in her lap. "I'm sorry, it's sort of heavy."

"I'm not touching this," she said, biting off half the blini.

Dino reached down and swept away the napkin. Underneath it were stacked ten bundles of hundred-dollar bills. "Happy Birthday!" he said.

She didn't touch the cash. "My birthday is five months away," she said.

"What does that matter?" he replied.

She nudge a stack of bills with a fingernail. "How much is this?"

"Each bundle contains one hundred thousand dollars," Dino explained. "There are ten bundles." He could see her lips moving.

"That's a million dollars," she said.

"Yours to do with as you wish."

She narrowed her eyes. "Dino, have you taken a bribe?"

"I have not. The money is honestly obtained."

"Have you embezzled from the Police Pension Fund?"

"Once again, I have not."

"Start at the beginning," she said, "and don't leave anything out."

13

Viv drained her champagne flute and allowed Dino to refill it. "You're going to want sex, aren't you," she said, and it wasn't a question.

"Of course, but not until you absorb all of this and tell me what you want to do."

"I want to go down to ABC and buy some really expensive carpets: old ones, tens of thousands apiece."

"What else?"

"I want silk draperies in this room."

Dino looked around. He liked the curtains fine, he thought. "Okay."

"I want a new car and a full-time driver. Wait, cancel that: I want a full-time couple, possibly live-in, and I want him to drive me whenever I like."

"Okay. What kind of car do you want?"

"A Bentley Flying Spur," she said.

"Like Stone's?"

"Yes, but silver, with red upholstery."

"You might have to order the car to get what you want," Dino pointed out. "It could take three or four months."

"We'll see about that," she said.

"What else?"

"I want to go to the Armory Antiques Show and buy a lot of expensive accessories for this apartment that will make it look like we've always lived here."

"Okay."

"What do you want, Dino?"

"I thought I'd wait for you to finish and see if there's anything left. I calculate that you've already spent more than a million dollars."

"My list won't be finished for a while," she replied. "I'll let you know as ideas pop up. Come on, what about you?"

"Well, we have a nice library, but I'd like a lot more leather-bound books—sets. I want to design and build a new bar in there, too. A welcoming one."

"Is that it?"

"For now."

"I thought of something else," she said.

"Shoot."

"I want to buy the little penthouse on the floor above us—the super says it's about to go on the market—then turn it into a master suite and install a stairway. And I want a Steinway grand piano in this room."

"That's doable," Dino said. "Maybe this would be a good time for the sex."

"You're on," she said, rising and flinging herself at him.

STONE CALLED DINO.

"Bacchetti."

"Would you two like some dinner?"

"Not tonight," Dino said. "We've started something we haven't finished yet."

"Talk to you tomorrow," Stone said and hung up.

THE FOLLOWING MORNING Stone was in his office when Joan buzzed. "The D.A. for you on one."

Stone picked up the phone. "Good morning, Ken."

"Good morning, Stone. I take it you've returned from your trip."

"I have."

"Where did you go?"

"To Switzerland, on business."

"I guess that's why they haven't found you yet."

"Why who hasn't found me yet?" Stone asked.

"They'll be unconnectable to the Thomas family, but nevertheless . . ."

Stone's stomach turned just a little sour. "And they're looking for me?"

"There's good news and bad news," Burrows said, "and the good news isn't all that great."

"Tell me all of it."

"Well, as you said in your call, Heather Thomas blabbed to her ex-husband."

"Right."

"The good news is, they don't know I have the Tommassini file."

"All right."

"The bad news is, they think you have it."

"Why do they think that?"

"Because that's what Heather told Jack Thomas. Fortunately,

she didn't know that you gave me the file, so Jack thinks you still have it."

"Well, I'll have to ring Jack up and disabuse him of that notion," Stone said, "and pass along your involvement."

"Don't do that, Stone."

"Why not? It's the truth."

"Because it would hinder the progress of justice."

"Oh, so a bullet in your head would hinder justice, but a bullet in mine would be okay?"

"Of course not. I just need time to make a case from what's in the file."

"How much time is that going to take?"

"A few weeks," Burrows said. "Possibly, a few months."

"And you think I can survive that long, with Jack's mob buddies after me?"

"Stone, you have the advantage of multiple homes and your own airplane. You can just disappear."

"You don't think the mob has access to transportation?"

"They won't know where to look," Burrows said.

"So, they'll look everywhere."

"That will take time, and I'll be building our case."

"Swell, I'm happy for you and your little army of ADAs."

"Something else they don't know."

"I'm happy to hear it," Stone said wryly.

"They don't know about the other eleven files."

Stone laughed. "The files on all those dead people?"

"'Those dead people' have progeny—children and grandchildren."

"What, no great-grandchildren? No cousins or nephews?"

69

"Well, now that you mention it . . ."

"What's your head count on the progeny?"

"Thirty," Ken replied. "Well, thirty-odd . . . but not all of them are in the family business. If we're talking made men, thirty's not a bad guess."

"And all of them are looking for me?"

"Well, not all of them. They still have loan collections to enforce, prostitutes to pimp, and legit businesses to subvert. My people's guess is that not more than ten are involved with, ah, speaking to you."

"Ken, you haven't gotten to the part about how you can protect me."

"Times is hard, Stone. I suggest you go private on that—you can afford it."

"Tell me, Ken, how many outstanding warrants do those ten made men have?"

"I'm not sure, but at least a few, I would suppose."

"Well, why don't you start by executing those warrants, and let's see how many we have left on the landscape looking to flame my ass."

"I'll look into that," Burrows said.

"Forgive me, if I can't detect urgency in that statement."

"As I say, times is hard. We'll do what we can." The district attorney hung up.

14

Faith walked into Stone's office and handed him a sheet of paper. "Here's the expense report on the trip to Switzerland."

"Give it to Joan, and tell her it's chargeable to the Bianchi estate."

"Certainly." She started to leave.

"Oh, and get ready for another flight," Stone said.

"Where to?"

"I haven't decided yet. Let me look at the weather."

"Just say when."

"Don't worry."

Joan buzzed. "Dino on one."

"Good morning," Stone said. "How'd she take it?"

"If we're talking money, she took it like a champ. I reckon I'm five million dollars poorer than I was this time yesterday. Oh, and she took the other thing just great, too."

"I didn't ask."

"Anyway, she's taking a couple of weeks off, in order to spread cheer among the New York interior furnishings community."

"What's she buying?"

"Ancient carpets, silk draperies, antiquities, and, oh, the penthouse upstairs. I forgot, I'm supposed to be talking to the super

71

about that right now, so we can steal it before it goes on the market."

"Call me back when you've stolen it." Stone hung up.

Joan came in. "Faith tells me you're off again soon."

"That is correct. Check the weather forecast for Penobscot Bay, will you? And call Charley Fox and ask him where the yacht is and in what stage of readiness it might be."

"Okay." She went back to her desk, where the phone was ringing.

Stone picked up. "Dino?"

"Yep."

"Have you stolen the penthouse yet?"

"Yep. The owner took a quick sale for two and a half million— and no broker's commission. And I have to write Richie a nice check."

"Who's Richie?"

"Our super—and sometime Realtor."

Joan buzzed.

"Hang on a minute," Stone said and pushed a button. "Yes?"

"The highs are in the upper sixties and the lows in the upper forties," Joan said. "And the yacht is done with its winter refit, ready to launch on twenty-four-hours' notice."

"I'll get back to you on that," Stone said, then pressed the Dino line again. "How would you and Viv like to take a nice vacation, say a cruise?"

"Like I said, she's already told Mike Freeman that she's taking at least two weeks off. The architect is due here this afternoon to get started on the new stairway to upstairs and the renovation of the penthouse."

72

"So you're available?"

"Where are we cruising from and to?"

"From Maine, where the temps are in the upper sixties; to wherever you want to go."

"South, I should think."

"You're on. How about day after tomorrow?"

"Let us talk to the architect, and I'll get back to you." Dino hung up.

Stone called Charley Fox, who was his partner, with Mike Freeman, in Triangle Investments, and who kept tabs on the use of the yacht, which the three of them had bought from the estate of the CEO of a company they had bought.

"Hey, Stone."

"Hey, Charley. Can we launch the day after tomorrow and have *Breeze* at my dock the following day—crewed and provisioned for a week, maybe two?"

"Sure. Destination?"

"To be determined."

"Are you running from somebody or are you just a free spirit?"

"A little of both."

"It shall be done."

"Thanks, Charley." Stone hung up and buzzed Joan. "Tell Faith we're flying to Maine the day after tomorrow, and she and I will copilot. Also tell her we'll be gone a week or two, and she can choose to stay at the Dark Harbor house or to sail with us."

"Tell me," Joan said, "is the purpose of this cruise pleasure or self-defense?"

"A little of both; have you noticed something?"

"Well, the same black SUV has circled the block four times in

73

the past fifteen minutes and slowed down at your front door each time."

"Did you get a tag number?"

"I will on the next circuit."

"Good." Stone hung up. He was sweating a little.

DINO CALLED BACK late in the afternoon. "Well," he said, "there's a perfect site for the staircase, and all the penthouse needs is painting and a redo on the bathroom and kitchen."

"Then you're up for a cruise?"

"Viv needs tomorrow to deal with the contractor and think of a few more ways to spend my money."

"Then we'll leave for Maine day after tomorrow, wheels up at two PM."

"You're on."

A minute later, Joan buzzed. "Dino's back, on one."

"What? Did you chicken out?"

"Something tells me I should have," Dino said. "What's going on?"

"I don't know what you mean," Stone said, defensively.

"This is all happening a little too fast," Dino said. "Not that we're not impulsive."

"Well . . ."

"I knew it. Tell me all, so I'll know what armaments to bring."

"A black SUV is circling our block, casing the house."

"Is there something to this, or are you just being paranoid?"

"A little of both."

"I've got a message on my desk from Ken Burrows," Dino said. "Should I call him back?"

"I'd appreciate it if you would. I'd like to know what he has to say."

"I'll get back to you." Dino hung up.

Stone buzzed Joan. "Have you seen my yachting cap?"

"It's in your office closet, perched on the top shelf, raring to go, along with your reefer suit and your mess kit."

"Thank you," he said.

"I got a plate on the SUV." She dictated it while he wrote it down. "And Dino is on one again. What's going on?"

"Never you mind." Stone pressed the button. "Dino, what did Ken have to say?"

"He says you're in imminent danger, and that I should supply you with round-the-clock cops, though not on his budget."

"We got a plate number on the black SUV," Stone said, dictating it. "Run it, will you?"

"Hang." Dino put him on hold. Two minutes of elevator music later, he was back. "The car is owned by Dominic Rentals, in Little Italy," he said. "Do I need to find out who owns the company?"

"I can imagine," Stone said. "Oh, bring a dinner jacket, and tell Viv you're bringing it, so she won't come to dinner in a slicker and Top-Siders. And I wouldn't mind a cop on the door here, day and night, until we have abandoned the premises."

"Done," Dino said and hung up.

15

Jack Thomas, CEO of H. Thomas & Son, picked up his phone in response to a buzz. "Yes?"

"Sir," his secretary said, "the chairman would like to see you—immediately, he says."

The younger Thomas immediately broke into a sweat. "Right," Jack said, and hung up. He grabbed a tissue, dabbed at his face and neck and walked out of his office into the vestibule with the private elevator and pressed the PH button. Moments later, he tapped on his father's office door and received the shout, "Come!"

Jack walked into his father's office suite, with its commanding view of New York Harbor, and found his father seated in his electric wheelchair next to the leather sofa, a bib tied around his neck, eating what he ate for lunch every day of his life: clam chowder and a glass of ale, followed by corned beef and cabbage from McSorley's Old Ale House, on East 7th Street, the oldest pub in the city.

"Sit," the old man said, as if he were a misbehaving dog.

Jack sat. "Good morning, Poppa," he said.

"Boy," his father replied, calling Jack what he always called him, "what's this about a Tommassini file that some lawyer has got hold of."

Jack was astonished that his father knew about this. Then

again, the old man had always had his own private intelligence network at his beck and call. "It's nothing," Jack said. "I'll take care of it."

"Oh? Then why haven't you *already* taken care of it?"

"The lawyer, whose name is Barrington, has been out of the country, in Switzerland, temporarily beyond our reach, but he's back now, and I am looking for opportunities to do this with some delicacy."

"I haven't heard the name Tommassini for more than twenty years, at least not applied to me and my family."

"It shouldn't concern you, Poppa," Jack replied, as if the matter wasn't worth his attention. "It will be dealt with."

"And how do you plan to handle it with 'delicacy,' as you put it?"

"An accident will befall him."

"I always knew that Bianchi was my enemy," Henry snarled.

"Poppa, he was your best friend. He loved you."

"If he loved me, why did he take notes on my life—and yours—and leave a file where others would find it after his death?"

"I don't understand it," Jack replied.

"*I* understand it," Henry replied. "He was always drunk with power, had his hands on every lever. He wanted power over me even after he had gone to hell. He loved himself more than anyone, even his children. You know who he loved? His son-in-law, that *policeman*. He left a lot of money in a Swiss account, and all of it went to that sonofabitch and his son."

Again, Jack was amazed and not a little appalled at what his father knew. "It's not so much," he replied. "His greedy wife is already spending it."

"So how will you handle this? A falling piano in the street?"

77

"Please don't worry, Poppa. It will be done soon and no one will suspect us."

"Boy," the old man said, "if that file is published, *everyone* will suspect us of *everything*. Don't you understand that? Sixty years of the most careful planning will be for naught. We will become pariahs. You will go to prison, and your son will never become president or even reelected to Congress. The presidency would be the crowning achievement of my plan. Can you imagine the power that would come to our family with that?"

"The family is doing very well," Jack replied, hastily adding, "with your brains and leadership."

"All of that will become dust, if the file becomes public."

"Only Barrington has it or even knows of it."

"You blithering idiot!" Henry shouted. "Don't you even know that the district attorney already has his hands on it?"

Jack did not know that, and he was shocked into silence.

"There are so many ways to bring pressure on him," Jack said, finally. "He would be destroyed. In fact, if someone must know of the file, he is the best possible person because we can control him."

"Now that is the first sensible thing you've said," Henry spat.

"And he has the only copy," Jack added.

"Why on earth do you think that? Is this Stone Barrington a complete fool?"

"Don't worry, I don't underestimate him."

"Unless he is a fool he will have made copies of that file—and the other files—and plans to distribute it, if an 'accident' should befall him."

"'Other files'? What others?" Jack asked, his voice trembling.

"All the old members of the ruling council and their families. This thing of ours would never recover!"

"That's impossible, Poppa—not after all the work you've done to make our power disappear."

"How many soldiers do you have on this?" Henry demanded.

"A dozen—top men, all of them, and with no Italian names."

"It's not enough," Henry said, seeming to grow tired. "Double it. Find Barrington wherever he is and cause him to disappear without a trace."

"I'm hard at work on it," Jack replied.

His father sagged. "I know where he is. Do you?"

"Tell me, Poppa, and he will disappear."

"In two days he will be on a beach somewhere, and that *policeman* will be with him. See that they don't return." He waved a hand dismissively. "Leave me."

Jack rose and bent to kiss his father on the cheek, but the old man turned his head in disgust. Jack got out of the office and leaned on the wall of the vestibule and took deep breaths while he waited for the elevator.

He was not a fearful man, but he was afraid of his father, and never so much as at this moment.

THE BLACK SUV, its windows darkened, parked on the street a few doors up from the Barrington residence. A young man named Terrence Pelham, *né* Tito Profini, sat at the wheel. He was startled to hear a sharp rap on the driver's-side window, which was so dark he could only see the form of a man. He pressed the button and lowered the window six inches. A uniformed policeman stood there.

"Open up! All of it!" the man shouted.

Pelham lowered the window to the sill. "Yes, Officer? How can I help you?"

"License, registration, and proof of insurance," the cop said.

"It's a rental, officer," Pelham replied, finding the document and handing it to him.

"Do you have a driver's license?" the cop demanded.

"Yes, of course."

"Then hand it to me."

Pelham got out his wallet and handed him the license. To his alarm, the officer swiped it over something in his hand, like a notebook.

"You're lucky it's genuine and that you have no outstanding warrants," the cop said, pressing a button on the device and printing out a sliver of paper. "Here's a ticket for parking in a tow zone. See that it's paid promptly." He turned on his heel and walked away.

This couldn't get back to his capo, he thought. He would pay it today. He got the SUV in gear and drove away, shaking.

16

The night before their departure for Maine, Stone rang Edith Beresford, whom he had been seeing once in a while.

"Well, hi there," she said warmly. "Are you back from Switzerland?"

"I am," he replied, "and about to depart again. I want you to come with me."

"What sort of clothes?"

"The sort of things you'd wear on a yacht in the Caribbean," he replied. "We'll be dressing for dinner."

"When do we leave?"

"You'll be picked up at noon tomorrow."

"How long will we be gone?"

"Perhaps as much as a couple of weeks. And you can't tell a soul you're traveling with me or where we're going."

"The last part is easy, since I don't know where we're going."

"You're very perceptive."

"I'm in. I'll be ready tomorrow at noon, my bags with the doorman."

"See you then." He hung up, relieved.

. . .

IT WAS NOT the first time Stone had needed to disappear for a while, and he outlined in his head the barriers he had to erect between himself and his seekers.

The airplane would be hangared in Rockland, the nearest airport to Islesboro that could accommodate the jet, safe even from prying satellites. No mail would be forwarded to him. Joan would tell anyone who called that he was sailing in the Caribbean, and then take a message. Fred would garage the Bentley and not take it out. The staff would be told not to mention his departure.

Joan came into the office with two small boxes. "All right," she said, "I've done as I was told." She handed him the latest iPhone. "This is registered in the name of Matilda Stone," she said, "and mine is in the name of Harry Flicker, Fred's father's name. Your e-mail address is matilda@stone.com, and mine is harry@flicker.com."

Stone turned on the phone to be sure it was working. "We will not communicate, except on these phones," he said. "You can forward e-mail, even documents, to me, and I can print them on the yacht, if necessary. We will not use each other's names during conversations: I will be Matilda and you, Harry. Understood?"

"Understood," Joan replied.

"None of us will be seen outside the house in Dark Harbor. We will board the yacht after dark. The Wi-Fi system aboard is new, we won't use the old one."

"You'll get to use your new airplane, won't you?" Joan asked.

Stone had weeks before bought a new Cessna 182, which was hangared at Rockland Airport, for the purpose of ferrying him and his guests to and from the island of Islesboro, where the runway was only 2,450 feet long, much too short for the jet. The aircraft was registered to Triangle Investments, as was the yacht.

At two o'clock sharp Stone eased back on the yoke, and the Citation Latitude rose into the air. He had filed a flight plan for Fort Lauderdale Executive where an outgoing international aircraft could refuel and clear out with customs, and a continuing flight plan to St. Martin, in the Caribbean, near St. Barts. As soon as they had climbed to 10,000 feet, Stone called Air Traffic Control. "New York Departure, November One, Two, Three, Tango Foxtrot.

"One, Two, Three TF, New York Departure."

"I would like to change my destination to Rockland, Maine, and my final altitude to flight level 190."

"What is the reason for your destination change?"

"The climate. It's too hot in St. Barts."

"Destination approved. Turn left, direct Carmel VOR, then direct Rockland. Climb to flight level 190."

Stone made the turn and the altitude change. Anyone checking online for his tail number would find the flight plans to Fort Lauderdale and St. Martin. He had long ago removed his tail number from FlightAware and other websites that allowed tracking of general aviation aircraft.

They set down a little more than an hour later at Rockland, and taxied immediately to the large hangar, where a lineman was waiting with a tractor to tow the airplane inside. Once sheltered from prying eyes, they unloaded their luggage and reloaded it into the Cessna 182. The airplane was noted for being able to carry anything that could be squeezed into it, and Stone had ordered only half fuel, so that their weight would be even lighter. His guests and copilot were sitting with their lighter luggage in their laps.

Fifteen minutes later they set down on Islesboro, where Seth Hotchkiss, Stone's caretaker, was waiting with the 1938 Woodie Ford station wagon, towing a small trailer, which took their luggage.

At Stone's house, they unloaded in the garage.

"What time are we boarding?" Dino asked.

"Just after sunset."

"Sounds good. Is Faith coming with us?"

"No, she decided she'd rather enjoy some solitude."

"So it's just the four of us?"

"That's right."

THEY HAD A SNACK at five o'clock, then relaxed around the house until after sunset. When it was fully dark they walked down to the dock. Seth had already taken their luggage down and placed it aboard the tender.

They boarded, then drove slowly through the moored yachts in the harbor and well out from shore, where the yacht awaited them with only minimal lights showing. They boarded, the tender was winched onto the upper deck, then they were under way.

Dinner had already been prepared in anticipation of their arrival, and they sat down to a fine meal.

"Now do we get to know where we're going?" Viv asked.

"You'll wake up tomorrow morning in Nantucket," Stone said.

"Why Nantucket?"

"Because it's not in Maine, where we might be expected to be, and the Nantucket Harbor will be filled with yachts, making us harder to spot from the air."

"Who would expect us to be in Maine?" Edie asked.

"I'm something of a fugitive from justice," Stone said. "Well, not legal justice—something more primitive."

"You're giving me chills," she said.

He leaned over and whispered into her ear. "I'll warm you up later. I promise."

"Oh, good," she replied.

17

Jack Thomas sat in his office and regarded the sleek young man across his desk. "Tell me," he said.

"Godfather . . ."

"Don't address me in that manner. Do you think you're in a movie?"

"Sir . . ."

"That's better."

"Sir, we checked the FAA website for a flight plan for an aircraft with the tail number N123TF, which is known to be flown by Stone Barrington. The aircraft filed two flight plans yesterday for Fort Lauderdale, Florida, which is an entry airport where he could refuel and check out with customs for his second flight plan, to St. Martin, which is a convenient airport for a short flight to St. Barts in a smaller aircraft."

"So he has a yacht in the Caribbean?" Jack asked.

"No, sir. Approximately ten minutes out of Teterboro the aircraft contacted New York Departure and requested a change of destination to Rockland, Maine. The request was granted."

"Ah, so now we come to the yacht?"

"Sir, the only yacht registered in the name of Stone Barrington anywhere in the United States is a small sailing vessel called a

Concordia, with an address in Dark Harbor, Maine. We checked, and that boat is being prepared for the season in a boatyard in that village. Our man saw it up on blocks in a shed, being varnished, perhaps a week or two away from launching."

"No, if he's hiding, it would be on something larger, more comfortable. You've already told me that Dino Bacchetti is out of his office, so they're likely together."

"We've also run a check on every Maine-registered yacht chartered for this period. It's early in the season, so there isn't much out there, making him easier to spot if he's cruising."

"Have you checked Maine-registered yachts owned by corporate entities instead of individuals?"

"That's being done at the moment, sir."

"Have you checked corporate entities that Barrington is associated with as an owner or board member?"

"That is being done as well, sir."

"When do you expect to have results?"

"Very soon, sir."

"What is your plan for when you find it?"

"A gas explosion is always good for destroying yachts and the associated evidence. We'll start there."

The young man's phone rang. "Excuse me for a moment, sir," he said, picking up his phone. "That could be news. Rance here," he said. Then he listened carefully. "Have you checked that against the registry?" He listened again. "Get back to me soonest." He hung up. "Sir, there are nine corporate entities that Barrington is associated with—most of them clients. There is something called Triangle Investments, too, and we're looking into what that is."

"Good."

Rance's phone rang again. "Yes?" He listened. "I want a search of Maine waters immediately." He listened yet again. "Get back to me." He hung up. "We got lucky, sir. Barrington is a partner in Triangle, and there is a large yacht registered to the company. The yacht's name is *Breeze,* and she's being prepared for the season at a boatyard in Camden. We'll have eyes on it soon."

"Now we're making progress," Jack said.

A SHAFT of early sunlight woke Stone in his cabin. He went to a porthole and drew back the curtain. There were hulls and masts as far as he could see. The brass clock on the bulkhead read 6:40 AM.

Edie sat up on an elbow, the sheet falling away to reveal a breast. "Is it time to do it again?" she asked sleepily.

Stone sat on the bed and kissed her. "Let's hold something in reserve, shall we?" he said. "We've got all the time in the world. Breakfast on deck?"

"Give me a few minutes," she said.

They showered together, then Stone shaved and dressed. A few minutes later they were on the fantail, ordering from a stewardess.

The captain, Todd, appeared and unrolled a sheet of plastic, holding it up for Stone to see. "Will this do?"

Stone read the banner: *Fantasia.* "Sure," he replied.

"We'll apply it over *Breeze* on the stern," Todd said. "Have it on in half an hour. We'll change the hailing port to Camden."

"That should give us some cover," Stone said.

A moment later Dino and Viv joined them and placed their breakfast order.

"What's going on astern?" Dino asked.

"We're changing the yacht's name to *Fantasia* and the hailing port to Camden."

"You're being really careful, aren't you?"

"I've also asked the crew not to seek provisions or fuel until we've moved to another port."

"Is someone really looking for us?" Edie asked.

"I'm afraid so."

"Why? Didn't you pay your taxes?"

"Nothing like that. It's more personal. It's better if you don't know any more."

"Are we in any danger?"

"We are not. That's why we're taking these precautions."

JACK THOMAS ARRIVED at his office at noon from a meeting to find Rance waiting for him. "What's up?" he asked.

"I have some photographs to show you."

Jack waved him to the conference table. "Tell me."

"First of all, we checked the Camden yard and *Breeze* was launched the day before yesterday but has not been seen since. We broadened our search to the whole Northeast, and early this morning we got some satellite shots of Nantucket Harbor, where there are many yachts moored."

"How could you spot her among so many?" Jack asked.

"By her size. *Breeze* has an overall length of 125 feet, and there were smaller and larger yachts moored there, but only two of that length." He unrolled a photograph with an eagle-eye perspective. "Here's one of them. Look, you can read the yacht's name on the stern."

"It says *Fantasia*," Jack pointed out.

"Yes, but we got a side view from a helicopter a while later." He pulled out another photograph that showed the yacht in profile. "Look at the tender on the top deck," he said, handing Jack a small magnifying glass.

"Ahhh," Jack replied. "*Tender to Breeze*, it says."

"Now, why would *Fantasia* have a tender aboard connected with *Breeze*? Did the boatyard put the tender aboard the wrong yacht?"

"I think not," Jack replied. "Now that you have her, get to work."

"Not just yet," Rance said.

"Why not?"

"Because she weighed anchor early this morning and left the harbor. Our satellite was out of position at that time, and the chopper had landed. We also checked with the provisioners ashore, and she bought nothing, not even fuel. She's gone, and we have to start a new search. And we don't know what course she took."

"What sort of range does that yacht have?"

"At normal cruising speed, about two thousand miles. But if she's running faster, a lot less—maybe as little as four hundred miles."

"She'll be moving fast," Jack said. "Search the Cape and Martha's Vineyard."

"Under way," Rance said.

18

By midmorning *Fantasia* was sailing down Buzzard's Bay, and soon she turned into Narragansett Bay, Rhode Island, and slowed as she approached Newport, which was, if anything, even more crowded than Nantucket. They motored past the French château–style mansion that is the Newport station of the New York Yacht Club, of which Stone was a member.

"Why don't we moor at the club?" Dino asked. "There's room, and you said we're having dinner there."

"We want a more crowded area," Stone replied, "so we're putting into Bannisters Wharf Marina, where we'll blend in."

Shortly they were docked, and the crew began another name change, to *Expensive.* Captain Todd came to Stone. "I'm afraid we made a slipup last evening," he said.

"How's that?"

"We neglected to change the name on the tenders. That's being taken care of now."

LATER IN THE DAY, Rance walked into Jack Thomas's office. "I'm afraid we've come up dry on Cape Cod," he said. "I think we should work our way south toward New York, port by port."

"That's going to be time consuming, isn't it?" Jack asked.

"I'm afraid so, since we have to wait for the satellite to move into position. We're having a look at Newport, Rhode Island, right now, and there's nothing the size of *Breeze* at anchor. We had thought that Barrington might pick up a mooring at the New York Yacht Club, where there is space available for a large yacht, but she's not there. We're searching the marinas now."

"If she's in a marina, we'll have to wait for her to leave," Jack said. "I don't want an explosion in downtown Newport, where there are hundreds, if not thousands, of tourists wandering around, buying T-shirts, and gaping at the yachts."

"I'm aware, sir. We're putting people out on foot now to canvass the big marinas."

"Don't forget Goat Island," Jack said.

"We won't, sir."

AT DUSK the two couples were ferried to the yacht club by the tender, and they slowly climbed the long flight of stairs to the house, set on a hilltop.

Stone took them into the library for a drink and to catch their breath.

"It's a beautiful house," Edie said. "Was it built as a club?"

"No, it was the home of John Nicholas Brown II, a scion of the famous Newport family—Brown University, etc.—and a former commodore of the yacht club. After his death, it was put up for sale, and a consortium of club members bought it. Then the club raised the money to buy it from them and renovated it for club use."

They moved into the club's dining room for dinner. The room was quite full. Stone spotted a few familiar faces but didn't approach anyone.

• • •

JACK THOMAS SAT in his library in his downtown house, sipping cognac and reading the *Wall Street Journal*, when Rance called.

"Yes, Rance?"

"We've searched the marinas, and there are half a dozen candidates, but no *Fantasia* and no *Breeze*. Tomorrow morning we'll move on to Block Island, and after that to Long Island and the Hamptons."

"Suppose they've gone north to Nova Scotia?" Jack asked.

"Very unlikely, sir. They're much more likely to move toward warmer weather, perhaps all the way to Florida, or even to St. Barts."

"It's not inconceivable that they could be hiding in Penobscot Bay, while we look south," Jack said.

"I'm afraid you're right, sir. The only way we could have been sure would have been to follow her by boat from her launching, but of course, when she was launched at Camden we hadn't yet begun our search."

"Call me when you've had a look at Block Island," Jack said.

WHEN THEY RETURNED to *Expensive* late in the evening, their lines were taken by two crew members who were unknown to Stone, but they were wearing blue jackets with the name *Expensive* embroidered on them. One of them introduced himself to Stone.

"I'm Hal, Mr. Barrington. Mike Freeman sent us, sir, at your request. We'll be aboard for as long as you need us, and we've brought sufficient firepower to defend the yacht, should it become necessary."

"Thank you, Hal," Stone replied. "I'm sure we'll all feel safer with you aboard. How long have you been here?"

"Long enough to spot a man and a woman checking out all the large yachts in the marina. They took no particular notice of this one, except to view her stern for name and hailing port."

"Then perhaps they've overlooked us," Stone said.

"I think that's a real possibility, sir."

"Perhaps we'll stay a day or two in Newport, then," Stone said.

"I think it would be a good idea to stay indoors or under canvas, Mr. Barrington. I have no doubt they have satellite surveillance at their disposal. If you go ashore, wear hats."

"I'll let everyone know, Hal."

Stone gathered everyone in the saloon for a nightcap and gave them the good news. "It looks as though we can stop running for a while," he said.

"You think they'll expect us to keep running, then?" Dino asked.

"I believe so. I'm not sure they would think we would hide in plain sight in such a busy place as Newport. We'll take our meals aboard, though. I wouldn't want to get spotted in a restaurant by some waiter in their employ."

THE FOLLOWING AFTERNOON Rance appeared at Jack Thomas's office.

"You look like bad news," Jack said.

"I'm afraid there's no good news, sir," Rance replied. "We've searched Block Island by satellite and on foot, and we've got people on the lookout in Montauk and the Hamptons. We'll get a call, if the yacht turns up."

"But you think we've lost them?"

"I believe we have," Rance replied. "They could have left the yacht anywhere along the way and gone to a hotel, or even back to New York."

"Then maybe you'd better pull in your people after another day or so and concentrate on the Barrington and Bacchetti residences. They have to come home sometime."

"Yes, sir. I'll do that."

Jack finished his brandy, dreading his report to his father the next day.

19

They spent a leisurely day aboard: had a good lunch, a nap, and Stone caught up on his reading—Sidney Blumenthal's *A Self-Made Man*, about the political life of Abraham Lincoln. He and Dino had a conversation about what to do next, and made a decision.

Stone called Faith at Dark Harbor. "How's your vacation going?"

"Very well, thank you. Seth and his wife, Mary, are taking good care of me."

"Well, it's about over," he said. "Find another pilot and move the airplane to New Bedford, Massachusetts, tomorrow. We'll meet you there and fly back to New York."

"I've got someone standing by," she said. "We can be in New Bedford by noon."

"See you then." They hung up.

THE FOLLOWING MORNING, Stone and his friends said goodbye to the crew, and Stone gave the captain instructions to leave Newport, then change the yacht's name back to the original. Stone's group traveled to New Bedford, a half-hour drive, in two taxis with one guard in each. The Latitude was waiting on the ramp for them, and they and the guards boarded for the short flight to Teterboro.

THEY WERE MET in Teterboro by Dino's car, as Stone didn't want the Bentley moved from the garage. "Can you ask for a drive-by at my house and make sure no one is lurking?" he asked Dino.

"Just another personal service by your friendly police department," Dino replied. They dropped Edie off at her apartment. Then, shortly before their arrival in Turtle Bay, Dino got a call. "Good," he said, then hung up. "There was a silver SUV parked across the street from your house," he said. "My guys gave them a ticket and shooed them off."

"Good," Stone replied. "Please ask your driver to pull into my garage, and I'll unload there."

Stone used his remote control to open the garage door. He was dropped off and Dino's car continued.

"I'm surprised to see you back so soon," Joan said. "We've had a squatter outside since you left, but the police scared them off a few minutes ago."

"Yes, and I'm going to lie low for a few days more," Stone said, settling into his chair to confront the mail and messages. There was one from the district attorney, and he returned the call.

"Good afternoon, Stone," Ken Burrows said.

"Afternoon, Ken."

"I thought I'd bring you up to date."

"I'd appreciate that."

"A couple of my staffers have reported having been drawn into conversations by various people regarding your files."

"Please, Ken, they're not my files, they're Eduardo's."

"Of course, but you are the only living person to whom they have been connected, outside the Thomases."

"You're forgetting about yourself, aren't you?"

"I'm not a person, I'm an institution."

"One that someone has attempted to penetrate."

"Don't worry, the files are safe, and they continue to be worked on by a select group of my staff. A young man named Rance Damien, a grandson of one of the subjects of a file, has been seen entering Jack Thomas's office a couple of times."

"Do you think he's leading the effort to lay hands on me?"

"That's our supposition at this point. I won't ask where you are at the moment, but you should continue to move about with caution."

"I've been doing just that," Stone said.

"Something else," Burrows said. "My father had lunch today with old Henry Thomas at his downtown office and, over corned beef and cabbage, received a veiled threat to my person, which he took as a joke. He's reported to me that Henry is in a sour mood and that his staff are tiptoeing around him."

"I'm glad his mood is soured," Stone said, "but what I need from you is some sort of move against the Thomases that would make it inadvisable for them to continue making me the subject of their unwanted attention."

"What do you have in mind?"

"How's your current relationship with the FBI?" Stone asked.

"They have a new agent in charge, and he's anxious to make a good impression."

"Can you get him to send a couple of special agents around to visit the Thomases and ask some leading questions? That might draw their attention away from me. I mean, a car containing two of their thugs has been parked outside my house for days."

"That's not a good thing," Burrows said. "But a visit from the FBI might be, along with an oblique mention of your name. Maybe that'll get them off your back. I'll see what I can do."

"I'd be grateful. That might save me a visit to the trauma center."

"I'll do whatever I can," Burrows said.

"I'd like to know what that is," Stone said. "Get back to me."

"I'll do that." They hung up.

JACK THOMAS PRESENTED himself at his father's office late that afternoon.

The old man waved him to a chair. "I hear you've had a visit from the federal authorities," Henry said.

How the hell did he know *everything*? Jack wondered. "Nothing to worry about, Poppa."

"I understand Barrington's name came up. I'm not surprised, after your failure to get to the man."

"It was mentioned."

"Pull your people off him for the time being. If something happens to Barrington now, we'd be high on their list of suspects."

"Yes, Poppa."

"Tell me, how could you not find a 125-foot yacht in an area as small as New England? Did somebody shoot down the satellite?"

"Finding it is not as easy as it sounds," Jack replied. "We do know, however, that it's back on its mooring in Dark Harbor, after having been missing for the better part of a week."

"Then Barrington is probably home again."

"The police ticketed the car we had watching his house this morning, so that's probably so."

"What I'd really like," Henry said, "is to bring his house down around his ears."

"I understand."

"I'm going to have to give the problem my personal attention," the old man said.

"Whatever you decide, Poppa."

20

The following day, Joan buzzed Stone. "Bill Eggers on one," she said. Eggers was a law-school friend, who had rescued Stone when he was booted from the NYPD and had given him a chance to use his law degree. Eggers was now the managing partner of Woodman & Weld, where Stone was a partner.

"Good morning, Bill," Stone said.

"And to you, Stone. How was your time off?"

"Very good. We just took a brief sail from Dark Harbor to Nantucket, then Newport. I got back yesterday."

"Dino, too?"

"And Viv and Edie."

"I can never understand how Dino gets so much time off," Eggers said.

"I can't understand it, either," Stone replied, "but I'm afraid to ask."

"I had an interesting phone call this morning."

"Anybody I know?"

"Someone who knows you, at the very least."

"Who might that be?"

"Jack Thomas, of H. Thomas & Son."

"What the hell did *he* want?"

"He said he's thinking of expanding his firm's legal footprint, and guess what? Your name came up."

"In vain?"

"Not in the least. He said he'd heard good things," Eggers said.

"From whom?"

"He didn't say."

"What did you tell him, Bill?"

"I made an appointment with him for this afternoon at three, in my office."

"I thought people like the Thomases got a nosebleed if they travel north of Wall Street."

"He said he had to be in the neighborhood anyway, so he'd drop by."

"Well, let me know what he has to say."

"Oh, he specifically asked that you join our meeting. I got the impression he wants to get a sniff at your backside."

Stone laughed. "To tell you the truth, I think he'd rather I got a knife between my shoulder blades."

"I didn't know you knew Jack. Do you two have a history?"

"Yes, but a very brief one. I think I'd better turn up half an hour early and brief you on that. It might have a bearing on whether you want to represent his firm."

"You mean there's some doubt as to whether we should take his business?"

"You can tell me that after we talk."

"Talk now."

"Not on the phone."

"All right. Then, join me for lunch at the Grill," Eggers said. The Grill had formerly been the Grill Room at the Four Seasons, before their lease had ended and the landlord had given them the boot. "Is one o'clock all right?"

"Since you're buying, you get to choose," Stone said. "See you at one."

THE ROOM HADN'T changed much since the new restaurant opened in the Seagram Building, which was where Woodman & Weld had its offices, but the New York Preservation Society was responsible for that. Eggers was already seated at what had always been his table, on the upper level, where he could gaze down on lesser mortals. He waved Stone over. "Martini?"

"I gave them up for bourbon years ago," Stone replied.

"Knob Creek, then?"

"Since we're meeting a Thomas, I think I'd better keep my wits about me."

They read the menu and both ordered the Dover sole, which had recently slept in the English Channel.

"All right," Eggers said, "let's hear it. And it had better be good. They're offering us a half-million-dollar annual retainer, and that could translate into multimillion-dollar business."

"Bill," Stone said, "I'm sorry to have to tell you this, but Henry Thomas and his son, Jack, and his grandson, Hank, are not who they seem to be."

"Horseshit," Eggers said mildly. "Henry has been a Wall Street fixture since before you and I were born."

"And a fixture elsewhere before that," Stone replied.

"'Elsewhere'? What are you talking about?"

"I'd better begin at the beginning," Stone said, then told him about the Excelsior safe and the files.

"'Tommassini'? That was the family name?"

"Yes."

"Lots of immigrant families anglicize their names," Eggers pointed out.

"You need to know the Tommassini history," Stone said, then laid it all out for him.

"That's the most fantastic thing I've ever heard," Eggers said. "And if you go around telling people that, you'd better be ready for a monumental defamation suit."

"I don't think that's going to happen. The Thomases think I'm the only man alive who has that information."

"What did you do with the files?" Eggers asked. "I'd like to see them for myself."

"I turned them over to the D.A., like a good citizen," Stone said.

"Then why do the Thomases think you have them?"

Stone told him about Mary Ann Bacchetti's conversation with Heather Thomas, and Heather's conversation with her ex-husband, Jack.

"Swell," Eggers said. "I never knew Mary Ann was such a blabbermouth."

"She wasn't when her father was still alive, but now . . ."

"Has she gone completely nuts?"

"I've been dealing with her on Eduardo's estate for a year and a half, now, and she always seemed perfectly sane, even sensible, to me. Dino, however, blew his stack when I told him I'd told her about the files. He predicted her subsequent behavior and Heather's, too."

"So what is this meeting with Jack Thomas about?"

"I think he's going to offer you some business in order to get leverage over me, to keep my mouth shut."

"If the Thomases are really the Tommassinis, why haven't they blown your head off?"

"I think they've given serious consideration to doing just that," Stone replied. "I've been running from them for the past few days, and every day I was gone there was a suspicious car parked near my house."

"What have you pulled me into, Stone?"

"Jack didn't call me, he called you."

"So, he thinks that by buying off Woodman & Weld, he can pressure me into keeping my foot on your neck?"

"I hope not literally, but that's about the size of it," Stone replied. "And once they've wormed their way into Woodman & Weld, there'll be no stopping them."

Eggers mopped his brow. "Holy shit," he said. "I've never dealt with people like this. We've always avoided them."

"Want some advice?"

"Sure."

"Go on avoiding them," Stone said.

21

Jack Thomas sat and surveyed Bill Eggers's office—the mahogany paneling, the cheerful fireplace, the sweeping views of Manhattan from the top of one of the city's most beautiful skyscrapers. Clearly, he was impressed.

"Coffee? Tea?" Eggers asked Jack from an opposite leather chair before the fire.

"Neither," Thomas said. There was a cut in his voice that disappeared when he said, "Handsome offices."

"Thank you," Eggers said. "I'll tell my former wife you said so." Eggers had two or three former wives, and their care and feeding had cut deeply into his assets for a while. "How can we help you, Mr. Thomas?"

"It's Jack, please."

"And we're Bill and Stone."

"So be it. To cut to the chase, we're beginning to build a new division of H. Thomas, though it won't be identified with the house."

Eggers avoided a frown. "What sort of division?" he asked.

"High-earning lending," Thomas replied.

"How 'high-earning'?"

"Loans with interest rates of twenty percent or more."

"More than twenty percent?" Stone asked. "That kind of lending has a name."

"And what name is that?" Thomas asked sharply, as if daring him to identify it.

Stone identified it. "Loan sharking," he replied.

"These days it's more respectable," Thomas said. "Pink-slip or payday lending."

"But not much more respectable," Stone said.

"It will be in the way we do it."

"And how will you do it?" Eggers asked.

"Our offices won't be in strip malls, and they'll look more like banks than loan companies. We'll even offer some banking services: savings accounts, auto and remodeling loans."

"Low risk?" Eggers asked.

"You might call them that."

"How many people will this new division employ?" Stone asked.

"About four thousand in the first year of operation," Thomas replied.

"How many of those will work at collection?" Stone asked.

"To be determined by necessity," Thomas replied.

"What will your hiring standards be for collection officers?" Stone asked.

"Women will staff the telephones for the first three calls. Men will knock on doors when personal contact becomes necessary."

"What sort of height and weight parameters will you specify for those *personal* collectors?" Stone asked.

"I'm not sure what you mean," Thomas replied.

"I mean, will they be of the gorilla class of collectors?"

"Let us merely say they will be persuasive," Thomas replied.

"In our telephone conversation," Eggers said, "you professed a particular interest in Stone's participation. In what capacity do you see him?"

"We had thought as president," Thomas replied.

"And who would be your chairman?"

"A young man of great promise, called Rance Damien."

Eggers made a note on the legal pad in his lap. "How is Mr. Damien currently employed?"

"He is a consultant for our firm."

"What is his area of consultancy?"

"Security."

"And Stone," Eggers asked, "would he actually work in an executive capacity, or would he just be the public face of the company?"

"Up to him," Thomas replied. "As for fees, we anticipate a half-million-dollar annual retainer, against your usual fees."

"Yes, you mentioned that on the phone," Eggers said. "Do you anticipate an initial public offering at some point in the future?"

"No, the company will be privately held by multiple investors," Thomas replied. "There would be an opportunity for your firm to participate, and Stone could, as well, on a favorable basis."

"So there would be no visible connection between the company and H. Thomas, if, say, an investigative reporter took an interest?"

"None whatever. I'm sure Stone could suggest a corporate ownership structure that would keep investors' names out of the media. Perhaps the company could be based in the islands?"

Stone managed a small smile.

"What sort of compensation do you anticipate for Stone's participation as president?" Eggers asked.

"A salary of two million dollars a year, with the usual CEO perquisites," Thomas said. "As a start."

"And how much of Stone's time would be required in management?"

"He would certainly have an office at headquarters, but I expect that most of his advice could be given to Rance Damien on the phone or in personal out-of-office meetings."

"Would Stone's name appear on letterheads and other corporate documents?"

"Of course. We can't have a secret president, can we?"

"So," Stone said. "Rance Damien would be the actual CEO, with me as a figurehead?"

"Precisely," Thomas replied. "We reckon that your personal reputation would lend authenticity to our operations."

"And what executive would be in charge of collections?" Stone asked.

"Rance will appoint a head of collections and security."

"So, your collections officers would also be security officers, which would allow them to carry arms?"

Thomas regarded his manicure. "That's a very good suggestion, Stone," he said. "I wish I'd thought of it."

"I'm sure."

"After all, collections can sometimes have an element of risk."

"Yes," Stone said, "but mostly for the debtors, I imagine."

"Those who pay on time will have no worries," Thomas replied.

"Well," Eggers said. "Thank you for coming in, Mr. Thomas. Is there anything else you wish to talk about?"

"Not today," Thomas said, rising.

"Then I will discuss this with my board of partners and give you an early answer."

The three men stood, shook hands perfunctorily, and Eggers escorted Jack Thomas to the door. Then he came back, sat at his desk, and rang for his secretary. "Come in, please, and bring your steno pad."

The woman appeared almost instantly and sat down across his desk.

"Take a letter, please: to Mr. Jack Thomas, CEO, H. Thomas & Son, fill in the address," Eggers said.

Dear Mr. Thomas,

Thank you for taking the time to visit our offices today, for your request for legal representation by Woodman & Weld for your new "lending" company, and, specifically, for the managerial participation of our partner, Stone Barrington.

Upon due consideration of our board of partners, we must decline to represent, in any manner, such a slimy business enterprise as you described to Mr. Barrington and me in our meeting. Furthermore, Mr. Barrington has informed our board that, as he so gracefully put it, "I wouldn't touch it with a barge pole."

If you have any further requests of this firm, very kindly go fuck yourself.

Yours most sincerely,
William Eggers
Managing Partner

Eggers turned toward Stone. "Can you think of anything else I should tell him?"

"I think you've touched all the bases, Bill," Stone replied.

"Then type that up on the firm letterhead for my signature," he said to his secretary. "And send it to him by registered mail, for his signature only."

22

Stone and Dino met at P. J. Clarke's and went straight in to dinner. After their drinks had arrived, Stone said, "Well, the Thomases have made their next move."

Dino's eyebrows shot up. "Did they take a swing at you?"

"Yes, but it was more like shadowboxing. Still, it was all aimed at my head."

"Tell me about it."

"Jack Thomas came up to Bill Eggers's office and outlined a new payday loan operation they're planning to start, one that will be made to look unconnected to H. Thomas & Son. I was at the meeting."

"You mean those pink-slip loans at huge interest rates?"

"Exactly."

"Why the hell would he go to Bill Eggers?"

"Ostensibly, for legal representation, but he wanted me to be president of the company."

"Ah," Dino said. "I begin to see the light. He wants to buy your ass and shut you up."

"I couldn't have put it more gracefully," Stone said.

"What did Eggers tell him?"

"He told him he'd bring up the matter with the board of partners and then give him an answer." Stone handed Dino a copy of Eggers's letter. "Then, without leaving his office for consultations, he dictated this letter to Jack Thomas."

Dino read the letter and let out a hoot. "This is wonderful! I'll bet you that no lawyer has ever written a letter like that to a prospective client!"

"Probably not," Stone replied.

"Did he mention actual money?"

"Half a million annual retainer for the firm. Two million a year salary for me, but I'd report to somebody named Rance Damien."

"Who dat?"

"I was hoping you could tell me."

"You want me to run the name."

"You're a regular clairvoyant," Stone said.

Dino got out his cell phone and tapped out an e-mail. "There you go."

"How long will it take?"

"A few minutes."

"Let's see what Google has to say about him." Stone went to his iPhone and typed in the name. "Nada," he said. "Absolutely nothing. How does somebody avoid Google?"

"By never getting his name in the papers, running a company, or getting written about," Dino replied. His phone made a noise. "And look at this," he said, "the guy's clean. We have absolutely nothing on him."

"I looked through Eduardo's files this afternoon, after our meeting. The only similar name I came up with was D'Amato. He had a son called Renato, who would be an old man by now."

"Well, the initials match, just like those of the Thomases."

113

"Dino, how do you keep tabs on somebody nobody's ever heard of?"

"With great difficulty, unless we can somehow lay eyeballs on him, then track him to his roost. You have any idea what he does for a living?"

"Jack Thomas says he's a security consultant to H. Thomas."

"Well, he probably wouldn't rate a mention in their annual report. Why don't you ask Mike Freeman at Strategic Services if he knows of anybody in the business by that name?"

"Good idea. I'll call him tomorrow."

"I'll ask Viv, too, when she calls in."

"Where is she?"

"Hong Kong. The good news is, when she gets back, she'll be too jet-lagged to spend any more money."

"How's that going?"

"Well, there's a great big hole in our living room ceiling, meant to accommodate a spiral staircase," he replied. "Someday."

"It's like that, is it?"

"You know something about the renovating arts, don't you?"

"I do."

"Well, it seems to be moving very quickly. The architect has drawn plans redividing the penthouse space so that we'll each have a bathroom and a dressing room."

"That may be the secret to a happy marriage," Stone said.

"We'll see. Right now we've got a thick layer of builder's dust in our whole apartment. We've had to bring in a commercial cleaning company to keep up with it."

"I hope you sealed off the master suite."

"In a matter of speaking. Every time we open a door, a cloud of dust blows in."

"Why don't you just move into a hotel until the work is done—downstairs, at least."

"The builder says he'll have the staircase in and sealed off in another week, so why bother. Anyway, Viv likes to come home, not to a hotel suite. And she deserves to experience what I'm experiencing, doesn't she?"

"Of course."

"Also, the apartment is full of boxes—stuff she bought at the Armory Antiques Show. God knows what's in them."

"The only good thing about this, Dino, is that you can afford it all. That, and the fact that someday, it will all be over, and you'll have a bigger home with more stuff in it."

"We bought a Steinway grand piano, too, at their factory sale. When they've finished reconditioning it, you'll have to come and play for us."

"Doesn't Viv play?"

"Sort of. I think she mostly wants it for parties."

"Parties? You give about one a year, don't you? Maybe two?"

"I have a feeling we'll be giving more parties from now on."

"How are you going to explain all this newfound wealth to the department?"

"Well, I already spilled my guts to the mayor. He'll see that the news filters down into the right places. I'll have a word with my chiefs, too."

"I'm happy to confirm your lawful good luck to anybody who needs knowing," Stone said.

"Thanks, I may need that."

"You know, I think our meeting with Jack Thomas could take the pressure off me."

"How so?" Dino asked.

"Well, the search for the yacht was covert. If they'd found it, they might have been able to sink it with all of us aboard, without the incident coming back to bite them on the ass. Now, though, the Thomases have a reason for animosity toward me, which adds up to a motive if anything happens to me."

"Well, then," Dino said, "we'd better devote some brain cells to their next move. I don't think they'll stop, do you?"

"Not for a minute," Stone said.

23

Since Dino's home was mostly uninhabitable, he went home with Stone for a nightcap. Stone lit the fire in the study and poured them each a cognac.

"You know," Dino said, swirling his brandy and inhaling the aroma. "If the full story about the Thomases and the other eleven families became public knowledge, they would have no further reason to come after you. I know an ace investigative reporter at the *Times* who would be thrilled to have a look at the files and who would know exactly what to do with them."

"Dino, if I exposed the Thomases and their allies, they'd have a whole new motive to off me: revenge. And that's what people like them do best, isn't it?"

"You have a point."

"Now, if somebody at the D.A.'s office leaked everything to your contact at the *Times* and kept my name out of it, that would be a different ball game."

Dino took a noisy sip of his brandy. "Do you have anybody in mind for the leaker?"

"How about Ken Burrows?" Stone asked.

"No, Ken would never do that. It would have to be one of his people."

"I don't know any of his people," Stone replied, "and even if I did, what would that person get out of leaking the story?"

"You have another point," Dino said. "It would have to be Ken himself. And once the story is out, they won't have the guts to kill a D.A."

"You have to consider the danger to your guy at the *Times*, too. He wouldn't be too big to go after."

"It's not a he, it's a she."

"What's her name?"

"Jamie Cox."

"She was one of those reporters who shared the Pulitzer for going after that movie producer, the sex maniac, wasn't she?"

"She was."

"No doubt she's looking for a brand-new subject to investigate."

"Absolutely," Dino said. "She called me yesterday and asked me if I had any ideas."

"So, if she wrote about the files, we could blame you."

"Don't go there, pal. I'm not going to be anybody's source."

"Is there still anybody watching my house?" Stone asked.

"Ask Joan. She's on station."

"I'll do that."

"What are you thinking?"

"I was thinking that I might invite Ms. Cox over for a chat."

Dino shook his head. "I don't think you can take it for granted that they're not watching you just because there's no suspicious car on the block. If you have any notion of pursuing this, you're going to have to do it with such secrecy that nobody will ever get a whiff of what you're doing. You can't invite Jamie over for a chat, and you can't meet her anywhere in public. You're going to have to pretend you're Lance Cabot." Lance Cabot was the director of the Central Intelligence Agency, and an acquaintance of both Stone and Dino.

"So where could I meet her and show her the files? I'm not going to leave this house with a heavy package under my arm," Stone said.

"No," Dino agreed. "You probably wouldn't make it to the next corner."

"How about this?" Stone said. "She enters the common Turtle Bay garden from Second Avenue, a block up from my street. There's a wrought-iron gate there, where she could be let in. Then she walks up the garden, not to my house, but to the house next door—where my staff live—and enters from the rear. Then it's a simple matter for her to walk through the passage to my house."

"How's she going to get through the gate from the street?"

Stone walked over to the desk, opened a drawer, and came back with a key and a tag. On the tag he wrote *Wine Cellar*, then he attached it and handed it to Dino. "Give her this," he said.

Dino looked at the key and the tag and smiled. "So you really want to do this?"

"I want to talk to her," Stone said. "Then I'll decide."

"I'll give her a call," Dino said.

"No. No telephone calls. You're going to have to pretend you're Lance Cabot, too."

Dino laughed. "If we don't meet, how am I going to get the key to her?"

"Up to you, Lance." Stone wrote down the number of the cell phone that Joan had bought for him for his cruise. It remained unused. "Find a way to meet with her and tell her just enough to get her interested, then tell her to call me at this number, but not from her office, home, or cell number. She can buy a throwaway."

"I'll see what I can do," Dino replied.

"Be subtle," Stone said.

"I will be the soul of subtlety."

THE FOLLOWING MORNING at his office, Dino buzzed for his assistant, an attractive female sergeant, Delta Hill.

"Yes, boss?"

"I need a throwaway cell phone, unused," he said.

"Yes, sir." Ninety seconds later she walked into his office and handed him a cell phone and charger. "The number's on a label on the back."

"Where the hell did you get this?" Dino said.

"We bought a dozen for an operation. This one didn't get used."

"Do you have any more?"

"Sure."

"Bring me another one."

The sergeant went away and came back with an identical phone and charger. "They're both fully charged," she said.

"Do you own any civilian clothes?" he asked.

"Of course, I do," she said. "Do you think I walk around seven days a week in a police uniform? I'd never get laid."

Dino laughed. "Okay," he said, handing her one of the cell phones. "I want you to put this into an envelope, then get into some civvies and go uptown to the *New York Times* building, call Jamie Cox down to the lobby and hand her the phone, along with a slip of paper with this other throwaway number, and a message from me. She's not to mention this to anybody."

"Gotcha," Delta replied.

DELTA DID as she was instructed and took the subway uptown. She walked into the *Times* building, then used the throwaway and called the editorial department.

"May I speak to Jamie Cox, please," she said to the woman who answered.

"Who's calling?"

"That's confidential," Delta replied, "but you can tell her it's official police business."

"One moment," the woman said, then put her on hold.

"This is Jamie," she said. "Who the fuck is this?"

"I'm just a messenger," Delta replied. "I'm downstairs in the lobby, and I don't want to come upstairs, but I have a package for you from an important person, and I'd like you to come downstairs and get it."

"Will it explode?"

"No."

"What do you look like?"

"I'll spot you," Delta said, then hung up and sealed the throwaway in an envelope.

24

Jamie Cox went back to her cubicle and opened the envelope. Inside were a cell phone, a key labeled *Wine Cellar,* and a hand-written note:

Meet me on the corner of 8th Avenue and 44th Street at two pm; I'll be in a black SUV with darkened glass. Very big story. You'll be out most of the afternoon.

She looked at her watch: ten to two. She sighed, stuffed the envelope into her purse, grabbed a jacket, and told her secretary to cancel an appointment she had made and not to expect her back today. She had no idea who this was: she was running on gut.

DINO SAW HER waiting from half a block away. As the SUV approached, he opened the back door. "Hop in," he said.

Jamie got into the vehicle and closed the door. "What the fuck, Dino? Are we spies now?"

"I am, and you're about to be if you like the story."

"What story?"

"All will be revealed soon, at our next stop. Harry, next stop, please." The car drove away.

"Okay, I'll bite," she said. "How big?"

122

"As big as the sex maniac story," Dino said. "If you write it right."

"I always write it right," she replied.

They made their way across town to Second Avenue in the forties, and the car stopped.

Dino pointed. "You see that doorway over there?"

"Yeah. There's probably a drunk asleep in it."

"No, there's a wrought-iron gate, leading to gardens on the other side. The wine cellar key will open it."

"Then what?"

"You'll walk over to the downtown side of the garden and a little more than halfway to the other end. There will be a patio there with a geranium in a pot sitting on a teak table. Knock on the back door, and you will be admitted for a meeting."

"Who am I meeting?"

"All will be revealed. Have a good time. And by the way, we never met or spoke, clear?"

"I've never seen you before in my life," she said and got out of the car.

JAMIE FISHED THE KEY out of her bag and walked through the doorway to the iron gate, then let herself in.

The gardens were lovely, she thought. What a nice place to live. She walked to the downtown side, then toward the Third Avenue end and saw the geranium. She went to the back door and tapped on the glass with her ring.

A woman in her fifties with gray hair answered. "Please follow me," she said, and Jamie did. She was led through a kitchen, then through another door into a garage. There were three cars parked there: a Mercedes station wagon, a Bentley Flying Spur, and something with a racy profile under a cover. They went on, apparently into the house next door.

STONE WAS SITTING on the leather sofa in his office, doing the *Times* crossword puzzle, when the woman entered, and the door closed behind her. She was fortyish, tall—five nine or ten—and slender, with ample breasts and long, tousled chestnut hair. He stood. "Good afternoon, Ms. Cox," he said, extending a hand. "My name is Stone Barrington."

She took his hand. "Call me Jamie," she said. "Half the world does."

"And I'm Stone." He waved her to a chair. "I was about to have some tea. Would you like some?"

"I'd prefer a double espresso, if it's available."

"It's available." He picked up a phone and said, "Tea for me, please, and a double espresso for my guest." He turned to her. "I'm sorry for the cloak-and-dagger arrangements."

"That's okay. I wouldn't have gotten into the car, if I hadn't known the occupant."

"That's wise. I admired your work on the sex maniac piece," he said.

"My work was indistinguishable from everyone else's who worked on it," she replied.

"Then my congratulations to you all."

Their refreshments arrived, via Helene, who had brought Jamie in, and she had put a fat cookie on each saucer. She set them down and departed.

"Now," Stone said, "to business."

"I'd appreciate that," she said. "I have an appointment."

Hedging her bets, Stone thought. "You're probably going to want to cancel it," he said. "But before you do, you must understand and accept the necessity of complete secrecy, and agree not to discuss this with any other person, including your colleagues and editors, without my prior agreement."

"Give me a hint first."

"Should you speak with anyone else about this, without permission, both my safety and yours would be in jeopardy."

"Go on."

"Not until I have your agreement on secrecy. At some point, you may stop me and leave the way you came, but your promise of secrecy remains in force."

"All right, enlighten me."

"I am an attorney . . ."

"I know that. I've seen your photograph on that *Times* page about social events that should be called 'Parties You Weren't Invited To.'"

Stone laughed. "You should suggest that to your editor."

"I have. It didn't work."

"As an attorney," he continued, "I am the executor of the estate of a very prominent businessman."

"Name?"

"Not yet. He was well-known in the business and arts communities, having sat on a number of boards in each world. For decades there were rumors that, in his youth, he had rubbed elbows with another community of gentlemen who were engaged in activities more nefarious."

"You're talking about Eduardo Bianchi," she said. It wasn't a question.

125

Stone didn't respond to her guess. "Sometime after his death, a large, concealed safe was discovered in his house." He stood up and beckoned. "Come with me." He led her into the storeroom next door and pointed. "This is the safe. No one could open it. But finally, a very old gentleman of German origin was found who had helped the builder construct the safe, and he was able to open it."

"What was inside?" Jamie asked.

He went back to his office, and she followed. "We're at the point where you have to make a decision," he said.

"But I don't know anything," she replied.

"And, thus, you are not exposed to any danger. You can leave, and we'll forget about it, as long as you don't tell anyone about our conversation or the existence of the safe."

"You said I could leave at any point."

"I said 'some point.' This is the point."

"How much of my time will this take?"

"All of your time—for weeks, perhaps months. And you may require the help of some of your colleagues."

"At the end of all that, what will I have?"

"Another Pulitzer, perhaps sole ownership. At the very least, a bestselling book. And, unlike with the sex maniac story, you will be in charge."

"I can publish everything I learn?"

"Everything you *want* to publish."

"May I identify you as a source?"

"You may not, and you may not mention Dino Bacchetti in that regard, either."

"What's your connection to Dino?"

126

"I used to be a detective on the NYPD. Dino and I were partners for some years. It would be helpful in protecting both you and me, if you could legitimately hint in your story that one or more of your sources is in the district attorney's office."

"I can't lie about that to protect myself."

"Certainly not, but I suspect you are already acquainted with people in that office, and that you might persuade someone to talk to you about it."

"All right, I'm in," she said, polishing off her espresso. "Let's get started."

25

They sat over their dinner dishes in Stone's study. Fred came and cleared them away, and Stone poured brandy. It was nearly ten o'clock, and they had never stopped talking.

"Whew!" she said and took a swig of the brandy. "Have I been here all my life?"

"It may seem that way," Stone said. "You've read the Tommassini file and had a good look at the others. What do you think?"

"I think it's potentially everything you said it was. I'm going to need a couple of people from the *Times*," she said, "and I'm going to need to get my editor's approval, so that I can have the time and resources to do the job."

"Then swear him to secrecy."

"I'll try. He may decline to assign me under those circumstances."

"I'm sure you're more persuasive than that," Stone said. "Tell him the *Washington Post* would probably like to one-up the *Times* on this story."

"I think I can talk him into it. Can I take him a file?"

"No. You can bring him here to see all of them, if that will help. But he has to arrive separately from you, and under similar circumstances."

She nodded.

"I'd like you to do something for me back at your office. While not disclosing why, I'd like you to research a name and give me everything you can find about him."

"What name?"

"Rance Damien." Stone spelled it for her.

"Never heard of him."

"Neither had I until yesterday. Neither the NYPD nor Google has anything on him."

"Then he must be a complete nobody."

"Being a complete nobody these days is hard work," Stone said, "if you've done anything of significance—legally or illegally."

"Do you know anything else about him?"

"Jack Thomas, in our meeting yesterday, told us Damien is a consultant for H. Thomas & Son, and his specialty is security."

"Sounds like a thug."

"I don't think the Thomases would employ anyone who looks or sounds like a thug. Had we bitten on their offer to represent their new business, this Damien would have been in charge."

"You would have reported to him?"

"That was what they wanted. While you're at it, you might see if you can find out if Jack was serious about starting this loan company surreptitiously."

"I can get somebody on the business desk to look into it."

"Under our secrecy rules, fine, but tell him not to leave any fingerprints. If the Thomases find out the *Times* is interested, they'll know the tip came from me or my law partner."

"Do they have a corporate name yet?"

"Jack didn't mention one. I gather it's a new idea, because he wanted me to set it up as an offshore business."

"That does indicate a start-up, doesn't it?" She sipped her cognac and looked thoughtful. "When I get my team together I don't think we should work in the *Times* building. Maybe I can get my editor to rent a hotel suite."

"I own the house next door, where you entered. My household staff live there, but they never seem to use the living or dining rooms. They're large and well-furnished."

"We can bring our own computers," Jamie said. "I can speak to our IT people about setting up."

"I'd rather you use my guy," Stone said. "He does both hardware and software, and he can set up a secure system for files and communications. His name is Bob Cantor. He's ex-NYPD and a genius at what he does, which is almost everything."

"We're going to need secure storage," she said.

"You can use the Excelsior safe. I don't know anything more secure."

"We'll need the combination."

"Only you, and only after practice. If you screw up too often, it will lock you out. There are only two people who can crack it, in that case: Bob Cantor is one, the other is 104 years old, and you'd have to spring him from an old folks' home and buy him an excellent dinner."

"We've got a genealogist at the *Times* who's wasted on obituaries. I'd like to bring her in to put together family trees of all of the file subjects. I'd like to know who and where the descendants are and what they're calling themselves these days."

"Good idea. I suggest you buy some more throwaway cell phones for your coworkers."

"I'll do that," she said. "My editor is going to want to meet my source. When can we do that?"

"Tomorrow is fine, but you know as much as I do now. Just think of me as a friend who will offer advice as needed, not a source."

"That's good," she said, "because I have an iron-clad rule against fucking my sources."

"Well," Stone said, "as a friend who offers advice, I think that's a very good idea."

"Is there a bed in this house, or do we have to do it on the floor?" she asked, standing up and shedding her sweater.

Stone stood up, too. "I don't think I want to wait long enough to find a bed." He began undressing. "There's a perfectly nice rug in front of the fireplace."

She unhooked her bra and tossed it on a chair, then started working on Stone's buttons. Shortly, they were naked and stood, kissing and caressing each other. They laid down on the rug, and she grabbed a cushion from a chair and put it under her hips. "There," she said. "Come to me."

THEY DID IT ONCE, then again, then lay before the dying fire, her head on his shoulder and her leg over his. "That," she said, "was the best sex I've ever had from a former source."

26

The following morning Stone called Bob Cantor early. "I need an immediate sweep of both my house and the house next door," he said.

"What kind of sweep?"

"Audio, video, and phones, and we may need to upgrade the alarm system next door."

"Sounds like you're . . ."

"Don't ask," Stone said. "When can you get here?"

"As soon as I finish my coffee," Cantor said.

"Drink fast."

The throwaway cell phone on Stone's desk buzzed. "Yes?"

"It's Jamie. What a nice evening!"

"Thank you, I thought so, too!"

"I got my editor out of his office and into a corner, and I de-scribed what we've got."

"What was his reaction?"

"Hot to trot," she said. "Can I bring him over this morning?"

"Yes, but not through the front door. Bring him to the Second Avenue gate, open it, give him the key, then enter as you did yesterday. Tell him to follow you in two minutes."

"He'll love the cloak-and-dagger part."

"He's new, isn't he? What's his name?"

"He is, and he wants a big story to hang his hat on. His name is Scott Berger. Around ten o'clock?"

"Fine. He can stay for lunch, if he likes."

"Let's see how it goes. See you at ten." She hung up.

BOB CANTOR ARRIVED soon and went to work. A half hour later he came back. "The alarm system next door couldn't slow down a drunken teenage burglar. What sort of system do you want over there?"

"One just as good as over here," Stone said, "and as soon as possible. When can you start pulling wire?"

"We don't pull wire anymore. It's all Internet and electronics. Let me get the phone checks done, then I'll start. Do you want the Wi-Fi system over there?"

"Yes, and we'll be setting up some mailboxes."

"I'll get started, then." As he was leaving, Jamie Cox came in from next door, and Stone introduced them.

"Oh, good," she said. "I'll want to talk to you later about our computer needs, Bob."

"Anything you want," Bob said, and went next door.

"Scott will be in shortly," she said.

At that moment Helene brought in a man who was younger, shorter, and more rumpled than Stone had expected. He wore a beat-up tweed jacket and had a bad haircut, along with stubble. He shook Stone's hand. "Good to meet you," he said, "tell me all about this."

"Jamie will do that," Stone said. "I'll open the safe for you." He led them into the storeroom.

"Jesus," Scott said, "where'd you get that thing?"

"Eduardo Bianchi had it custom-made in Berlin before World War II." Stone opened the safe and left them to it.

Dino called. "How'd it go yesterday?"

"For an answer to that question, call me on the other phone," Stone replied, then hung up.

The throwaway rang immediately. "Hi, there. It went exceedingly well. The executive editor of the *New York Times* is in the storeroom now, and Jamie is taking him through the files."

"You think he's going to go for it?"

"Jamie says he will. He's new and wants something big."

"Dinner tonight? Viv is back, and she'll want to hear about this."

"Sure. I want to talk to her about some security, too."

"Patroon at seven?"

"Good." They hung up.

IT WAS NEARLY NOON before Jamie and Scott returned to Stone's office.

"You hungry?" he asked them.

They both nodded.

He called Helene and ordered some lunch. "Have a seat," he said to the two journalists. They sat down, and he waited.

"As far as I'm concerned, the *Times* is in," Scott said, "but I've got to get money and resources from the publisher. I've got an appointment with him at two o'clock, and Jamie will come with me. I want to take one of the files with me."

Stone shook his head. "If you want this story you're going to have to put security first: no document leaves this house; no document will be copied, except by my secretary; no phone calls or e-mails will be executed, except on secure phones and computers. If your publisher wants to see the files, bring him over here, the same way you arrived."

"Okay, let me call him," Scott said, reaching for his cell phone.

"Hold it," Stone said. He tossed him the throwaway. "Security starts now. Tell him that. You can call from the storeroom."

"Be right back," Scott said.

"He's thrilled," Jamie said when he had gone.

"I hope your publisher is thrilled, too."

Scott came back. "He really doesn't want to leave the office," he said, "but I think he'll want the story when he sees what we've got."

"Tell him if he wants it to get his ass in gear and get over here, or I'll take it elsewhere."

Scott sighed and went back to the storeroom.

"Okay, one of us will meet him at the gate."

"Return one at a time," Stone said. "Clear?"

"Clear," Scott replied.

Helene arrived with sandwiches, salad, and iced tea.

"What do we need to do about security?" Scott asked.

"I've got a man next door installing a new security system as we speak. He'll sweep both houses for recording devices, cameras, and bugs. I'll want to hire some personnel from Strategic Services."

"I've worked with them before. Fine with me."

"We're going to have to find other ways to get people in and out of here," Stone said. "I don't want a daily parade through the gardens."

"Whatever you want. You sure you don't want me to set up secure facilities at the *Times*?"

"No, that would just cause talk in your offices, and we don't want that."

They talked through lunch, then shortly before two, Jamie said, "I'd better go get our man."

"Send him in first, and alone. And I don't want a limo parked at the back gate."

"Gotcha." She left the room.

"What do you want out of this?" Scott asked.

"The estate will take a cut of film, TV, and book rights, and it will pay me my usual fees," Stone said.

"That sounds all right with me, but you're going to have to discuss it with the business side."

"The business side just arrived," a deep voice said. "I'm Jeremy Green."

Stone rose to greet him and offered him a seat. "Lunch?"

"Already ate," he said. "What the hell is going on that's so important?"

Stone gave him an abbreviated rundown, then asked Jamie to take him into the storeroom and show him the files.

"He's married to a member of the owning family," Scott said when they had gone. "But he's all right: smart as a whip, and a good guy on top of it."

"I'm glad to hear it," Stone said.

"I've told him some of your demands, and I think he'll buy that when he's seen the files."

• • •

GREEN AND JAMIE were back in a half hour. "All right," Green said, "the *Times* is in. Tell me what you want from us."

Stone got a legal pad and made notes as they talked.

"Agreed," Green said. "Now what's this about the estate?"

"The estate gets twenty percent of any income from TV, books, and reprints in other publications. All I want is whatever my costs turn out to be. The estate will pay me for my services."

"Agreed," Green replied.

"Also, I think we're going to need a legal department that works only on this story. I suggest my firm, Woodman & Weld. We're going to have to set up a defense for any problem that arises. For instance, if the Thomases get wind of this they'll sue to try to stop publication. We have to be ready to counter that or anything else that comes up."

"Agreed," Green said.

"Jamie and Scott can tell you what else they need from the paper."

Jamie handed both Scott and Green a single sheet of paper. "Here's who and what we need," she said. "Anybody who works on this in any way, does it here, not at the paper. Stone has brought me to appreciate the need for absolute secrecy. Everybody will sign nondisclosure agreements."

Green addressed Stone. "Do you think the Thomases could be dangerous, if they find out what we're doing?"

"I think it's a distinct possibility," Stone said. "We have to devote all our energies to ensuring that they don't get wind of what's happening."

Green turned back to his people. "All right, I can manage to fund your list and Stone's. Try not to come back with other, more expensive requests."

They talked until five o'clock, trying to anticipate problems, then the guests left, one at a time, the way they had come.

Stone felt exhilarated. Now he wasn't alone in this.

Jamie stuck her head back through the door. "Why don't we work late?" she asked.

"I'll be back by eleven," Stone said.

27

Stone met Dino and Viv at Patroon for dinner.

"You look excited," Viv said.

"I am excited," he replied. "Now that we've got the paper involved. I met the editor and the publisher today, and once they saw the files they couldn't have been more enthusiastic. They've agreed to let Strategic Services supply security."

"When do we start?"

"Have your people come and survey the premises tomorrow morning," Stone said.

"I'll do it myself," Viv replied.

"You think you're going to be able to stay out of the sack with Jamie Cox?" Dino asked.

"Dino," Stone said. "Shut up." He turned to Viv. "I hear you've been doing some shopping."

"Just a bit," she said. "The upstairs is coming along nicely, though. I've had them working in two shifts."

"You'll have to have a housewarming," Stone said.

"I'm already working on the guest list."

LATER, STONE WAS in his study when Jamie walked in.

"Drink?"

"Let's take it upstairs," she said. "I still have rug burns."

They did so, and got into bed. "Except for the Pulitzer, this has been the best day of my career," Jamie said, setting down her drink and kissing him.

Stone set down his drink, too, and paid attention.

"Do you think we can keep this from your staff people?" she said.

"I don't see why not, as long as they're gone for the day."

"Oh, good."

"Viv Bacchetti, Dino's wife and the COO of Strategic Services, is coming over in the morning to survey our needs, so you'll need to be gone by eight AM."

"I'm always at work by eight," she said. "That gives us nine hours."

They had only used up one by the time they fell asleep.

VIV ARRIVED AT TEN. She accepted a cup of coffee and took it on their walk-around. Bob Cantor was at work next door and greeted her warmly.

"Stone," Bob said. "I've got something to show you." He led them down to the garage to where a sheet of drywall had been pulled loose, revealing a door. "I had to pick the lock," he said, opening it to reveal a tunnel and shining a flashlight down it. "This leads all the way to Third Avenue, under the houses. I saw how your people were coming and going—this will be less noticeable. I can change the locks and give everybody a key. All it needs is a good sweeping and some fresh lightbulbs."

"That's great, Bob," Stone said. "I was beginning to worry about attracting too much attention from the other residents who use the garden." He left Viv and Bob to discuss security, then went back to his office. Joan was waiting for him.

"You want to tell me what's going on around here?"

"We're going to have some guests working next door for some time," he said, then he brought her up to date. "We need to get Helene some kitchen help to make lunch every day and keep a pot of coffee going in the dining room next door. Tell everybody that they'll be working there and in the living room. Nobody uses those rooms anyway, since they have self-contained apartments."

"Sure thing," Joan said. "I know just the lady to help Helene."

"Somehow I thought you would," he said. "She has to be able to keep her mouth shut."

"Goes without saying," Joan replied.

He went back to his office to find Jamie waiting for him, all changed and fresh.

"The others are going to start arriving this afternoon," she said, "but I wanted to tell you about Rance Damien."

He sat her down and gave her coffee. "Shoot."

"You were right. He wasn't traceable through the usual routes. We were finally reduced to going through college yearbooks at our library at the *Times*."

"Did you find him there?"

"We did: Lawrance V. Damien. He has a superb education: Groton, MIT, where he got an electrical engineering degree and an MBA, then Harvard Law School, where he was second in his class."

"Ancestry?"

"He's a great-grandson of one of our file subjects, Vito D'Amato."

141

"Ah!"

"He lives on the Upper East Side in a prewar building and keeps a Mercedes coupe garaged nearby. No wife, but the doorman hinted at regular female traffic in and out of his place."

"Any connection to the Thomases?"

"Nothing visible."

"That's both expected and sinister," Stone said. "Don't start asking around their offices. We don't want anyone to know we know about him."

"Okay, hands off at H. Thomas & Son."

"I'd like to know if he turns up at class reunions at any of his schools, though."

"Why?"

"He may have connections with old boys who could prove useful to us."

"We'll check into it."

"Can you use the public library for references? I don't like the idea of anybody working on this where your colleagues could get wind of it."

"As you wish," she replied.

"Also, can you get somebody to follow him when he leaves his apartment? I'd like to know where he works."

"Sure."

"Bob Cantor is working next door; go talk with him and figure out what sort of computer setup you need. He can supply equipment and install it."

"Okay." She disappeared.

Viv came back. "Bob has got a grip on everything," she said. "All I need is to supply some warm bodies to keep an eye on both houses and the neighborhood. They'll find out if the same people keep showing up."

"Great, Viv, and thanks."

"I have to make an appearance at the office," she said. "It lets people know I'm still employed there." She gave him a peck on the cheek and departed.

Stone went to the Excelsior and fished out the file on Vito D'Amato. The name change to Damien came with Vito's grandchildren, so Rance had never been named anything else, and Jamie had not come up with any siblings. He was of particular interest to Stone, because he was the only descendant of the files that they had found to have a present-day connection to the Thomases. There must be more, he thought.

28

The next week went smoothly. Bob Cantor completed his work, including a local area network for the *Times* people's computers. They worked on laptops that were isolated from outside computers, even those of the *Times*. Only one computer could make that connection and all e-mail was sent or received by that machine.

There were two or three *Times* people there every day, sometimes as many as four, and they had all been supplied with keys to Bob's newly located tunnel to Third Avenue. This way no one was seen entering or leaving Stone's residence or office, except those who would do so normally, like staff and clients.

Jamie was spending so much time in the house that Stone let her stay in Peter's old suite, which suited her well. It was at the other end of the top floor, across from the master suite, which suited them both nicely.

Jamie walked into Stone's office one morning. "Good news," she said. "We've found out where Rance Damien works." She handed him some photos of Rance, who was tall, handsome, beautifully dressed, and barbered, going in and out of the H. Thomas building on Wall Street. "He occupies a suite of offices a couple of floors down from where the Thomases roost. The name on the door is LVD Consultants, and there may be as many as twenty people working in his rooms, mostly under forty years of age."

"Any word on what transpires there?"

"We don't keep specialists in breaking and entering on staff at the *Times*," she said. "And it's in all of our employment contracts that we must not do anything illegal while in the paper's service, so we're going to need some sort of freelancer for that. You're going to have to supply him and not tell me or any of my people anything about it."

"I'll speak to Bob Cantor about it," Stone said. "If he can't handle it, or doesn't want to, he'll know who to call."

"There, you see, I didn't want to hear that name. And I don't want any details of how it's done."

"Do you think you can tell me what you want from those offices without sullying your moral code?" Stone asked.

"Photographs of the premises, downloads from their computers to high-capacity thumb drives, names and addresses of the employees and their duties and any familial connections to the twelve files."

"Gee, is that all?"

"For the moment. You'll also have to find an impenetrable way of billing me for such services."

"And you'll have to find cash with which to pay the bills."

"The *Times* does not like dealing in cash for anything more boisterous than cab fare or an occasional corned beef sandwich."

"Then tell Jeremy Green he's going to have to pass the hat and take up a collection, because people who do this sort of work don't take checks or credit cards—not even from the august *New York Times*. And they like to be paid on the day, if not in advance."

"Can you dig up cash and somehow bill us for legal services, or something?"

"I'll see what I can do, without getting disbarred," Stone replied.

"Don't tell me anything about it."

"Yeah, yeah, yeah. And by the way, I want to know if Rance Damien has any siblings or first cousins with business connections to him."

"Didn't I tell you? He has an older sister named Evelyn, known as Eve to her friends, who attended Mount Holyoke College and got an English lit degree, and a younger brother named Paul, sometimes known as Paulie, who also has a law degree from Harvard. Nothing on their employment."

"No, you didn't tell me any of that, and why not?"

"In all the excitement, I forgot."

"I'd give you better than even money that they both work out of LVD Consultants' offices."

"You know what would be interesting?" Jamie said.

"What?"

"Where the family gathers for Thanksgiving dinner."

"That would be interesting, but Thanksgiving isn't for months."

"Our genealogist is making progress on the family trees. Once we have those we can set up a computer watch on the *Times* marriage announcements. Maybe we can plant a few people at a wedding or other family occasion and take some snaps."

"Now that's the kind of devious thinking I want to hear from you," Stone said. "Look for deaths, too, so you can attend the funerals."

"Listen, at what point are we going to call in some branch of law enforcement?" she asked.

"Dino is being kept informed, and if we get to the point where we can prove that federal crimes are being committed, we will call in the FBI or the U.S. Attorney for the Southern District of New York. You should try to be ready to publish when that happens because, suddenly, a lot of other people are going to be involved, and that will greatly increase the possibility of leaks to somebody other than the *Times*."

"That's a good point. Scott and Jeremy will be happy to know we've thought of that."

"Have you started on your book, yet?" Stone asked.

"Well, now, that's impish, isn't it."

"So you have started."

"I've written only the first chapter."

"Where does that chapter live?"

She winced. "On my laptop, I'm afraid."

"House it on one of the computers next door, and encrypt access to it. Then ask Bob Cantor to permanently erase it from your laptop, along with anything else relevant to what you're working on."

"Do I really have to be that careful?"

"What happens if you leave it in a cab, or have it lifted when you're walking across Times Square?"

"Oh, all right."

"Do it right now, and make sure none of your colleagues is keeping any kind of files anywhere but on our computers."

"Geez, I'm going to be so popular," Jamie said.

"You're still very popular with me," Stone said. "Especially when everybody's gone for the day."

"Hearing that makes me feel all aglow," she said.

147

"You're a hard-boiled newswoman, remember? You don't feel all aglow."

"Then what's that little thing I'm feeling when you talk that way? It's not supposed to happen until after my first scotch."

"I've got some scotch around here somewhere," Stone said. "Check back with me when they're all gone."

"Will do," she said, opening the door.

"And try to hang on to that little feeling!"

"Fear not." She closed the door behind her.

29

When Jamie had gone, Stone reached out for the phone to call Bob Cantor, then he stopped. He had used Cantor for such purposes before, but only in tightly contained circumstances where he was the only one with a need to know. Now, if he made that call, he would turn himself into an illegal arm of a newspaper, and they would expect to hear what he learned. He did not want to be in the position of having to tell them, if he didn't feel like it.

HE WAITED UNTIL the end of the day, when he and Jamie had adjourned to his study for her scotch and his bourbon. "I didn't call Bob Cantor," he said, "and I'm not going to. Not to find out the things you want to know."

"You're going to chicken out, are you?" she taunted.

"You've already done that for me."

"How so?"

"Because your newspaper requires you not to do anything illegal, and you are unwilling to violate their policy. You want me to do it for you thereby putting in jeopardy my law partnership and my license to practice, not to mention the serious possibility of my going to prison for doing your bidding."

"I thought you'd have more guts."

"I thought you'd have more sense," Stone replied. "I certainly do. I've laid a huge story in your lap and helped convince your paper to pursue it, but I haven't broken the law so far, and I'm not going to start now."

"Then how are we going to investigate LVD Consultants?"

"You're the investigative reporter, you figure it out."

She downed the remainder of her scotch and went to the bar for another one, then sat down again.

"You're right," she said finally.

"At some point, when you've put the genealogies together and know the structure of these families, you can go to the Thomases and start asking them uncomfortable questions."

"We can't do that until we can establish criminality."

"Right. Then you can go to the D.A. or the FBI and demand an investigation."

"At the first sign of an investigation," she said, "the cockroaches will all scurry back into their crevices and put themselves out of reach. Anyway, the D.A. already has the files."

"He's having the same problem you are: he doesn't have the evidence to put any of these people in prison. The worst he could do is to call you in, give you the story that you already have, and ask you to write about it, then see how they react. Somehow, I doubt Scott and Jeremy would go for that."

She moved over from her seat to his lap and kissed him on the ear. "I so admire clear thinking in a man. It makes me hot."

Somehow, a nipple found its way out of her clothing, and he kissed it.

"That makes me hot, too."

"I know," he said, and located the other nipple.

THE NEXT DAY, Jamie called Stone to the dining room next door, and he found an array of large sheets of paper taped to the walls, twelve of them.

"These are the family trees of the male subjects from the files," Jamie said. "As you can see, the names begin to stop being Italian at the point of the second or third generation. The younger male members all attended Ivy League colleges, except for the women, who attended Seven Sisters colleges. Only in recent years have the women gone to the Ivy League, as the rules changed. There are thirty-two in the third generation, and a dozen of them have law degrees."

"As befits a group of families who are going to need lawyers," Stone said. "You know, I think it's time we got the district attorney over here to see all of this; it might spur him into action."

"I have two concerns about that," Jamie said. "The first is that the possibility of leaks will increase if he tells his staff. The other is, what if Ken Burrows has already been corrupted, then where are we?"

"Fucked," the genealogist said. Nobody laughed.

"All right," Stone said, "let's get the D.A., the police commissioner, and the agent in charge of the FBI's New York Bureau here and show them this stuff all at the same time."

"We still don't have any evidence of wrongdoing," Jamie said.

"That's the job of those three agencies," Stone said. "They have the power to obtain search warrants and issue subpoenas; they also have the power to assign personnel to dig into these people's lives, residences, and places of business."

Everybody seemed a little disappointed.

"I know," Stone said. "You wanted to break a complete story, but we don't have the means to get at it. You're going to have to let law enforcement inside, if you want a story at all. As it is, you can only show that members of twelve families have changed their names, presumably to avoid discrimination, and sent their progeny to the finest American colleges and universities, where they excelled, and none of that is criminal in nature. Much of it is even admirable."

Jamie looked around the room at her people. "All right," she said, "keep at it, and I'll go and talk to our bosses."

Slowly, people shuffled back to their computers. Jamie left via the tunnel, and Stone went back to his office.

30

Stone was in bed, watching Lawrence O'Donnell's show, *The Last Word*, when Jamie came into his bedroom, undressed, and slithered into bed next to him. "All right," she said.

"Would you like the lights out?" Stone asked.

"Never, but that's not what I'm here to talk about. I poured my heart out to Scott and Jeremy, then Jeremy got on the phone and invited Dino, the D.A., and the U.S. Attorney to dinner at your house, tomorrow night—six-thirty for drinks. He and Scott will be here, too. You're on the hook for dinner."

"I can handle that," Stone said.

"After dinner, when everybody is lightly toasted, we'll trot in our placards and decorate your dining room with them, then I'll make our presentation."

"Better you than me," Stone said.

"Don't worry, I'm very good at that sort of thing."

"It's your breasts," Stone said, kissing them. "Everybody looks at them and forgets what you're saying."

"That's a dirty, sexist remark," she said. "Not just because I believe you could be right. At least they get my audience's attention, then I can divert it to more important things."

"There are no more important things," Stone said, fondling one of them.

"There you go again with the totally unacceptable remarks that I just love hearing." She reached down to fondle him. "Oh, I hadn't expected it to be so ready."

"Your presence in my bed makes that happen," Stone said. "Let's find a nice, cozy place for it." She rolled over onto her back, and they did.

THE FOLLOWING EVENING Dino arrived a half hour early and found Stone in his office. "How the hell did you get all three of us around the same table?" Dino said. "That's never happened before in a group of less than a couple hundred people in a hotel ballroom."

"Jeremy Green did it," Stone said. "By the way, who is the AIC at the New York Bureau these days?"

"It's a woman," Dino said. "The New York Bureau's first. Her name is Gillian McCarthy, known to her friends at Gilly, but don't call her that until she asks you to. She's not much more than five feet tall, but you know what they say about dynamite."

"How long has she been there?"

"About a month, I think. The last AIC had a heart attack, and she popped out of the deck."

"Where had she been before?"

"She was an assistant director in Washington. This is the first time she's commanded a bureau."

"Anything else?"

"She's an Irish Catholic girl from Philadelphia. What else can I tell you? Oh, she went to Notre Dame, then to Fordham Law

School—law review, first in her class, and all that. Divorced, with a daughter in school at Notre Dame."

The doorbell rang. "We'd better go upstairs," Stone said.

Fred had seated Gillian McCarthy in the living room. Stone introduced himself. "I expect you've already met Dino," he said.

"Oh, yes," she said, "at a dinner given by the archbishop for Catholic law enforcement. Dino was a great embarrassment to us all."

"How's that?" Stone asked.

"Well, first, he was an Italian at an Irish event."

"What, Italians aren't Catholic?" Dino said.

"And then he monopolized the archbishop. None of the rest of us could get a word in edgewise. It was a disaster for everybody but Dino."

"That is a string of gross exaggerations," Dino said. The doorbell rang again just in time, and Ken Burrows joined them. Right behind them, from the *Times*, were Scott Berger and Jeremy Green, with Jamie Cox in tow.

They were called in to dinner, before anyone could get to a second drink. An hour later, over port and Stilton, Jeremy Green took charge. Without standing he gave the guests a concise rundown of what had been discovered in Eduardo Bianchi's secret safe, and Jamie handed around samples of the files for everyone's perusal—that was to say for the perusal of Gillian McCarthy, who was the only law enforcement official present who had not had wind of them.

The placards were trotted out, and Jamie began a tour of them for the guests. None of them, except the *Times* people, had seen any of this.

When Jamie had finished, Gillian McCarthy was the first to speak. "Well," she said, "all this is just fascinating, but I'm afraid I missed the part about the crime they've committed."

"Well . . ." Jamie said.

"I mean, crime is what we all do, isn't it? What have these people done?"

"We're not sure," Jamie said.

"'Not sure'?"

"We don't have the slightest idea," Jeremy said. "But what we seem to have here is a first-rate Mafia conspiracy, and we suspect that its tentacles reach into a lot of so-called legitimate businesses. But my people don't have the authority or the resources to dig that deep; that has to be done by law enforcement, hence my invitation to you."

"What, exactly, do you want from us, Jeremy?" Ken Burrows asked.

"Ideally, a combined task force to investigate everybody on these family trees, living or dead. There's a crime there somewhere," he said, "maybe a great many crimes, and we think it's a good use of your time, resources, and budgets to find out."

"You're being very generous with our time and resources," Ken replied.

"Not in the least," Jeremy said. "We've done all the work so far with *our* time and resources. Imagine how much that has saved you and your people. But we're at a dead end, without the search and subpoena resources of law enforcement."

"Well," Burrows said, "if we wait long enough, they'll make a mistake, and then we'll be all over them."

Stone spoke up. "They haven't made a mistake for four generations," he said, "but if they should, it would be pretty embarrassing for your agencies that you knew all about them all along and did nothing."

"Ah," said Gillian McCarthy, "the screw."

"And who do you want screwed first?" Burrows asked the table. Silence.

"Take your pick," Jamie said, finally.

LATER IN BED, after exhausting themselves, Jamie said, "Well, that was a complete bust."

"I did the best I could," Stone replied, reprovingly.

"Not you. You did very well, as always. I mean the dinner was a bust."

"Not entirely," Stone said. "Now you at least have their attention, and since everybody was at the table, nobody can deny knowledge of all this. You just have to wait for the Thomases to make a mistake."

"In another four generations?" she asked.

"Well," Stone said.

31

Stone sat at his desk and looked across at Bob Cantor.

"What?" Bob asked.

"I need you to do something," Stone said.

"Well, that's what I do. What do you have in mind?"

"I wish I could be more specific, but I can't, since I don't know enough."

"What do you want to know?"

"Enough. Enough to reveal a criminal conspiracy in all its glory, so search warrants can be served and indictments demanded of a grand jury."

"What is the nature of the crime?" Bob asked.

"I just told you: I don't know."

"You want me to find out if somebody has committed a crime?"

"Exactly. Well, approximately."

"Usually, the way this works is a crime is committed, then you figure out whodunit."

"This time, it's the reverse."

"Who are we talking about, here?"

Stone took him through the whole business from the files in the safe to the *Times* investigation.

"And they've come up with nothing?"

"Let me narrow this down for you, Bob," Stone said.

"Please God, you should do that."

"The Thomases have got several high floors of their own building for their offices, but on the ground floor something else is going on that has nothing to do with their banking business. At least, that's what I believe."

"You want me to find out what they're doing on the ground floor?"

"Yes."

"I'm not available for the rest of my life," Bob said. "How long is this going to take?"

"You take a look at it, then you tell me."

"Who's paying for this?"

"I am. I can't involve the *Times,* and I don't want Dino, the D.A., or the FBI to know what you're doing until I've got something—maybe not even then. I just want to show them some evidence."

"I don't want any of those people to know what I'm doing—ever," Bob said.

"I understand. Just take a hard look at it, okay?"

"Okay." Bob got to his feet. "I'll let you know when I know something." They shook hands, and Bob left.

Joan came into the office. "You want to tell me what you and Bob are cooking up?"

"No, I don't."

"Why not?"

"Because I don't want you to know," Stone replied.

"I smell something in the air," she said.

"What?"

"I think it's desperation," she replied. "You need something that only Bob can give you, and that sort of thing is usually illegal."

Stone sighed. "It's not illegal yet," he said, "but if it turns out to be, you're better off being ignorant."

"Yeah," she said, "but I don't like ignorance. I prefer knowing everything, good or bad. I can always lie about it later."

"Not this time," Stone said. "Now go back to your office and try getting over it."

Joan went, but reluctantly.

BOB CANTOR DRESSED in a business suit with a necktie and put a briefcase in his truck. He drove to the Thomas building and parked in the underground lot, near the elevators. Then he put on some horn-rimmed glasses, a fake mustache, and a fedora, took his briefcase, and got into the elevator, where he discovered that he couldn't go above the mail lobby without a key card. This meant clearing security. First, he had to go to the reception desk.

"Picture ID," the security guard said.

Bob handed him the Florida driver's license he had made for himself earlier that day.

"And who did you wish to see?"

"Congressman Hank Thomas," Bob replied.

"I don't know if he's in New York today," the man replied.

"He's been in the building since early this morning," Bob said. "He asked me to meet him here."

The guard handed him back his license and a guest security badge. "Wear that," he said. "Take the elevator to the fortieth floor, that's where his New York congressional office is."

160

"Right," Bob said. He went through a metal detector while his briefcase was X-rayed, then went to pick it up.

A guard was staring at an object inside his briefcase. "What's that?" he demanded, pointing at the screen.

"A ham and Swiss on rye with mustard," Bob replied.

"What?"

"A sandwich. I'm on a diet, and I eat only what my wife prepares."

"Okay," the man said, "go on up."

Bob picked up the case and had a good look at the building directory, checking for ground-floor offices. The word "Private" was the only name that appeared on the ground floor.

He got onto the elevator and pressed the button for forty; when he reached that floor, he immediately switched to a down elevator. You didn't need a pass going down.

In the garage, he got into his truck, which was a Mercedes Sprinter, took off his jacket, and ate his sandwich. At noon, people began to enter the garage and drive away. Upstairs, he figured people were leaving their offices for lunch. At a quarter to one, he got into some coveralls and a baseball cap, and, keeping the mustache and glasses, took his toolbox and located a spot near where the private offices were, a floor above. There was an entry door, which was locked.

Bob made short work of picking the lock, then let himself in, wearing his visitor's badge. The stairway, he noted, had a half dozen thick cables leading up from somewhere below, and he recognized them as concealing bundles of many smaller cables. He made his way upstairs and found a woman sitting at her desk, eating a salad. "Yes?" she asked.

"I'm here to fix the copying machine," he said.

"We don't use copying machines much," she replied. "There's only the one."

"Then that must be the one," he said. "Where would I find it?"

"Go over there, take a left, and there's a door at the end of the corridor, with a sign saying 'Admittance to Authorized Personnel Only.'" She opened a desk drawer and handed him a key.

"Thank you," he said. "This is going to be a full service, so I'll be at least an hour."

"If I'm not here when you get back, just put the key in this drawer." She pulled it open to show him, revealing many other keys.

"Sure thing." Bob followed her directions, and walking down the hallway he could see through a glass wall into a large room filled with people at long tables, working on computers, with supervisors looking over their shoulders.

At the end of the hall he let himself into the restricted room and looked around. "Bingo," he said aloud to himself.

AN HOUR AND A HALF later Bob returned the key to the woman at the desk, thanked her, and went back to his truck. Two hours later he pulled into Stone Barrington's garage.

32

Stone stared across his desk at Bob Cantor. "You're looking very smug," he said. "What did you find?"

"Everything and nothing," Bob replied.

Stone stared at the ceiling. "Jesus," he muttered. "All right, Bob," he said. "In your own time."

Bob told him how he had gotten into the building and held up a key ring with two keys attached. "These open the downstairs door from the garage and upstairs, which turned out to be a room full of computers and electronics. The computers are stacked in rows, and put together, they approximate a supercomputer. There are fifty of them."

"If you want a supercomputer, why not just buy one instead of stringing together fifty other computers?"

"They're making themselves a semi-supercomputer because buying a supercomputer isn't all that easy. First of all, they cost tens of millions of dollars, and people like IBM are not going to take an order for a supercomputer from some schmuck who wanders in off the street with a checkbook. The government wants to know who owns these things and what they're doing with them. The National Security Administration, down at Blackstone, in Virginia, wants to know about them, too, because they're going to want to break into the new supercomputer at the first opportunity and find out what's in it. On the other hand, anybody can buy a bunch of desktops from a dozen suppliers and build their own semi-supercomputer. And they may not need a supercomputer for their specific needs. Something less will do nicely for thousands of applications."

"Now we're getting somewhere," Stone said. "Why do the Thomases want their own semi-supercomputer?"

"Well," Bob said, "I found a schematic of their systems, which I copied on the copying machine I ostensibly went there to service, which didn't need servicing. There are actually two semi-supercomputers in the building—one serving the upper floors, where the banking business is operated, and another one serving a big room on the ground floor where there are thirty or forty computer stations hooked up to it, with as many people working like beavers on them."

"For what purpose?" Stone asked.

"You remember a couple of minutes ago, I said I found everything and nothing?"

"Yes."

"Well, the everything part is the two semi-supercomputers. The nothing part is what they're doing on them."

"Well, shit," Stone said.

"Now, don't get your shorts in a twist," Bob said. "I have a plan."

"What is your plan?" Stone asked.

"I'm going to add another computer to the downstairs semi-supercomputer, one that I can use to operate the whole thing and see everything that's going on in there."

"I like the sound of that. How are you going to do it?"

"I'm going to buy a computer just like the fifty they're work-ing on, copy their operating system and files to it, and make my-self a system operator, which will allow me inside."

"Can you be up and running tomorrow?"

"Hey, wait a minute! I've got a ton of work to do there, includ-ing establishing a wireless link from the semi-supercomputer to my pirate computer, and I've got to locate that somewhere and make it impenetrable to their system operators if they sniff out the pirate, who is me, and impossible to locate. I also have to not get caught fucking with their computers while I'm setting up this stuff. For all I know, they may have a torture chamber buried in the bowels of that building, where intruders go to talk, then die."

"All right, all right. Give me a timeline."

"First, I've got to go home and study their schematic until I've got it memorized."

"Go on, how long?"

"I might be up and running by the end of next week."

"Oh, shit."

"Hey, what's the hurry here? You want this done right, and find out what they're doing? Or do you want it fucked up and me floating facedown in the East River?"

"I want you alive and well and pumping information out of their semi-supercomputer and into yours, and I want a detailed description, in writing, of what they're up to."

"Eventually, we'll get there, but please remember that the Thom-ases probably spent a year getting that place up and running, and with an unlimited budget. Don't expect the same from me in a week on your dime."

"Bob, you don't have to reinvent what they've done."

"I know I don't or I'd be asking you for two years and a few million bucks."

"As it is, what are you asking?"

"Ten days and two hundred grand, and I'll need half up front, to buy stuff."

"Done." He buzzed Joan.

"Yes, boss?"

"Write Bob Cantor a check for a hundred thousand and bring it to him in my office."

"Now you've really got me curious," she said.

"Don't ask any questions of either Bob or me," he said.

"Oh, shoot!" She hung up.

Stone hung up. "Joan always wants to know everything I'm doing."

"Stone," Bob said, "Joan already knows everything you're doing. She'll figure this one out in no time."

"She better not."

"Now, I need a place to work that's not in my home or office. How about your home or office?"

"Well, I've got the *New York Times* investigative journalism department camped next door in my living and dining rooms, but I can put you upstairs in a bedroom. It's important that the *Times* people not know about you and what you're doing. If they are ever asked by a grand jury about it, it's best that they can truthfully say they don't know what the D.A. is talking about."

"Secrecy is all right with me," Bob said. "After all, it's going to be my dick in the wringer if I get caught."

"Bob, I can't stress too much that, if it's a choice between your getting caught and our getting this information, you come first. Feel free to cut and run at any moment."

Joan came in with a check, flapping it and blowing on it as if there were ink to dry. She handed it to Stone for his signature, then gave it to Bob. "Here you are, sir," she said. "Go buy whatever your heart desires."

"That will be all for now, Joan," Stone said wearily. "Leave Bob alone with his money."

"I've got to put something in the 'for' space on the computer, so the accountant will know how to deduct it," she said.

"Put in 'tech support,'" Stone said. "Now beat it."

Joan beat it, and Bob headed for the garage and his truck.

33

Late that same afternoon, Congressman Henry Thomas II, known as Hank to his constituents and to everybody else, walked into the H. Thomas building and gave the security man at the front desk a cheerful wave.

"Afternoon, Congressman," the man yelled. "Did you just get into town?"

Hank stopped, then went over to the desk. "Yes, Bernie, why do you ask?"

"Well, you had a caller around lunchtime who said you'd been here since seven AM and that he had an appointment."

"At seven AM I was having breakfast in D.C.," Hank replied. "Did you send him up?"

"Yes, sir," Bernie said. "I thought it best to, since there was no one else in the office at that hour."

"Did he come back downstairs?"

Bernie took a look at the hooks where the visitors' passes were stored. "Yes, sir, he did." He consulted his logbook. "Funny, his pass is there, but he wasn't logged out."

"Where were you at the time?"

"At lunch, in the employees' cafeteria."

"Describe the man."

"About forty to fifty, five-nine or ten, pretty solidly built, glasses, a mustache, and a hat. Suit and tie. Briefcase, too, with a ham sandwich inside, according to the X-ray."

"Okay," Hank said, then strode through security without pausing and took the elevator to the top floor, then walked to the receptionist's desk. "Sheila," he said, "did I have a visitor this morning?"

"No, sir," she replied. "You were in Washington."

"I know where I was. I want to know about a visitor."

She checked her logbook. "No, sir, no visitors."

"Anybody get off the elevator?"

"Yes, sir, but he didn't check in with me; he got right back on a down car. I guess he came to the wrong floor."

"Describe him."

Her description matched Bernie's.

"He didn't go into my office, did he?"

"No, sir. He got right back on another elevator and went down."

"To what floor?"

"I don't have any way of knowing that."

"Do the elevators produce an electronic log of their stops?"

"I don't know, sir."

"Find out, and see if it recorded where that man got off the down elevator."

"Yes, sir, right away." She picked up a phone.

Hank went into his office and had a good look around. Everything seemed in order, and his safe was locked. He walked back into reception, took the spiral staircase to the next floor up and

169

asked if his father was alone. He was, so Hank knocked and walked into the big office. "Good morning, Dad," he said, giving his father a kiss on the cheek.

"Morning, Hank. How are you?"

"Pretty good, actually. How's Poppa?"

"As cantankerous as ever."

The phone rang, and the elder Thomas picked it up. "Yes?" He handed it to Hank. "For you."

"This is Hank."

"Sir, the elevator log shows that the man was one of three people who traveled from this floor to the garage floor."

"Thank you." Hank hung up and turned to his father. "Someone may have tried to breach our downstairs office," he said.

"Why do you think that?"

Hank told him about the bogus visitor.

"I wouldn't worry too much about that," his father said.

The phone rang again, and again it was for Hank.

"Yes?"

"Sir, I checked with reception downstairs, and the only outsider to enter the downstairs floor today was a copy machine repairman, here to do a routine servicing of their copier."

"Did he have an appointment?"

"No, sir, those people just turn up every few weeks and service the machines. Keeps them running smoothly."

"Did she know the man by sight?"

"No, sir, they don't often send the same man twice."

"Thank you." Hank hung up.

"Well?" his father said.

"Could have been a copying machine repairman."

"There you go."

"Are we set for tomorrow?" Hank asked.

"The day after tomorrow. A red district in south Georgia that's threatening to turn blue, where the Dems have a hot young man who scared the pants off our candidate in their one debate. It's tailor-made for our operation."

"I can't wait to hear the result," Hank said.

"We've been running models for weeks, but this is our first real-time, hands-on shot at something real, even though it's only a special election for a vacant seat."

"Do you still think it's the right move for me to run as an independent?" Hank asked.

"I do. The Republican Party is dead on its feet, and it's going to take a real pasting in November. It looks like Secretary of State Holly Barker is going to announce for the Democratic primary, and she has very high approval ratings, in the sixties among all voters. You'll have a better shot at stealing Republican votes as an independent."

"By giving their members a conservative independent to vote for."

"Exactly, and it could be the first step toward building a new party."

"I hope you're right."

"Even if I'm not, it won't hurt your chances. You're the fresh face the center-right needs at this time."

"Again, I hope you're right. Should I go and say hello to Poppa?"

"Sure, he's up there."

Hank took the staircase up another floor and knocked on his grandfather's door.

"Come, godammit!" the old man yelled.

Hank let himself in. "Hello, Poppa."

The old man stood and embraced him. "You're a fine sight for these rheumy old eyes," he said, holding his grandson at arm's length and looking at him. "Have a seat. It's not too early for a drink, is it?"

"A small scotch would go down nicely," Hank replied.

His grandfather loved tending bar, and he came back with two glasses of amber liquid, each containing one very large ice cube.

"Now, tell me everything," Henry said, raising his glass.

Hank told him about the test run two days hence.

"If this works," Henry said, "we can say goodbye to gerrymandering."

"Maybe some," Hank said. "And we're still not going to know if we can upscale from a special election in one district to the general election's popular vote."

"Do you realize what it will mean for us if this thing works?" Henry asked.

"I certainly do," Hank said.

The two of them sat and watched the tugs and liners come and go in New York Harbor, then they had a second drink.

"How big a swing are you going for?" Henry asked.

"It's pretty close already, so we think a three percent swing will put things right. And we'll leave some Russian fingerprints on the hack, just in case."

Henry raised his glass. "Here's to three percent," he said.

34

Stone went upstairs to change for dinner; he and Jamie were going to Daniel, the marvelous French restaurant uptown. The phone rang, and he picked it up. "Yes?"

"It's Holly," she said.

He warmed to the call immediately and sat down on the bed. "It's so good to hear from you."

"I warned you it would be a while. I have to keep my distance from you until after the election."

"So I'm political poison, am I?"

"In a manner of speaking, but anybody but the dullest man would be poison, and you're not dull. We want the press focused on experience and policy, not my love life."

"Such as it is."

"Well, yes. Hang on to your hat."

"You're announcing."

"Tomorrow."

"Wow. I can't get my head around this."

"You've had plenty of time to get your head around it, Stone," she said. "And I want to thank you for being so understanding about the distance I've kept. God knows, I'd rather be in bed with you every time I go to bed alone."

"That's flattering."

"No, it's just the truth. You should be happy about being kept in the background. The press would make your life hell between now and the election."

"Who's the opposition going to be?"

"In the primary, nobody of consequence, but in the general, who knows? I'm getting vibes that Hank Thomas is going to leave the party and run as an independent."

"He'd have a better shot without you to run against in the primary."

"And as an independent, he'll have no opponent, so he can cuss the candidates for both parties."

"Do you have any polling on you versus Hank?"

"Yes, and I have a solid eighteen-point lead with him as an independent. Bigger, if he were in the Dem primary."

"That's a good start," Stone said.

"Yeah, but I'm going to run as if it is a close race. He'll get a big bump if the Republicans pick a weak candidate."

"What time tomorrow?"

"Noon on the Capitol steps, then I fly to Warm Springs for a live shot at Roosevelt's Little White House on the evening news shows. I'm going to let my opponents run against me with FDR as my running mate."

"Good choice!"

"Also, I'll do all the Sunday shows this weekend from my office at State."

"Are you going to resign from State right away?"

"No, I want to be seen as handling both my job and the campaign at the same time."

"Who do you want for a running mate?"

"You, but I suspect you're not available."

"Correct. Who do you want that is?"

"I'll probably wait until the convention to name somebody. I'll see how they all behave until then."

"How about Peter Rule?" Peter was President Kate Lee's son from her first marriage. He was also the junior senator from New York.

"That's an interesting idea, but it might look like too much sucking up to Kate."

"A good point. Have you talked with her about it?"

"Only obliquely. She knows Peter's a serious candidate, but she's not sure whether it's the best move for him. He's young enough to wait his turn, and that would give him time to do some good work in the Senate before running."

"Will Lee would make a great running mate."

"He would overshadow me. You know what I'm thinking?"

"What."

"If I'm elected, getting Will to run for Speaker of the House."

"But he's not a House member."

"Most folks don't know that you don't have to be. Anybody at all can serve as speaker."

"I'm one of those who didn't know that."

"Stone, what are you doing with yourself? Anything exciting?"

"Yes, but I can't talk about it on the phone. I'll tell you when—or rather, if—I see you before the election. You'll find it entertaining, I think."

"I'll look forward to it. Well, I have a speech to memorize."

"Use the teleprompter, like everybody else."

"I've gotten by so far without that. I have an excellent memory."

"It will be an impressive sight to see a politician speaking extemporaneously, while not making a fool of herself."

"That's the idea," she said. "Now, you go and make love to somebody, and pretend it's me."

Stone laughed, but she had already hung up. He decided to take her advice.

THEY ARRIVED at the beautiful restaurant on East 65th Street and settled into a good table. They were still looking at the menu when the wine waiter brought over an ice bucket with a bottle of Dom Pérignon resting in it.

"What's this for?" Stone asked.

The waiter placed a business card on the table, and Stone read it.

"Who's it from?" Jamie asked.

"Rance Damien, but pretend you don't know who that is."

She shrugged, and Stone looked around. "Which table?" he asked the waiter.

"Three o'clock. The handsome young couple."

Stone looked at the card again, then at the indicated table. "I don't know the gentleman," he said. "Please take the bottle to him with our thanks, but tell him I've already chosen a wine."

"As you wish, Mr. Barrington."

"Why are we pretending not to know who he is?" Jamie asked.

"Because he has seen me in the company of someone from the *Times,* and I don't want him to think that our dinner has anything to do with him. As far as he's concerned, you've never heard of him."

"Okay, I get that."

"Whatever you do, don't look at him again," he said. "Just look at me."

"That will be easy," she said, and they went on with their dinner. By the time they were ready to leave, Damien had already left the restaurant.

35

The following day, Stone and Joan watched the noon news together and were given an abbreviated version of Holly's announcement speech on the Capitol steps.

"I'd call that short shrift," Joan said.

They liked better what they saw on MSNBC just after six o'clock. Holly stood on a small platform set before the main entrance to Roosevelt's Little White House, in Warm Springs, Georgia.

"We've had some good presidents, some great presidents, and a very few bad ones," she said, "but to my mind, we've had only three very great ones. They are: George Washington, who saved the Revolution; Abraham Lincoln, who saved the Union; and Franklin Roosevelt"—she paused—"who saved the world." She got a standing *O* from the crowd for that. When they had calmed down, she went on, "I think a Democratic president could do a lot worse than to model her administration on Roosevelt's twelve years in office. Thank God we don't have a world war in our laps, but many of our problems are very similar to those Franklin D. faced. Among them are the state of public education in our land, the lack of fully comprehensive health insurance for all Americans, and a national infrastructure that is very near being worn out. Barak Obama made a valiant effort to fix the infrastructure, but the Republicans in Congress cut his request for funds in half. That meant we could fix the potholes and save a few bridges from collapse under the weight of our cars, but while we were doing that, too many other problems arose and went unsolved.

"Roosevelt created the Works Progress Administration, which built roads, bridges, and airports that we are still using today: the Golden Gate Bridge and LaGuardia Airport come to mind. I want to see a new, up-to-date version of the WPA hard at work again, curing our infrastructure sins of the past and building for the future, at the same time. I expect to pay for it all with a reasonable increase in the gasoline tax, something Congress hasn't had the guts to deal with, but something that will see that the costs are defrayed most by those who use our infrastructure most. A permanent, nonpartisan national infrastructure commission will decide which projects to take on and which ones come first. But, for the time being, my running mate is going to be Franklin Delano Roosevelt."

Holly talked on for another five minutes, then thanked everyone, and the TV switched to a panel of pundits, who seemed mostly in favor of what she had said.

"Much better," Stone said. Stone sent a short e-mail to Holly's private mailbox, which read:

You done good.

"Are we sending a campaign donation?" Joan asked.

"I think that group of us who gave Kate's political action committee a million dollars each can expect to hear from Holly's campaign soon. When that happens, send them a check."

"What if she asks for more than a million?"

"Good point," Stone said. "We'd better start freeing up some cash in anticipation of being asked. Call Charley Fox at Triangle Investments and tell him to put together five million, with due attention to capital gains taxes and offsetting them with any losses we may have."

"Surely she's not going to ask those people for five million each?"

"If she doesn't, she'll need more as we approach the convention and the election, and we'll contribute then."

"As you wish, boss." Joan went back to her desk and made the call.

DOWNTOWN, THE THOMASES—grandfather, son, and grandson—watched Holly's performance.

"Shit!" Hank said when she was done.

"I take it you're not going to vote for her," his father said.

"That speech made me want to," Hank said, "but I fought off the urge. I think we'll wait until next week to announce, after her appearance has had time to cool off in the public mind."

"Good idea," his grandfather said. "What do you hear from the special election in Georgia?"

"It's too early," Hank replied. "We'll know something before bedtime, though, I think."

THE FOLLOWING MORNING, Stone turned on *Morning Joe* at breakfast and got a report on the Georgia special election. Chandler Dodd, who had been leading the polls by a point or two going into the election, had lost by two points.

• • •

STONE WAS at his desk at eleven o'clock, thinking about lunch, when Joan buzzed.

"Somebody named Dodd is calling from Georgia, something about an election."

"I'll speak to him," Stone said, pressing a button. "Mr. Dodd?"

"Yes, Mr. Barrington. I'm calling to thank you for the generous campaign contribution you sent us a few weeks ago. It helped us almost bring it off, but as I expect you've heard, not quite."

"You're very welcome for the donation, Mr. Dodd, and you have my condolences on your race."

"Call me Chan, please. The other thing I called about is: I think we're going to bring a lawsuit to set aside the vote and demand a recount."

"Well, that's a daunting prospect," Stone said. "What grounds do you have?"

"We're not sure yet, but something very peculiar happened yesterday."

"What was that?"

"Every polling station, across the board, had a last-minute surge of three percent for my opponent."

"Every one? Three percent?"

"Exactly three percent."

"Well, that certainly does sound fishy."

"I wonder if you'd be interested in taking our case?"

"No, I think you'd get a more generous hearing from the public if you use a Georgia attorney—a local one, if you've got someone who can handle it."

"You have a point."

"If you set up a fund to challenge the election, I'd be glad to make a contribution."

"I'll take you up on that," Dodd said. "I think maybe I know an old law-school classmate who might take our case."

"You're going to need some tech help, too, to make sense of the count."

"I've already got someone on the campaign who can handle that—in fact, she's the one who spotted the last-minute shift in voting. She's a seventeen-year-old high school student."

"That will look very good in the papers," Stone replied. "Make sure she gets a lot of TV interviews."

"I'll work on that."

"Keep me posted on your progress."

"Thank you, Stone. Goodbye."

Stone hung up wondering what the hell was going on in Georgia.

36

The following morning Stone was reading an account in the *Times* of the three percent anomaly in the Georgia special election, when the "Breaking News" sign began flashing on the TV screen. They did that so often that he was reluctant to pay attention, but then the image of a beefy, balding man in a suit came on the screen, and he was standing before a podium emblazoned with the name CAMERON.

"Ladies and gentlemen, my name is Arnold Cameron, and last night I was elected to Congress in your district." Scattered applause. "The problem is, my computer people believe I was elected fraudulently. Shortly after the polls closed it was pointed out to me that my vote totals in almost every district showed a late three percent surge. *Exactly* three percent, in *every* district. My people spent the night digging into this, and they have found traces of Russian hacking into the county systems. So it would appear that, for some reason, Vladimir Putin has some interest in my election." Groans and moans.

"Well, I am not going to sit still for this. I have written to the county board of elections and asked that my total vote be reduced by three percent, leaving my opponent, Mr. Dodd, with a victory by an overall margin of one point two percent, too high

183

to effect a mandatory recount. I am standing aside in favor of Mr. Dodd. The board of elections, on viewing the evidence, has accepted my decision. I thank everyone who voted for me, and I hereby take this opportunity to declare my candidacy for the seat in the next election. Thank you."

He walked off the platform, and the cable networks went nuts. They were on every channel, praising Cameron and damning Vladimir Putin.

HANK THOMAS WENT UPSTAIRS for lunch with his grandfather and father. The old man could barely contain himself.

"Young man, what the hell went wrong?" Henry demanded.

"We've spent the morning working on that, and we've traced it to a single station in our operation. A young and inexperienced operator misunderstood his instructions and simply enlarged the vote at every voting station by three percent. Naturally, this was noticed almost immediately. Arnold Cameron, our candidate, refused to be elected that way and stepped aside in favor of Dodd."

"I assume your computer operator has been fired," his father said.

"Certainly not. We can't have him walking the streets knowing what he knows. He's simply being retrained. Also, in the search for what went wrong we discovered a hack into our system, which I had thought impossible. It bears the hallmarks of one of the Russian groups who do that sort of thing. So, on balance, it's turned out well for us, since we discovered a weak link in our software, which has already been repaired."

"Well, after all," the old man said, "this was just a test run, and it's just as well we did it. At least, no one has traced this incident to us."

"I agree," Hank said. "Work continues apace."

UPTOWN, STONE MET with Bob Cantor. "You've seen the news, I suppose," he said.

"Seen it? I *am* the news," Bob replied.

"You've been found out?" Stone asked, incredulous.

"Just the opposite," Bob said. "I discovered a little bit of code that took three percent of the vote and added it to Cameron's vote, proportionately adjusted to each district. I adjusted the vote totals to a flat three percent across the board and routed my code through one of their stations. I also planted what appears to them to be a Russian hack to their system. They've found it, as I intended, and removed it from their system, but I've got two other hacks of my own still operating."

"So you're in?"

"I'm in. I just don't know yet what I'm dealing with. Oh, I found the election thing—no problem. But there's more than that going on, and I haven't yet figured out what they're up to. All I know is it's really big. They're using very nearly the maximum capacity of their system to work on it."

"The general election?"

"No doubt," Bob said, "but there's something else. They're writing a ton of code, but they've broken it up among three dozen operators so that not even their people know exactly what they're working on. Right now, I'm working on the passwords to their sysops. They're very complex, but I've written some software to search them out."

"How long is that going to take?"

"Longer than I'd hoped," Bob said. "I've taken to sleeping in the bedroom you've given me, so that if I wake up at night I can check progress. It's easier then because they're not working after midnight. They've got a guy who comes in at midnight and sweeps their system for hacks or attempts at hacks. I've managed to dance around him, though, so he's not on to me."

"This is making me nervous," Stone said.

"Me, too," Bob replied.

STONE AND JAMIE were having dinner in his study. "You're looking discouraged," he said to her.

"Does it show?"

"There are two little wrinkles between your eyes that show up when you're unhappy."

"You're very observant. We seem to be at a dead end, and I'm having trouble convincing Jeremy and Scott that we need more time."

"I thought something like that might happen," Stone said.

"Why did you think that?"

"Because I've got somebody else working on it, too, with a whole different skill set than your people are working with."

The two little wrinkles appeared again.

"Tell me about it," she said.

Stone shook his head. "If I told you about it you'd have to tell Jeremy and Scott, and that would put your investigation at risk."

"I don't have to tell them about it," she said.

"That would put you in an impossible position. Sooner or

later they'd know the truth, and they would know you can't be trusted."

"That's my problem," she said.

"It's mine, too. I don't want to see a brilliant career destroyed because you had to keep secrets from your bosses."

"Then why are you telling me about it?"

"Because it's the only way I can get you to shut down your investigation—at least, for a while."

"That would make me look very bad."

"Only for a while. If this other thing works out, you'll have a bigger story than either of us had imagined."

"But what am I going to say to Jeremy and Scott?"

"Tell them the truth: you've gone as far as you can until you get a big break, and you don't want to waste any more of the *Times*'s money. That will impress then. After all, you've cracked half the story: you know all about the Thomases. You just haven't found out what they're guilty of."

"But you're confident that this new thing you're doing will crack the whole thing?"

"'Confident' is too strong a word," Stone said. "*Hopeful,* is a more appropriate one."

37

Stone came back from lunch the next day to find Joan on the phone.

She pressed the hold button. "It's that nice Senator Sam Meriwether, from Georgia, for you. He's Holly's new campaign chairman. I just love this guy."

"I think I know what that's about," Stone said. He went into his office and picked up the phone. "Sam, how are you?"

"Never better, Stone. I wanted to call and thank you for the million-dollar check that came in from you."

"Yeah, sure," Stone said. "How much more do you want?"

Meriwether took a deep breath. "Five million from each of the President's Council members. That's what we're calling it."

"Let me shake loose some cash, and I'll have another four million on the way by tomorrow," Stone replied.

"That's fantastic, Stone."

"How many of the others have come through?"

"Well, to tell you the truth, you're the first one I've called. Can I use your name with the others?"

"Sure, go ahead."

"Something else. I heard that your buddy, Dino Bacchetti, has come into some money. Should I hit him up?"

"I don't think you should ask a public servant for that kind of money, even though it would come from his personal fortune. There are certain parts of the media that would report it as stolen from the Police Pension Fund."

"I guess you're right, Stone. You'd think I would have thought of that."

"I'll talk to him about making a smaller, but substantial, contribution during one of your TV drives. He can call it in."

"Great idea. I'll leave it in your hands."

"Give my best to Holly." Stone hung up and called Dino.

"Bacchetti."

"It's Stone. Are you sitting down?"

"Uh-oh."

"It's not a bad thing. I've committed you to joining a special committee on Holly's campaign called the President's Council. You're going to love it. You'll get the best seats to the inauguration, tickets to the ball, and a free hotel suite and limo for the week."

Dino sighed. "How much is it going to cost me?"

"Only five million dollars."

"*What!!!*"

"That's what each member of the council contributes. You can manage that, can't you? Sam Meriwether will call you for confirmation and to give you wiring instructions."

"*Have you lost your fucking mind?*"

"Relax, Dino, you'll have a stroke."

"Why do they think I even have that kind of money?"

"Word has gotten around about your recent inheritance, so they know you've got it."

"I'm saving that to buy a retirement place somewhere."

"Dino, your country needs it more than you do."

"*Nobody* needs it more than I do! Now you call them back and tell them you've made a mistake."

"Okay, I'll tell them you want Hank Thomas for your next president."

"I didn't say that! I want Holly!"

"Well, they're never going to believe that if you demand your money back. Holly will hear about it, too. Tell you what, how about if she appoints you the director of the FBI?"

"What?"

"Interesting, huh?"

"You think she'd do that?"

"Who would be better?"

"Well, nobody, of course, but everybody will think I bought myself the job."

"Gee, I hadn't thought of that. I'll cancel the contribution, if, the first time you see one of Holly's TV commercials, you call in and donate a hundred grand. How's that?"

Dino was cooling down. "Well, I guess I can do that," he said. "I mean, I was going to give her ten grand, but . . ."

"Careful what you say, Dino. This line could be tapped. You might hear yourself buying the directorship of the FBI on Fox News."

"Holy shit."

"You don't want to be heard saying that, either. Well, I'd better get busy calling some more folks for campaign contributions. On Holly's behalf, I thank you for the hundred thousand dollars."

"Don't mention it."

"Not ever again?"

"Wait a minute," Dino said suspiciously. "You didn't tell them I'd give them five million, did you?"

"Of course not. I wouldn't hang you out to dry for five million—just for a hundred grand. See ya!"

Stone hung up the phone laughing so hard that Joan came in to find out what was going on.

"What's going on?"

"I just told Dino I'd committed him to five million for Holly's campaign."

She burst out laughing, then stopped. "He didn't agree to that, did he?"

"Of course not, but I got him up to a hundred grand, instead of the ten grand he thought he was going to get away with."

Joan howled with laughter. "Oh, I wish I could have seen his face!"

"I can tell you, from the sound of his voice, that it was *puce!*"

THAT NIGHT, Dino and Viv were watching the evening news, when a clip of Holly's Warm Springs speech came on, followed by an 800 number for contributions. Dino picked up the phone.

"Who are you calling?" Viv asked.

"I thought I'd make a contribution to Holly's campaign."

"Good idea. Make one for me in the same amount."

"This is the Holly Barker campaign," a young woman's voice said. "Would you like to make a contribution?"

"Yes, I would," Dino replied.

"May I have your name and mailing address, please?"

Dino gave it to her.

"And your phone number and social security number?"

He gave her that, too.

"Now, you must state that this is a private contribution from your own funds and not from a corporation or business, and that you're over eighteen years of age."

"I so state," Dino replied.

"May I have your credit card number?"

Dino gave her the number of his new black American Express card. "Oh, and my wife wants to contribute, too." He gave her Viv's card number and confirmed her information.

"And how much would you like to contribute?"

"A hundred thousand dollars," Dino said.

Viv sat up straight in her chair.

"Each."

"Oh, wow!" the young woman said. "Hey, everybody, I've just scored two hundred grand!" There was cheering in the background. She came back on line. "Mr. Bacchetti, my supervisor tells me that's more than the legal limit for a couple, but you can make the donation to Holly's political action committee. I can handle that for you."

"Fine, you do that. Gotta run."

"Goodbye and thank you so much!" she yelled.

Dino hung up.

"What have you done?" Viv asked.

"I told you I was making a campaign contribution, and you asked me to make one for you in the same amount."

"You gave them a hundred thousand dollars?"

"Yes, and another hundred thousand from you."

Viv's jaw was working, but no sound was coming out. Finally, she spoke, "From now on, I'm charging you for sex—ten thousand bucks a pop."

"Hey, wait a minute."

She stood up. "Come on, let's go upstairs. You have a hundred thousand dollar credit."

He followed her upstairs.

38

Stone was watching the news the following morning, when he learned how successful Sam Meriwether's fund-raising had been. He had gathered twenty-one contributions to Holly's PAC of five million dollars each.

"As a sideline," the news anchor said, "the Holly Barker PAC revealed that it has received two contributions of a hundred thousand dollars each from Police Commissioner Dino Bacchetti and his wife, Vivian." Dino's face appeared on the screen in a shot from outside his office building. "It came from our own personal funds," he said. "Please note that I did not rob the Police Pension Fund."

"Do you think you'll be considered for director of the FBI, if Secretary Barker is elected?"

"Who knows? I do know that I can't afford the attorney general's job."

Stone got a good laugh out of that.

Jamie sat up across the bed. "Was that Dino?"

"Yes, it was. Good line, huh?"

"I hope it made the *Times*," she said, picking up the paper from the breakfast tray and leafing through it. "Nope."

"That's because he just said it. That was a live shot from One Police Plaza."

"Oh, well." She reached for him.

"Not now," he said. "Breakfast will get cold." They ate quickly.

When he went downstairs, Stone walked into the living and dining rooms and looked around. All the paraphernalia from the *Times* investigative team was gone, and the place was as neat as a pin.

Jamie passed him on the way out. "Gotta run to work," she said. "I'm taking the tunnel." She vanished.

Stone went downstairs to his office.

"Did you see Dino on TV?"

"Yes, I did."

"He was great, wasn't he?"

"He won't have thought of it," Stone said, "but I'll bet no other candidate for head of the FBI will have made a two-hundred-thousand-dollar campaign contribution."

The phone rang, and Joan picked it up. "Oh, hi, there! Congratulations on your announcement. He's right here." She handed the phone to Stone. "Holly."

Stone took it. "Good morning."

"And to you. This is an official campaign call," she said. "I want to thank you for your wonderful contribution."

"It couldn't go to a better cause," Stone said. "I understand Sam did very well last night."

"Didn't he, though? Oh, I saw Dino on TV this morning—he was great."

"I'm sure he thought so, too."

"You know, he would make a terrific choice for FBI director. Do you think he'd do it?"

"Not a chance," Stone said. "Dino is a New Yorker all the way through, and he could not tolerate Washington. However, he'd love to be asked, then he can spend the rest of his life telling people that he turned down the job."

"I'll be sure and ask him," Holly said.

"I'll tell you what would be good for him, though."

"What's that?"

"Appoint him to the President's Intelligence Advisory Board. After all, he already runs the largest intelligence operation outside the federal government."

"That's ideal!"

"Well, I expect you have twenty other calls to make," Stone said, "so I won't keep you."

"Thank you for understanding. Bye." She hung up.

DOWNTOWN, HANK THOMAS sat with his father and grandfather. "So, she's already got over a hundred million dollars in her campaign war chest," he said, dejectedly. "Do you think we could do something similar?"

The old man laughed. "I don't know twenty people with that much money who don't already hate us."

"Don't worry about it," his father said. "You will not lack for funding."

"And where will the money come from?" Hank asked.

"It's better if you don't know."

"Are we going to report it?"

"Of course, and appropriately dressed up. It wouldn't be fruitful to spend the money to get you elected, only to have you impeached because of a campaign funding scandal."

"I'll leave it to you and Granddad, then."

The middle Thomas started making some calls.

"Good morning, Harvey," he said to a giant of industry.

"Morning, Jack. To what do I owe the pleasure?"

"I just wanted to give you a heads-up. Next week you're going to be appointed to the board of Hank's presidential campaign."

"Yeah? How much is that going to cost me? Business hasn't been so good, you know."

"Not a dime, Harvey, but you'll be on a published list of people who donated ten million dollars to the campaign."

"Maybe I didn't make myself clear . . ."

"No, Harvey, you just didn't listen clear. You don't have to make the donation, just take public credit for it."

"Oh? How does that work?"

"Perfectly legally, Harvey. And the next time you need financing for another takeover, H. Thomas will smile on you—as long as this is completely under your hat."

"That seems fair," Harvey said. "Who else is being so blessed?"

"Nineteen others. You'll know when the list is published, but not until then. And you'll be acquainted with a lot of the others, who will have made the same deal you have, so don't discuss it with any of them."

"When will this be announced?"

"Right after Hank's speech from the Capitol rotunda, right under the dome."

"I'll look forward to it."

"Oh, one other thing, Harvey."

"What's that?"

"Hank is going to announce as an independent candidate. Staying affiliated with the party would be a millstone around his neck."

"That's a ballsy move, Jack. You think he can get away with it?"

"Let me put it this way: I think he has a much better chance of being elected as an independent."

"Then good luck to him. I'm sick to death of those party sons of bitches."

"Expect some calls from the press for comment."

"Don't worry, I'll have something pithy for them."

Jack hung up and went to the next name on his list.

39

The executive editor of the *New York Times* looked up from his desk to find his publisher standing in the doorway.

"Good morning, Scott," Jeremy said.

"Good morning, Jeremy. Come in and have a seat." Jeremy went in and sat down on the leather sofa on one side of his editor's office, and Scott took the facing chair. "What's going on?"

"That's not a question I expect my editor to ask me," Jeremy said. "It should be the other way around."

"Well, given that you don't spend much time in this office, I deduce that you know something I don't."

"No, not really. I'm just here to ask a question you don't seem to be asking."

"What is your question?"

"My question is: What the hell is going on with this Stone Barrington character?"

"In what respect?" Scott asked calmly. He had found it best to be super calm when his publisher was asking questions like that.

"Why, after all his promises, did he shut down our operation?"

"I don't recall him making any promises," Scott said. "What he did was show us the Tommassini files, then he helped us try to find out what they mean."

"Oh, all right, but how did this latest thing happen?"

"Stone told Jamie that nothing was going to happen for a while, but something would later on. He advised her, for the meantime, to stop spending your money on further research. Why would you object to that?"

Jeremy got up and began to pace. "He's shut us out," he said, waving an arm for emphasis.

"No, he's just advised us to take a breather while he awaits further developments."

"I don't like being out of the action," Jeremy said.

"Have you calculated how much it was costing us every week to have the core of our investigative team working at his house in secret?"

"It's just salaries," Jeremy said, "and Barrington wasn't charging us rent for the space."

"I've never heard you employ the phrase, 'just salaries,' Jeremy, when discussing budgetary matters."

"Do you have any idea, or does Jamie, what Barrington expects to learn that will be so tremendous?"

"I do not, and he refused to tell Jamie, as well."

"God, I hope it's good!" Jeremy replied.

"Hoping is okay, Jeremy, but I think we have to accept that it's out of our hands for the moment."

"There's still the story of what's in those files," Jeremy said. "We could do a hell of a series on that."

"Jamie believes, as do I, that having the whole story would be much better. Publishing now would just put the Thomases in defensive mode, and we'd have to fight them before we're ready."

"Speaking of the Thomases," Jeremy said, "a friend phoned me this morning and told me something hair-raising."

"What was that?" Scott asked.

"You know this thing that Sam Meriwether did for Holly Barker, collecting more than a hundred million dollars in one go?"

"Yes. Senator Meriwether did the same thing for Kate Lee when she announced, only back then it was a million a head, instead of five million."

"Well, my friend told me that he and a bunch of other movers and shakers are going to contribute ten million each to Hank Thomas's PAC when he announces next week."

"Well, *that's* a story we can run now and beat the world!"

"No, we can't."

"Why not?"

"Because my friend made me promise not to—not just yet, anyway."

"Swell," Scott said, then muttered something under his breath.

"What was that you said?"

"I was just thinking out loud, wishing you wouldn't make promises like that—ones *I* have to keep."

"Well, you wouldn't know about it, if I hadn't promised."

"Then, we can start on the story, so that when they announce, we'll be on top of it. Did your friend mention who the other contributors are?"

"No, but I can guess half a dozen."

"We can't print guesses," Scott said.

"Here's a list of my guesses," Jeremy said, shoving a piece of paper at him. "Why don't you have a reporter call each of them and ask if he's making a ten-million-dollar contribution?"

"Then we could print the denials?" Scott asked. "I can see the lead: *'Six zillionaires deny making ten-million-dollar contributions to Hank Thomas's campaign.'* Does that sound like all the news that's fit to print?"

"Oh, all right. It was just a thought."

"Why don't you buy your friend lunch, get him outside a couple of scotches, and press him for the other names."

"What would motivate him to tell me?"

"What motivated him before? Tell him you've heard that another paper has the story, and they're going to go ahead with it without knowing everything. You're giving him the opportunity to let the horse's mouth speak."

"You want me to lie to him, Scott? The *Times* doesn't lie."

"All right. *I've* heard a rumor that *New York Magazine* has the list, and it's going to be next week's cover story."

"Is that true, Scott?"

"Probably. But I can promise you that it's true that Hank Thomas hates that magazine, since they published a story about him screwing a secretary at H. Thomas. The mention of the magazine's name ought to get you the list of contributors."

"All right, I'll discuss it with my friend over lunch. But I'm not going to lie to him."

"Jeremy, I wouldn't want you to bust your cherry this late in life. Let me know what he says."

JEREMY GREEN MET Bobby Tarnower for lunch at the Metropolitan Club, a beautifully preserved relic of the gilded age, on Fifth Avenue. Bobby ran a rapacious hedge fund that was on a buying spree, snapping up tech start-ups and the like, in the hope of hitting the jackpot two or three times during the next five years.

They started with a drink in the bar, and that time was taken up by Tarnower bragging about what he had bought and how cheaply. Jeremy waited until they were seated in the dining room before changing the subject.

"Bobby, I've heard a rumor that *New York Magazine* is going to do a cover story on you and your colleagues who are donating all that money to Hank Thomas's campaign."

"Oh, horseshit, Jeremy," Tarnower said. He took a sheet of paper from his pocket and handed it to him. "There, that's the list. Twenty men who are contributing ten million dollars each."

Jeremy read the list and smiled. "And I can publish this?"

"Yeah, you can, and you didn't have to make up that ridiculous lie to get it."

"I didn't make it up," Jeremy replied, omitting that his executive editor had.

40

Stone opened his *New York Times* and read it at his desk, with his second cup of coffee.

Joan buzzed. "Bob Cantor is here."

"Send him in."

Cantor came in and sat in his usual chair.

"Have you seen the *Times* this morning?" Stone asked.

"That's why I'm here," Bob replied. "I don't believe it."

"What don't you believe?"

"The money. It's too much."

"You're not keeping up with inflation, Bob. I just gave Holly Barker's PAC five million. Last time, when Kate first ran, they were asking for a million."

"I've had a look at their banking practices," Bob said.

"You can see that on your tap into their computer system?"

"I can, and they're transferring large sums from bank accounts in the Cayman Islands to accounts in the United States."

"How much?"

"Fifty million, so far, and they've made deposits to equal that into the Cayman accounts."

"So the Thomases are giving money to people who are then giving it to Hank's PAC?"

"I can't tell you that for sure," Bob said, "but I think it's the best explanation for what I'm seeing. I'm grateful to the *Times* for explaining it to me."

"That's not what the *Times* explained."

"It's close enough to what I'm seeing to fill in some blanks for me."

"Are they transferring from the Caymans directly to the people on the *Times* list of donors?"

"That's what I can't tell. I suspect that there is a chain of bank accounts set up in different places that are handing off the money that comes from the Caymans. Maybe four or five times each."

"Is the money being deposited in the Cayman accounts coming from H. Thomas?"

"No, they'd be crazy to do it that way. They're taking in the money the same way they're distributing it, through a chain of bank accounts: no names, just numbers."

"Hoping nobody will notice huge amounts of money being wired here and there?"

"Exactly. It's too complicated for ordinary hackers to penetrate. I just happen to have a line into their computer system, which gives me a big advantage."

"Where do you think the money originates?"

"I think they're stealing it, but I don't know how or from whom yet."

"Maybe this is too big for us, Bob," Stone said. "Maybe we should turn it over to the Treasury or the FBI."

"Then they will come and take me away," Bob pointed out. "What I'm doing isn't legal, you know." He slapped his forehead. "Why am I telling a lawyer?"

"Well, there is that."

"No, there is not. If I get a whiff of the feds around this, I'll unplug and take my gear home, leaving no trace of my presence. I'll disappear up my own ass."

"I could hardly blame you," Stone said, "and they'd be coming after me shortly thereafter."

"You think I'd rat you out, Stone?"

"No, Bob, I don't. But they can bring an awful lot of pressure to bear."

"Then let's not invite them in. Anyway, they'd take years to digest what I'd tell them, and by then Hank Thomas would be president and giving them their orders."

"That's a depressing thought," Stone said.

"Yeah, I'm pretty depressed, myself."

"What do you want to do, Bob?"

"I want to keep on doing what I'm doing. Every day, what I see makes a little more sense. I want to see it through. Maybe I'll even steal some of their money for myself, if I get the chance."

"I'm sorry, there was a car backfiring in the street, so I didn't hear that."

"Hear what? I didn't say anything."

"That's what I thought. Anything else that will depress or elate me?"

"Next time, I'll try to bring a little elation your way," Bob said. "Oh, there's another thing."

"What's that?"

"The scale of this thing—the size of the deposits and transfers—are the sort of stuff that people will kill for."

"I expect that's so."

"I didn't mean it in a general sense," Bob said. "I was thinking of me—and, of course, you."

"That's a sobering thought," Stone replied.

"I'm glad you think that. Bye." Bob left.

Stone sent Holly a text message: *I need to communicate with you in a secure manner. How?*

A LITTLE MORE than an hour later, Joan came into his office, carrying a package. "This was hand-delivered from the New York office of the State Department," she said. "You want me to open it?"

"No, I'll do it," Stone said. "There might be a bomb inside."

Joan set down the package gingerly and hurried back to her desk.

Stone found a box cutter and opened the package. Inside was an iPhone with a phone number on a Post-it stuck to the screen. Stone tapped in the number.

"Hi, there," Holly said. "You now have a secure line to me."

"Can you talk now?"

"I've just kicked a dozen people out of my office, so go ahead."

"You've seen the *Times* this morning?"

"Yes, and I hate it when I read things like that. Hank has one-upped me—not to mention doubling what I have in the war chest."

"He may be doing it illegally," Stone said.

"I would be delighted if that were true. Tell me all about it."

"No, I'll tell you as little as I can while giving you the message."

"Oh, all right, but that doesn't sound like much fun."

"Maybe later. I know someone who has some knowledge of the inner workings of Hank's campaign."

"I won't bother to ask who, because I don't want to know."

"Exactly."

"My acquaintance believes that the money those donors are giving to Hank's PAC is being stolen from somewhere—he doesn't know where—and transferred through a chain of numbered, offshore bank accounts into the accounts of the donors, who are then sending it to Hank's PAC."

"That's an interesting idea. Is your acquaintance out of his fucking mind?"

"No, he is a moderately sane person who has a much stronger grasp than you or I of how computers and banking work."

"Can your acquaintance prove this in a court of law?"

"Not yet, but he's working on it. In any case, I think he would prefer to take it to a newspaper of note rather than to the U.S. Attorney for the Southern District of New York."

"That works for me," she said. "Tell him to get a move on."

"I have already done so."

"Just so you know, when we hang up, no record of this call will exist anywhere. Cute, huh?"

"Pretty cute."

"See you around one of these days. In the meantime, keep me posted." She hung up.

So did Stone, after memorizing her number.

41

Stone lay in bed with Jamie Cox; they had thrown off the covers to cool down after their exertions, which had been considerable.

Stone turned onto his side for a better view of Jamie's body. "You are a beautiful woman," he said.

"It's all right to say, 'girl,' in that context," she replied, turning toward him and giving him a wet kiss.

"I'll keep that in mind."

She fondled him. "Is it too much to hope?"

"At my age, yes."

"What age is that?"

"A day older than yesterday. Give me a few minutes."

"Then you'll have to give me something to think about, other than your genitalia," she said, "with which my mind is currently occupied, to the exclusion of all else."

"All right, but this is off the record and neither printable nor reportable to your superiors."

"Will there come a time when those restraints will be lifted?"

"If we're lucky."

"Who's 'we'?"

"'We' is me and an acquaintance of mine and, incidentally, you. We'll all need to be lucky."

"And I can't tell Scott or Jeremy?"

"You may not."

"They're getting antsy, especially Jeremy."

"The publication of Hank Thomas's donor list should keep them feeling good for a while."

"It will wear off soon, and they'll be on my ass again."

"Who can blame them? It's such a nice ass."

"Come on, cough it up."

"You agree to my limitations?"

"Yes, if not wholeheartedly."

"There's something hinky about the origin and destination of the funds being contributed to Hank's PAC."

"Define 'hinky.'"

"It's a cop term for something that doesn't look, smell, or feel right."

"Continue."

"My friend has a theory about all of that."

"Oh, good."

"I emphasize that it's a *theory*, nothing more and maybe less."

"Less than what?"

"Less than real, possibly imaginary on his part."

"Okay, let's start with origination: Where's the money coming from?"

"The theory is, it's being stolen."

"From whom?"

"The theory ends before we arrive there."

"We're talking about tens of millions of dollars. Wouldn't someone miss that?"

"It's not money until it can be spent. Up until then it's just a lot of ones and zeros out there in cyberspace, being moved around. It's not like the victim will look in his safety-deposit box and find it empty."

"This is all beyond me."

"It's beyond me, too," Stone said. "The ones and zeros are being gathered in a number of offshore bank accounts, then transferred to a number of computers, and from there to a number of other computers."

"But eventually, they arrive in Hank's PAC?"

"Yes, but first they go into the accounts of the donors, who then contribute the funds to Hank's PAC."

"Hold on a minute," she said. She rolled over onto her back and closed her eyes. Half a minute passed before she opened them. "Let me see if I understand the upshot of all this: Hank's campaign is running, or is going to be running, on stolen money that is laundered through the contributors?"

"That is the theory."

"I just love that," Jamie said.

"You love it?"

"It's a reporter's wet dream, and I think I just came."

"I'm sorry I wasn't of more help."

"You did just fine. You know what's wrong with this theory?"

"Tell me."

"It's just too fucking good to be true. If it were true, and if I could substantiate it, it would surpass Watergate as a story. It would win every journalism prize in existence and make me more famous than Woodward and Bernstein."

"Is that such a bad thing?"

"No, it's too much of a good thing. Things like that don't happen to me. My stars are just not aligned that way."

"Things like that don't happen to anybody," Stone said, "until they do."

"I am not, repeat, *not*, going to think about this anymore."

"That would be good, if you can do it."

"I can't do it," she said. "I'm going to think about nothing else until this happens, if it ever does. Why did you tell me this?"

"Well, at the moment, everything is sort of stalled. I thought it might cheer you up."

"Cheer me up? It terrifies me! If it happens, I'll never have a life again."

"Of course you will. It just won't be the life you have now. It could be infinitely better than the life you have now."

"Jesus, I'm in bed with this lovely man. I've just had my brains fucked out—repeatedly—and I'm neck deep in the afterglow. What could be better than that?"

"Put your mind at rest," he said. "You don't have to give that up."

"It's sweet of you to say so. However, I'll have to move, I'll have to change my phone numbers and my e-mail address, and I'll have to buy an entirely new wardrobe for television appearances."

"Is the thought of that really painful?"

"I thought things couldn't get any better than they are now," she said. "I'm unprepared for a big improvement."

"May I suggest a way of calming yourself?"

"Shoot."

"If and when this all happens, you're going to have to write a book about it. Don't wait until then: start now. You'll have it half done when you learn about the rest, and that's a great head start. Lose yourself in the book."

"Can I put you in the book?"

"No."

"Why not?"

"I'll have to think about that. The experience will be different for me."

"How so? Are you afraid you won't get any credit?"

"I don't want any credit. I want my life to continue as it is. I'm not going to win any journalism prizes or get promoted to editor or write a bestselling book, but I'll be in danger of never having any privacy again. I'd have to leave the country."

"I see your point," she said. "But where would you go?"

"I have properties in Paris, London, and the English countryside, so where to go isn't a problem. I just wouldn't be able to stay here, and here is where you are. I couldn't even be seen with you in public, or there would be a howling pack of paparazzi at my front door. It would upset the neighbors and my Labrador retriever."

"I see your point."

"And before you publish, I want a head start. I don't want to be in New York when that issue of the *Times* hits the doorsteps of the city's denizens."

"I'll guarantee you a head start," Jamie said. "In fact, I might even come with you."

"Don't make any promises you can't keep," Stone said.

42

Scott was at his desk, editing a story, when Jeremy Green rapped on his door and ushered himself in.

"I'd offer you a seat, Jeremy," he said, "but you've already taken one."

"Thanks," Jeremy replied. "Do you think Jamie Cox is being diddled by Stone Barrington?"

"'Diddled'?" Scott asked. "I haven't heard that word since junior high."

"All right, fucked."

"I've no idea."

"Do you think they might be doing it?"

"Fucking?"

"Yes, isn't that what we're talking about?"

"I have to be sure what we're talking about when I'm talking to you, Jeremy."

"Never mind that. Do you think they're getting it on?"

"Now we've jumped backward from junior high to the sixties, have we?"

"I just want your opinion, Scott."

"I work hard not to form opinions until I'm presented with evidence," Scott said.

"You're evading the question."

"I'm glad you noticed."

"Do you think it's possible that they're fucking? Each other?"

"Assuming that they both have the required working parts, of course it's possible. It's also none of my business, nor yours, for that matter."

"Of course, it's my business," Jeremy said. "Yours, too."

"I'd be interested to know the route you took to believing that."

"This paper is ours—yours and mine—more than it belongs to the people who own it. If one of our reporters is screwing a major source for a major story, it would be derelict of us to allow that to happen."

"First of all, Barrington is not currently our source, having surrendered copies of the files, which is everything he had. But if you're correct about their behavior, it has already happened, so we can't prevent it. What's the next step, matching chastity belts?"

"If this thing blows up in our faces there is going to be a massive amount of scrutiny from every other news outlet everywhere," Jeremy said.

"I don't see what we can possibly do about that, except not talk about it, for fear of being overheard."

"We can fire Jamie," Jeremy said.

"We certainly cannot fire Jamie," Scott shot back. "She's the most effective investigative reporter we have, and we can't afford to be without her. Not to mention that firing her would open a new can of worms."

"Why?"

"Well, if we fired Jamie, do you think she would just walk away and wish us luck?"

"You mean she could sue us?"

"She could, and she would probably win a big settlement, but she will also walk into another job within a matter of hours, and she would take this enormous story with her. Do you want to be reading about it in the *Wall Street Journal* or the *New Yorker*?"

"That's a depressing thought," Jeremy said.

"Jeremy, we're dug in to this thing up to our armpits. All we can do now is wait for facts to emerge and make sure that everything is triple sourced. I hope you understand that."

"Sure, I do, Scott. I just needed to be told by somebody other than myself."

"Jeremy," Scott said, "has it ever occurred to you that this office and your office and Jamie's office and all our telephones could be bugged?"

Jeremy sat bolt upright. "Do you think that's possible?"

"I do."

"Well, let's get somebody in here to find out!"

"That's your department, not mine. I just edit."

"All right, I'll get somebody in."

"Who?"

"I'll call Mike Freeman at Strategic Services right now. There's nobody better at this stuff."

"How are you going to explain the expense to the board?"

"Routine security. We'd be negligent not to scrub the place clean." He stood up and headed for the door. "I'll make the call now."

"Bye-bye, Jeremy." Scott gave him a little wave.

. . .

MIKE FREEMAN GAZED across the desk at the publisher of the *New York Times* as Viv entered the room. "Jeremy, have you met Vivian Bacchetti?"

The two shook hands. "In passing only," Jeremy replied.

"I understand your concerns about keeping this work quiet, so I thought it would be best if Viv, who is our chief operating officer, could handle it personally, since she already knows about it through her husband, Dino."

"Good idea, thank you."

Viv produced a notebook and a pen. "Now, Jeremy, how large an area are we talking about?"

"The editorial department, which occupies all of one floor and part of another."

"Then we should sweep all of that?"

"Yes, I think so. Also, my office, on the floor above."

"Only your office on that floor?"

"I'm the only person on that floor who knows what we're working on."

"If there's something new, beyond the files, do you want to tell us what that is?"

"Not unless I have to. I'm just concerned that there is no electronic surveillance of the two areas I've mentioned. If, in the course of things, you should discover conversations about our current story, then we can talk."

"Well, you seem to be devoting a lot of space to stories about Hank Thomas's expected announcement."

"Correct. That's certainly relevant. Is H. Thomas a client of yours? Would that be a conflict?"

"No, H. Thomas keeps all its security operations in-house. No conflict."

"Thank God," Jeremy said.

"I assume there are people working twenty-four/seven in your editorial department."

"Yes, but only a few at night."

"I suggest that you pick a four-hour period and announce that there is going to be a visit from a pest control company, who will spray the area with gasses that humans would find offensive or even caustic. That will clear them out for a time."

"Let me discuss it with our editor and ask him for a recommendation on when to empty the floors involved."

"Good. We'll send an eight-man crew in with their equipment. That should be adequate for the sweep, and they'll be dressed in coveralls bearing the name of a pest control company. They'll also be carrying tanks and masks which will convey to your staff that they won't want to breathe the air while we're present. They'll arrive in two vans in your garage, and the vans will bear the company name, too."

"That sounds good," Jeremy said. "I'll call you this afternoon about the schedule."

Everyone shook hands and Jeremy departed. He was in the backseat of his driven car before it occurred to him that he had not asked what this service was going to cost. Oh, well.

43

Bob Cantor sat in an upstairs bedroom of Stone's house and worked his way from right to left at the bank of computer monitors he had installed there. He had installed his three software bugs on the sysop machines in the computer room at H. Thomas, which covered all fifty computers, and which connected to the secret website he had set up. Three signals appeared on three different monitors, which indicated that all the Thomas computers were being employed in some sort of exercise. He concentrated everything he had on receiving, recording, and decoding their output.

FOUR HOURS LATER, exhausted, he fell into bed and went to sleep nearly instantly. He was awakened by the television receiver, on which he had installed a timer, which was now turning it on at seven AM.

He had displayed six muted screens: NBC, CBS, ABC, CNN, FOX, and MSNBC, and after an hour or so all six suddenly displayed a single image, that of Congressman Hank Thomas. Bob switched on the sound.

"Good morning to all of you," Hank Thomas said, revealing

very fine dental work. "I'm grateful to all the networks for giving me a couple of minutes of their time to make an announcement.

"For a long time I have been troubled by the direction the country has taken during the years of the two Lees, who have successively served as president. They have exhibited the behavior we have come to expect from the Democratic Party: soft on defense and immigration; wild overspending on things like PBS, the arts, and medical care; and cutting our military to the bone and beyond. The result has been a weaker nation, one constantly taken advantage of by our enemies and even our allies. I have also been disappointed in the actions of the Republican Party, and so, as I today announce my candidacy for President of the United States, I do so as a conservative independent. I want to come to this election unstained by the continuing political warfare we have seen so much of.

"These are the things I promise you: a stronger economy than this country has ever seen; a military that can handle three wars simultaneously anywhere in the world; a sensible medical insurance program, which will cover much of every family's healthcare costs; trade policies that will keep our unemployment down and our wages up; absolute support for our Second Amendment rights; and finally, a constitutional amendment that will ban abortion in all its evil forms. I also promise you a major upgrading of our cybersecurity tools and weapons. No longer will any nation be able to attack our vital computer systems. There will be much more, of course, but those are the bones and structure of my campaign.

"I look forward to personally meeting a large number of you in every corner of our country: urban, suburban, and rural.

"Finally, I have another announcement. A committee of twenty of our nation's most prominent business, technology, and financial leaders have each contributed ten million dollars to my political action committee, which will allow me to wage the strongest possible campaign against my Democratic and Republican opponents. The list of those contributors is being released to the press as I speak.

"Thank you for your attention and, I hope, your support."

BOB TURNED HIS ATTENTION to his computer monitors and found that whatever task they had undertaken had been completed while he slept. What the task was baffled him.

He got out of bed, showered, shaved, and dressed, then returned to his monitors. When he was satisfied that he had seen what he was looking for, he went downstairs to Stone Barrington's office.

"YOU LOOK TIRED, Bob," Stone said as Joan brought them coffee. "I hope you didn't work all night."

"No, I got a few hours of sleep, but my computers did not. I believe the Thomas installation completed its task of moving money into their own accounts and out into the accounts of their contributors, then out again into the Thomas PAC."

"You *believe* that is what happened?"

"I still cannot prove my theory to the extent of duplicating it, but I feel stronger than ever that the theory is accurate. But there is something else very peculiar going on."

Stone leaned back in his chair and sipped his coffee. "Go ahead, tell me."

"I've explained that I think the funds are being stolen from accounts around the world, then run through the Thomas systems."

"Yes, I understand that," Stone said.

"What's peculiar is that the funds do not seem to exist before entering that system."

Stone's brow wrinkled. "If the funds don't exist, then how can they be transferred, then spent?"

"I've misstated my theory," Bob said. "What I mean is that the transaction is somehow wiped clean at the origination point."

"How is that possible?"

"It's ingenious, but not impossible. I believe they're withdrawing huge sums of money, then erasing that fact from the accounts they took it from."

"That's a frightening supposition," Stone said.

"It certainly scared me shitless," Bob replied. "I went over all the transmissions that I recorded, and I have concluded that it really happened."

"Are you going to be able to learn where the money was taken from?"

"I can only deduce," Bob said.

"And what do you deduce?"

"There is a central banking account that receives and disburses funds from virtually every bank in the world. If I'm wiring you money, I first send an authorization to my bank. They verify the authorization, then they wire it to the central account, where it remains until it is withdrawn and wired to other accounts. First, your bank has to prove to them that the transfer is properly authorized, then the receiving bank makes an application to the central account to collect the funds, after having identified themselves properly, and the funds are sent to them. Those banks could wire the funds to other accounts in other banks, perhaps many of them."

"So, where in this process do you think they are diverting the funds?"

"They aren't diverting the funds, they're just following the rules, but when the transaction is complete, they're erasing all trace of it having happened and that they've digitally restored the funds."

"How can they do that?" Stone asked.

"If I could tell you that, I would be living in the lap of luxury on a private island somewhere warm."

"So how can we prove this?"

"Unless you can wring a confession from the people who wrote the code, it can't be proven, only deduced."

"Will you explain your theory to the Treasury and the FBI?"

"If I do, I'll be arrested for cyber crimes."

"Yes," Stone said, "there is that."

"I think it's time for me to get out of town," Bob said.

44

Stone and Dino met at P. J. Clarke's for dinner.

Dino looked at him closely. "All right," he said, "let's have it."

"Have what?"

"Whatever you're going to ask me for."

"You think that's what this dinner is about?" Stone asked, sounding hurt.

"That's what I think. Only this time, it's bigger. It has to do with the Tommassini files, doesn't it?"

"Before I tell you about this and ask your advice, I need to know that what I'm about to tell you stays between us."

"Advice? That's all you want?"

"That and your solemn promise that it stops here."

"My 'solemn promise'? Won't a carefree promise do?"

"I want you to swear on whatever Catholic cops swear on—your mother's grave or something."

"How about my mother's mortal soul?" Dino asked. "Will that do?"

"It would, if you had title to it, but I believe it's in other hands."

"You have my word," Dino said. "That used to be good enough for you."

"It still is. The reason I'm being so careful is that spreading this information puts another party in jeopardy."

"Which other party?"

"A mutual acquaintance."

"Well, that narrows it down to a few hundred people we both know."

"I'm not going to mention his name, but you'll know who I'm talking about."

"So I won't need to go through my Rolleiflex?"

"You mean Rolodex. A Rolleiflex is a camera."

"No shit. You think I didn't know that?"

"What, did you say Rolleiflex just to annoy me?"

"I would have, if I'd thought of it. C'mon, spit it out."

"Our mutual acquaintance gained entrance into some offices on the ground floor of the H. Thomas building and discovered a huge computer installation that is unconnected to the banking firm."

"So what are the Thomases doing with that? Sending out their Christmas cards?"

"No, they're stealing tens of millions of dollars from the global banking industry and laundering it through Hank's PAC."

"From the global banking industry?"

"Yes."

"The whole thing?"

"Sort of." Stone took him, step by step, through Bob Cantor's theory.

"That sounds impossible," Dino said.

"It's not impossible," Stone replied. "Our acquaintance got into their system and copied what they were doing."

225

"So, he can prove this?"

"That's the impossible part," Stone said. "He says it can only be deduced from the available evidence, not definitively proved. They've covered their tracks too well."

"Well, that's just swell. You're reporting a crime of earth-shaking proportions, but you can't prove they did it, or even that they thought about doing it."

"What can be proved is that a list of twenty contributors received ten million dollars each, then contributed it to Hank's PAC."

Dino thought about that. "Why is it illegal for them to receive ten million dollars and then give it to a PAC?"

"It's illegal if the reimbursements were stolen money."

"But you can't prove it was stolen."

"No, but I'll bet the FBI's or the NSA's computer geeks could figure it out, using the data our acquaintance copied."

"And where is the data?"

"In a guest bedroom at my house."

"Is Bob living in your house?"

"He was, sort of, for a while. He left all his equipment there."

"So the NSA or some government agency should just send somebody over there to take a look at it?"

"I guess that's how it has to start. The trouble is, if the feds get involved, it could take them years to get to the point where they could get an indictment, and by the time they fully understand what happened, Hank could be President of the United States, and those agencies would be working for him."

"Somehow, that sounds familiar."

"Well, yes."

"Maybe we should start with something a little more modest, say tax evasion."

"The money's not going through Hank's hands. It goes to the PAC, which doesn't pay taxes."

"That's not what I mean."

"What do you mean?"

"I mean that the donors who received the funds have to pay taxes on them, right?"

"I see your point."

"Then I'm sure the IRS would be interested in examining their records."

"But, if they paid the taxes, we're back where we started," Stone pointed out.

"Yeah, but they're not going to have done that."

"Why not?"

"Well," Dino said. "It sounds as though Hank persuaded them to contribute, because it wouldn't actually cost them anything. It's not their money in the first place."

"You think they're dumb enough to run ten mil through their bank accounts and not worry about the taxes?"

"I think at least some of them might just kind of overlook paying taxes," Dino said.

"I think you could be right," Stone said, "but the IRS would have to go through a whole investigation, and that would still eat up all the time before the election."

"Here's a thought," Dino said. "We could forget about the criminal charges and just crucify them and Hank."

"I trust you're not speaking literally."

"No, but the next best thing: we can crucify them in the *New York Times*, which is already on the case, right?"

Stone's eyebrows went up. "This is why I came to you, Dino. I knew you'd come up with something sneaky, but effective."

"Isn't the *Times* waiting for something like this to come up?"

"Yes, they are, but they're going to want proof, too."

"Well, sure, but maybe Bob's computers would be enough to convince them. After all, we don't need proof beyond a reasonable doubt, just enough to get this on the front page of the *Times*. They've had a lot of experience with cooking people's gooses."

"They have," Stone said. "And once they've exposed the scheme, the feds can step in and investigate, take as long as they like."

"And Hank's campaign sinks like a huge stone," Dino said.

"Good," Stone said. "I think I can choke down a steak now. I'll call the *Times* people in the morning."

"You'd better have Bob there to explain it to them," Dino said.

"Ah, well . . ."

"You don't want Bob there?"

"Bob has, uh, taken a vacation."

"I believe the proper term is 'taken a powder,'" Dino said.

"I'm afraid you're right."

45

Scott, Jeremy, and Jamie emerged into Stone's house through the tunnel entrance, and they had another fellow with them who appeared to be a teenager.

"This is Huey Horowitz," Scott said to Stone. "Huey is our director of digital services."

Stone shook the young man's hand, which felt more like that of a young girl. "Hello, Huey." He refrained from asking his age.

"I'm nineteen," Huey said. "I graduated from high school when I was eleven and from MIT, with a master's, when I was fifteen."

"Congratulations on both," Stone said.

"You wanted me to look at some computers?"

"Come with me, all of you," Stone said. He took them up to the third floor, to the guest room where Bob had been working. "All this was bought and installed by an acquaintance of mine," Stone said, "who is probably almost as smart as Huey."

That raised a giggle from Huey. "Do you have any idea what he was working on?"

"Before I tell you that," Stone said, "I need a promise from each of you that his name will never be mentioned in the *Times*, nor will any references be made that might connect him to this work."

"Is whatever he did legal?" Jeremy asked.

"Let's just say that a court would have to determine that," Stone replied.

"So it's illegal?"

"I didn't say that, and anyway, it's irrelevant."

"Okay, we agree to your terms," Jeremy said.

"I'm all in," Huey said. "What was he working on?"

"He discovered an enormous computer installation on the ground floor of the H. Thomas building downtown, what he called a semi-supercomputer, made up of fifty PCs all connected."

"Cool," Huey said.

"Stone," Jamie interjected, "this is Bob, right? Not your Labrador retriever, the geek?"

"We can call him that for the sake of convenience," Stone said.

"Why isn't Bob here to tell us about this?" Scott asked.

"He felt a strong urge to be somewhere else," Stone explained.

"Ah."

Stone recited what Bob had told him and what he had repeated to Dino.

"Holy shit," Jeremy said when Stone was done.

"I'll say," Huey echoed. "But we can't prove where the money came from."

"Why not?" Scott asked.

"Because the code these people wrote erased all trace of itself after the funds had been transferred."

"Huey," Jeremy said, "can you backtrack through all this and see if you can discover the source of the funds? We'll give you whatever support you may need."

"Well, one guy discovered this, so I can backtrack through the recordings he made and understand it, but I doubt very much if I'm going to be able to nail the source of the money."

"As Bob likes to say, it can't be proven," Stone said, "but it can be deduced from the available information."

"He's right, I think," Huey replied. "I'm going to need some time alone with this installation."

"How much time?" Jeremy asked.

"All the time I need," said Huey. He sat down at Bob's desk. "I'll get back to you."

Dismissed, they all went down to Stone's study.

Jeremy turned to Scott. "Can you write about this in a way that will allow us to expose these people, without claiming that we can prove it?"

"Jeremy," Jamie interjected. "We write stories like that every day. Anyway, I'll be doing the writing."

"She's right," Scott said. "I'll confine myself to editing and we'll get a lawyer on it, too, so we're sure of not stepping over a line."

Huey appeared at the study door.

"Already?" Jeremy asked.

"I'm already finished," Huey said, "and Bob was right about what he said. He's set himself up as a system administrator of that system, but I don't have the passwords. They're going to be at least twenty digits and symbols, so I can't crack them quickly. Can you get in touch with Bob, Stone, and ask him for them?"

"I'll try," Stone said. "Be right back." He went down to his office and found the throwaway cell phone Bob had given him, then dialed Bob's own throwaway. To his surprise, Bob answered. "Speak your name," he said.

231

"The *Times* people are here, and they brought a kid named Huey with them."

"Huey Horowitz?" Bob asked.

"How'd you know?"

"The kid is famous, a prodigy."

"He wants your sysop passwords."

"Has he been into the bedroom where I was working?"

"Yes."

"There's a safe in the closet, like a hotel safe. The passwords are in there, and the safe combination is 7070."

"Good. You okay?"

"I'm enjoying myself."

"Huey may want to speak with you."

"It would be an honor to hear from him."

"I'll give him this number."

"Good. If I don't answer immediately tell him to leave a message with a secure number I can use."

"Will do." Stone went back to the study and handed Huey a slip of paper and his throwaway cell. "There's a safe in the closet. This is the combination. The passwords are in the safe. You can call Bob on this cell phone, but not on your own phone or one in my house or at the *Times*."

"Cool," Huey said, then went back upstairs.

"Bob knows who Huey is," Stone said to the group, "and he's impressed."

"We've been talking," Jeremy said. "I'm willing to print the story with what we know now, if we absolutely have to, but I want Huey to have a shot at determining the source of the funds first."

"Actually," Stone said, "Bob deduced the source: it's this central clearinghouse. He just doesn't know where the instructions came from."

"Whatever," Jeremy said. "I want Huey to have a shot."

"Well, now we have Huey and Bob working together," Stone replied. "That's got to be a good thing."

They had lunch and sent a ham and cheese sandwich up to Huey, since, apparently, that was all he ate.

LATE IN THE AFTERNOON, Huey came in and flopped down on a sofa in the study. "Okay, Bob and I have figured it out."

"Tell us," Jeremy said.

"The reason we can't backtrack to the origin of the instructions to the central banking office is simple, really."

"Simple enough for us to understand?" Scott asked.

"Sure. The instructions didn't originate in the Thomas computer system. They came from another computer that just called it in. Somebody's laptop, maybe, or somebody's iPhone. If we want to prove all this definitively, we need that computer."

46

They all stared disconsolately at Huey. Jeremy finally spoke up. "So we have to find this laptop or iPhone?"

"That would be helpful," Huey said. "I'd like to point out that there are fifty people working in that big room that Bob described, and I would think that all of them have a laptop *and* an iPhone."

"Maybe you could have someone mug each of them as they're on their way home from work," Jamie said brightly.

"That's not funny, Jamie," Jeremy said.

"It's what you'd have to do," Huey said. "Of course . . ." He stopped talking.

"'Of course' what?" Jeremy asked.

"Of course, the code is probably not on a computer or iPhone. Those devices are too easy to lose or have stolen. It's much more likely to be on a key chain."

"What are you talking about?" Jeremy asked.

"A thumb drive," Stone said.

"The kind you can hang on your key chain," Huey said, holding up a key chain of his own, thumb drive attached. "I keep all my personal records and files on this and a chip imbedded in my neck, in case I'm ever kidnapped."

"You're worried about being kidnapped?" Jamie asked.

"Certainly," Huey replied. "That or being assassinated. The stuff I do is very annoying to the people I do it to. They pay a lot of money to geeks, who try to figure it out. Eventually, someone is going to decide that it's faster and cheaper to just eliminate me from the scene."

"Huey," Scott said, "you have personal security assigned to you."

"I do?" Huey asked. "News to me."

"We thought you'd be more comfortable if you didn't know."

"Uh-uh. I feel more comfortable knowing. What do they look like?"

"A man and a woman in business clothes."

"Isn't this program too big to fit on something like your thumb drive?" Jeremy asked.

"No, it's a fairly small program. You would load it into the Thomas system, use it, then delete it. All it does is communicate instructions to the central banking facility, then erase its own tracks."

"Well," Jeremy said, "it's going to be a lot harder to locate a thumb drive than a laptop or an iPhone."

"There's a way we can avoid mugging all those people," Huey said.

"Oh, good," Jamie said, laughing. "How?"

"We wait until they're going to move some money. When they've copied the program into their system, I steal it."

"I like it," Stone said. "Nobody gets hit over the head."

"That is devoutly to be wished," Jeremy replied.

"How big a window are you going to have between when the

software is loaded into their computer system and when they erase it?"

"That depends on how many transactions they want to accomplish," Huey said. "Of course, they have a semi-supercomputer to work with, and that's fast, but it can't be faster than the time the central banking system takes to request and authenticate the instructions. If it's one transaction, it would take substantially less than a minute, but if it's a taller order, they could be exposed for much longer."

"How will you be able to tell when they're transacting?"

"Well, Bob has already implanted his hardware, so I can write some code that will send us a message when their computers are working full tilt."

"So, you're just going to sit there in front of a monitor and wait for it to warn you?"

Huey turned toward Stone. "Can I move into the room where Bob's setup is?"

"Certainly," Stone said. "It's ready for occupancy."

"Cool," Huey replied. "Now I can sleep, and the computer will wake me when the activity increases."

"I'll tell Helene, the housekeeper, to keep you in ham and cheese sandwiches," Stone said. "If you want anything different, just tell her."

"Cool," Huey said. "I'd better get upstairs and write some code." He gave them a little wave, then left the room.

"That kid is quite an asset, Jeremy," Stone said.

"He certainly is. And he's not just a geek, he knows how to manage his department, too. He's the only person in our building who has three assistants, who work hard to keep up with him."

"One of these days he's going to take your job," Stone said.

"I'm not worried," Jeremy replied. "My job would bore him silly."

"I suppose you have to keep him excited and interested."

"He doesn't seem to get excited, and he finds *everything* interesting."

LATER IN THE DAY, Stone went up to the master suite to get something, and on his way back downstairs he knocked on Huey's door.

"Come in!" Huey called.

Stone opened the door. The first thing he saw was Huey sitting at the computer console, apparently naked.

"Everything okay?" Stone asked. Then he saw the lump in the bed.

"Their system is idling along at about eight percent of the computing power available to them," Huey said.

The lump in the bed moved. The covers were thrown back, revealing a lanky young woman with lots of blond hair—just as naked as Huey.

"Forgive me," Stone said, backing toward the door.

The girl got up and trotted into the bathroom, apparently not noticing Stone.

"It's all right," Huey said. "She's not shy. Actually, she has an exhibitionist streak in her."

The toilet flushed, and the blonde trotted back to the bed and dived in, noticing Stone for the first time. "Oh, hi," she said, then pulled up the covers.

"Hi," Stone replied.

"Stone, this is Trixie. Trixie, Stone."

"Hi, again," she said from under the covers.

"How do you do?" Stone replied.

"She does very well," Huey said. "I'll call you, if the pot starts to boil."

Stone let himself out and continued downstairs, shaking his head. Young Huey did pretty well, too, he thought.

47

Stone took Jamie, and they met Dino and Viv at Patroon. Everybody air-kissed.

"I hear you met Huey Horowitz," Viv said.

"I hear your people have been following him."

"Yes, and with the greatest difficulty. The kid never stops moving, and he moves at the speed of light."

"He apparently takes that trait to bed with him," Stone said.

"Oh?"

"I stopped into his room to see how he was doing, and there was a smashing blonde with him, running around naked."

"Oh, good," Viv said. "Maybe he'll burn off some of that energy and make our work easier."

"I hear he has three assistants trying to keep up with him."

"Actually, it's four," Jamie said. "He employs the fourth himself, and she's in charge of running his life."

"It's hard to imagine a nineteen-year-old life that requires four assistants."

"Yesterday, he went up to Turnbull & Asser and ordered a dozen shirts made. He also got measured for some suits."

"Suits? For a nineteen-year-old? How can he afford that shop on a *Times* salary?"

"He probably doesn't need the salary," Jamie said. "He does all sorts of other stuff. He's written half a dozen apps for the iPhone that are heavily used. He gets something like a quarter or fifty cents for each sale, but the sales are in the millions. He also does a lot of stock trading, buying and selling from wherever he is on his iPhone."

"How does he do with his trading?"

"Nobody knows, except his personal assistant, I guess, and his accountant."

"Well, I'm glad Huey is working on our side, instead of with the Thomases."

"Me, too," Jamie said.

They ordered.

"How DID YOUR SWEEP of the *Times* offices go, Viv?" Stone asked over dessert.

"We found three bugs," she said.

"Where?"

"I don't think I can say," she replied.

"Let me say it for you, Viv," Jamie said. "All three were in Jeremy's office."

Stone tried not to choke on his crème brûlée.

"You've never seen anybody so embarrassed," Jamie said.

"Well, his instincts were good," Stone replied. "There were bugs after all."

"He's been reconstructing his conversations from his diary and his memory, trying to figure out what the bug might have picked up," Viv said. "Fortunately, nearly all his sensitive conversations for the last few weeks have been conducted in Scott's office or the conference room, both of which are clean."

"Jeremy has instituted regular sweeps," Jamie said.

"He's also started to spread some disinformation," Viv allowed, "hoping to throw whoever is listening off the trail. He has pointedly said that the investigation into the Tommassini files bore no publishable fruit."

"Do you know who's doing the listening?"

"No. The signal goes to the Internet, but we haven't been able to figure out what the website is called. From there, the listeners can recall whatever he may have said within listening distance of the microphones."

"Once Huey has solved the big problem he's working on," Stone said, "put him on tracing the bug. Somehow, I don't think it would be hard for him."

"Have any of the Thomases visited Jeremy in his office?" Stone asked.

"I don't know," Viv replied, "but I'll find out. That's one way the bugs could have been planted."

ONCE HOME, Stone stopped by Huey's room to check on him. He was sitting up in bed, watching Rachel Maddow. "This woman is very smart," he said to Stone.

"Where's Trixie?"

"Oh, she's got an early-morning shoot at *Vanity Fair* tomorrow morning."

"She models?"

"She used to. Now she's a photographer, and she makes a lot more money than a model does."

"Good for her. Nothing yet from the semi-supercomputer?"

"All quiet," Huey said.

Stone said good night and went to join Jamie in bed.

THE FOLLOWING MORNING as Stone sat at his desk, he heard the sound of a telephone ringing, but muffled. He traced the noise to his desk drawer and found the State Department phone Holly had sent him.

"Hello?"

"I thought you weren't going to answer," she said.

"I had to find the phone. How's the campaign going?"

"Very well, thanks. We had a little of the wind taken out of our sails when Hank Thomas revealed his list of super-contributors."

"I don't suppose any of them are contributing to you, too."

"You don't suppose correctly. Listen I've heard a rumor that the money all those people contributed came right out of the Thomases' hands and into their accounts, and were then donated to Hank's PAC."

"Where'd you hear that?"

"From an overseas source, oddly enough."

"How far overseas?"

"Let's just say a Caribbean island. Have you heard such a rumor in New York?"

"I never listen to rumors," Stone said, avoiding the lie.

"I'd love to nail him doing that," she said. "I'm not sure it's illegal, but it would greatly embarrass his campaign."

"It would be illegal if the contributors didn't declare the money as income."

"Now *that's* an idea I can do something about."

"Are you going to sic the IRS on them?"

"I'm not going to do a thing, but somebody might put a flea in their ear."

"You should have been a mafioso," Stone said. "Or whatever the female of that is."

"*Mafiosa*, I expect," Holly replied. "Well, I'd better go find somebody who can transport a flea to its destination."

"Good luck with that, and everything else, too."

"Bye-bye." She hung up.

48

Stone was watching MSNBC the following morning when their ace poll-interpreting guy, Steve Kornacki, began putting up screens with numbers on them.

"These represent the first polls we've seen where several candidates from both parties, plus one well-known independent, are the subjects. Holly Barker is leading the Democratic candidates with 57 percent of her party backing her, along with 21 percent of Republicans. Her Democratic number is smaller than we might expect, since she's the best known of the candidates, and her Republican numbers are higher than we might expect, which is very interesting.

"None of the candidates for the Republican nomination has more than 35 percent of the Republican vote because of this guy." He put up the numbers for Hank Thomas.

"Congressman Thomas is getting 41 percent of Republican votes and 18 percent of the Democrats. When we get the race boiled down to fewer candidates, this is all going to get a lot more interesting."

Stone mulled this over, and he was not displeased with Holly's showing.

Huey Horowitz rapped on his office door and entered.

"Anything?"

"Nothing," Huey said. "However I think I may know the reason for the lack of traffic on the semi-supercomputer."

"What's that?"

"The transfers for the twenty giant contributors are complete, so now they're waiting for something else."

"Do you know what that is?"

"In some of their e-mails they call it the BO," Huey said.

"Do you know what that means?"

"I'm just guessing, but I think it could mean the Big One."

Stone poured Huey some coffee. "That sounds ominous."

"I mean, if this were North Korea talking about nuclear testing, we'd know what the Big One is."

"Have they taken in any other deposits, except the contributors'?"

"No, just those."

"And you think they stole those funds from the banking system, but covered their tracks?"

"I do."

"Then maybe the BO is something they've been building up to. They've tested the system with the contributors' accounts, and it worked, right?"

"Right."

"Maybe they're planning to pull off a heist," Stone suggested. "The Big One."

"What, the two hundred million they've stolen isn't enough?"

"That was for Hank's campaign," Stone said. "Maybe now they want a little something for themselves."

"By 'little something,' you mean a lot."

"Right," Stone said. "Tell me, are there any limits to what they can steal and get away with?"

"That depends on how they've written the code we're trying to intercept. In theory, they could steal anything they want. However, at some point the drain on the system would be noticed by somebody, who might start questioning the transfers. The central account probably has a limit on individual transfers and/or the total number of daily transactions, or the amounts of those transactions."

"They'd be crazy not to," Stone said.

"They certainly would."

"Is there any way to find out what the limits are?"

"Maybe Jeremy knows somebody in the international system," Huey said. "I could ask him."

"Do that," Stone said.

"In the meantime," Huey said, "I'm getting a bad case of cabin fever, so I'm going to set up the system here to send me an e-mail if anything starts to happen. Then I can get some fresh air."

"You're in charge, Huey. We'll do it any way you want."

Huey shifted in his chair but didn't rise. "Stone, may I ask your advice about something? This is personal advice."

"Sure, Huey, if you think I can help." He reflected that Huey didn't need advice about women, if Trixie was his standard.

"Over my years at the *Times* I've also dabbled in other things: I've written some apps, which have been lucrative, and I've done some consulting work, also lucrative. As a result I've built up a portfolio, doing the trading myself, which has grown into quite a pile."

"Is the pile mostly from your cash contributions or from portfolio growth?"

"Mostly my contributions," Huey said.

"If you don't mind my asking, because the question bears on the advice I might give you, how much is in the pile now?"

"About three and a half million."

"Have you paid taxes on all of it?"

"Yes, I'm scrupulous about that."

"Well, let me tell you how I handle my pile, as it were. A few years ago I formed an investment company with two friends, Mike Freeman . . ."

"From Strategic Services?"

"Yes."

"I've got some of their stock, it's done well. Who's the other guy?"

"His name is Charley Fox. Previously he was one of Goldman Sachs's youngest partners. Charley does our investing, along with any tips Mike and I might pick up, and he's done better for us than I was doing with a private bank. Perhaps you and Charley should sit down together and discuss how you're going to proceed."

"I'd like that," Huey said. "Will you set it up?"

"Maybe a lunch sometime soon."

"That would be great."

"Do you own a suit?" Stone asked, even though he already knew the answer.

"I do. I don't wear these jeans all the time, though they may look like I do. Helene made me let her launder my stuff."

"I'll speak to Charley and get back to you."

"Okay, just use my regular cell phone."

"I'll do that." Huey excused himself and left.

Stone called Charley Fox.

"Hey, there."

"Hey. I think I may have an investor you might want to meet," he said. "He's not a big one, yet, but he's very promising."

"Tell me about him."

Stone did. "I think he might also be a source for tips on the tech market," he said. "He's into that." He gave Charley Huey's number.

"I'll do a little research on him, then give him a call," he said.

"See you later." They both hung up.

49

Charley Fox looked up from his table to see a very young man in a suit, shirt, and tie that had never been worn before, standing in the doorway. He waved, and the youngster came over. Stone had not told him he was a high school student.

Charley stood and offered his hand. Huey Horowitz took it—his grip was firm but his flesh was soft. These hands had never strayed far from a computer keyboard, Charley reckoned.

Huey sat down. "I'm nineteen," he said. "I graduated from Groton at eleven and from MIT, with a master's, at fifteen. I always try and get that out of the way up front."

"Understood," Charley said, handing him a menu.

"What is this place?" Huey asked. "There was no sign out front, just a number."

"It's a private club that doesn't like to advertise its presence," Charley replied. "Stone is a member, too."

"I see some familiar faces," Huey said, looking around. "Politicians, the police commissioner over there."

"That's Dino Bacchetti, Stone's best friend."

"Oh. What are the membership requirements here?"

"Just one: that the candidate knows ten people who are

members and who like him enough that they are willing to write enthusiastic letters supporting his candidacy."

"I see."

"There's no minimum age," Charley said, to put his mind at rest.

"I wonder how many members I know," Huey mused.

"Well, let's see: you know Stone, then there are your executive editor and publisher at the *Times*. Then there's me. That's four."

Huey nodded and looked at the menu. "What's good?"

"Everything," Charley said. "If you're in the mood for fish, there's Dover sole today. I recommend it."

"Sounds good," Huey said.

"Would you like something to drink?"

"No, thanks, but you go ahead."

A waiter came and took their order.

"Well," Charley said, "Stone tells me you've built up a nest egg."

Huey laughed. "I think of it as my fortune."

"And so it is," Charley replied. "What are your ambitions for it?"

"To turn it into ten million."

"How quickly?"

"Well, it took me four years to save the three and a half, so I don't expect it to be overnight."

"That's a healthy expectation," Charley said. "How much are you saving a year?"

"About a million dollars," Huey said.

"Not from your *Times* salary, I take it."

"No, I have outside income from writing apps and consulting on computer matters."

"Let me tell you how we work," Charley said. "Stone and

Mike already had considerable fortunes when we began. Mine was more like yours, perhaps a bit more. I'm tracking the market, of course, but I'm always on the lookout for a good start-up or a moderately successful company that we can buy outright. Sometimes there's a good income stream from the business, other times they're losing money but have an initial public offering in their future."

"So there's always the chance of making a killing."

"A chance, yes. No guarantees, of course, but we're averaging annual value gains of around twenty percent per annum."

"That's spectacular," Huey said.

"Any questions?"

"Can I withdraw funds at any time? Like if I want to buy a house or a boat?"

"You can, but it's better to borrow at current rates and pay back from profits. We can usually arrange favorable financing for special purchases."

"I like it," Huey said. "Am I a satisfactory investor for your purposes?"

"You are," Charley said. "You seem to have a bright future."

"I believe so," Huey said. "Then I'm in." He offered his hand. Charley shook it.

Huey produced a checkbook. "Who do I make the check out to?"

Charley smiled. "I'll send you some documents to read and sign, then you can send the check. I stress that it is important that you read them before you sign."

"I'll look forward to receiving them," Huey said, handing him his *Times* business card.

• • •

AT MID-AFTERNOON, STONE took a call from Charley Fox. "How'd it go?"

"I love him," Charley said. "I'd adopt him, if he were a little younger."

"Is he on board?"

"Yes, and we're lucky to have him. I've already e-mailed him the documents."

"Good."

"I think he's going to be a good candidate for the club, too, once he meets a few more people."

"I'll write a letter."

"What are you working on with him?"

"I can't tell you, but if it happens, it will knock your socks off."

"I'll look forward to the day," Charley said.

STONE TOOK JAMIE to the River Café, under the Brooklyn Bridge, for dinner that evening. Stone ordered half a bottle of a good champagne.

"What a beautiful setting." Jamie said, watching the tugs and ferries go up and down the East River.

"It is, isn't it? You look excited about something else, though."

"I am. I've written three chapters of my book."

"That was quick."

"The best thing the newspaper business has taught me is how to plant my ass in a chair every day and write two thousand words, whether I feel like it or not."

"A valuable skill," Stone said.

"An essential one, if you ever hope to make a living as a writer—and I hope to make a fortune at it."

"Put me down for a couple dozen copies," Stone said. "I'll send them to friends."

"Consider it done."

"Where are you working?"

"Anyplace I can, except the *Times*. I don't want them to be able to say that I wrote it on their nickel."

"A good policy."

"It's in my contract that they get to fact-check any books I write based on my reporting, and they get to approve the pub date, so that it doesn't interfere with something else they're working on."

"That seems fair."

"How long before we can go to your house and climb into bed?" Jamie asked.

"How fast can you eat?" Stone replied.

50

Joan buzzed. "Huey Horowitz to see you."

"Send him in."

Huey walked in wearing a well-cut suit.

"Nice ensemble," Stone said, indicating his clothes.

"I told you, I don't wear those old jeans all the time. In fact, I'm thinking of not wearing them at all anymore."

"Good idea," Stone said.

"Thanks for your tip on how to dress for lunch."

"Glad to be of help."

"I was very impressed with Charley Fox. He's a no-bullshit guy."

"He was impressed with you, too."

"Mind if I go up and check the computers?"

"Please do," Stone said. "I'll buy you a drink when you're done."

HUEY WAS BACK in fifteen minutes. "Still perking along, nothing big yet."

Joan came into the office from the supply room. "I can't open the Excelsior," she said.

"Find the printed checklist and give it another go," Stone replied, and she went back.

"What's an Excelsior?" Huey asked.

"It's an old safe, made in Germany before World War II." Stone told him the story of how he came to possess it.

Joan came back. "No good."

"It's complicated," Stone said to Huey.

"You know something I discovered from my wardrobe change?"

"What's that."

"Women look at me differently, like I'm a man, instead of a boy."

"Then the clothes are worth the investment," Stone said.

"I have a feeling I'm going to start meeting more interesting people."

"Are you free for dinner?" Stone asked.

"Sure."

"Would you like to meet someone interesting?"

"Why not?"

Stone got out his phone and looked up Solomon Fink's number.

"This is Sol," the old man said.

"Sol, it's Stone Barrington. How are you?"

"Still alive, that's an accomplishment."

"It is. We're having trouble opening the Excelsior. If I send my car for you, can you come over and deal with it?"

"What else do I have to do with my time?" Sol asked.

"Can you stay for dinner? There's an interesting young man I'd like you to meet."

"I didn't know there were any interesting young men," Sol said. "I'd be delighted to stay for dinner."

Stone looked at his watch. "My car will be there in three quarters of an hour, traffic permitting. You'll remember my driver, Fred."

"Of course. I'll see him then." Sol hung up.

Stone asked Joan to send Fred to pick up Sol.

"Who's Sol?" Huey asked.

"He worked for the safe maker who made the Excelsior, in Berlin, shortly before the war."

"Was he a Nazi?"

Stone shook his head. "He was then and is now a Jew. His name is Solomon Fink. He's a little over a hundred years old and lives in a fancy old folks' home in Brooklyn. I think you'll enjoy him."

"I've never met anyone that old. My grandmother is only sixty-six."

"Let's go up to the study and have a drink."

"I'm not old enough," Huey said.

Stone got some cash from his other safe to pay Sol's fee, and they went upstairs.

"This is a beautiful room," Huey said when he walked into the study.

"My father built it, and all the other woodwork in the house. He was a cabinetmaker and a furniture designer."

"Lots of books. I read mostly on my iPad."

"A nice device," Stone said, "but e-readers make lousy interior decoration. What would you like to drink?"

"What are you having?"

"An excellent bourbon called Knob Creek, the place where Abe Lincoln was born in a log cabin. It's the patriotic thing to do."

"I'll have that," Huey said.

Stone mixed them a drink and sat down and lit the fire.

"I've got a loft downtown," Huey said. "It's pretty industrial. I think I'll redesign the interior to look more like this."

"Have you ever done any woodworking?"

"No, but I've admired it, as I do this."

"I inherited this house from my great-aunt, my grandmother's sister. I did most of the renovation myself, except for the parts that required a license, like plumbing and electrical. It's the most satisfying thing I've ever done."

"How did you learn to do it?"

"I grew up in my father's shop. By the time I went to college I could do almost anything he could."

"I'd like to learn."

"If you're going to redo your loft, hire a good woodworker who will let you help him. That's a good way to learn."

"I watch *This Old House* on TV; I admire those guys."

"Woodworking would slow down your mind, make you think in a different way. You're used to everything happening instantly, with your computers; woodworking is about next week and next month, not right now."

"You're full of good ideas, Stone."

"Thank you."

Joan buzzed him. "Sol Fink is here."

"Show him where the safe is, and send him up here when he's done. Tell Helene we're three for dinner."

It was a half hour before Sol appeared in the study. He sat down heavily. "Whew!" he said. "That was a workout."

"Is it open?" Stone asked.

Sol nodded. "I changed the combination." He handed Stone a slip of paper, and Stone pressed the cash into his hand. He tucked it into an inside pocket without counting it.

"What would you like to drink, Sol?"

"One of your single malts, I believe."

Stone looked through the bottles in his bar and picked one. "How about a Macallan 18?"

"Sounds perfect."

Stone poured the drink and handed it to him. "Why did you have to change the combination, Sol?"

"Because somebody who didn't know what he was doing tried to open it," Sol replied. "And it locked up."

Stone froze. "Joan tried."

"This happened before she tried. How long since you opened it?"

"A few days, maybe a week."

"Well, my boy, you've had a yegg in your house."

"What's a yegg?" Huey asked.

"A safecracker," Sol replied.

51

Dinner was served before Stone could ask further questions. "Sol," he said finally, "tell me why you think there was a yegg in the house."

Sol took a sip of his wine and nodded approvingly. "There's only one thing that can lock up the mechanism that way: someone entered the wrong combination twice."

"How do you get it to open after that?" Huey asked.

"Only two people know how to do that," Sol said. "I'm one of them, and the other is Bob Cantor, who I instructed in the art."

"And there's no other way to open it?"

"Not without destroying the contents. If you were after gold bars, you could simply blow the door off, although that wouldn't be easy. The gold might be scarred, but it would still be gold."

"Where do you get a safe like that?" Huey asked.

Sol looked at him sharply. "Are you in the market, son?"

"Yes, I am," Huey replied. "I have a lot of data records—disks, hard drives—that need securing."

"Well, there used to be half a dozen companies with them in New York, going back to the thirties, of course, and I serviced them."

"Are those companies still in existence?" Huey asked.

"Let me go through my old logbooks and see what I can find," Sol said.

"I'd appreciate that," Huey replied.

"Where do you keep those records now?" Stone asked.

"In the vault at the *Times*. I have a lockbox there, but it's pretty much full."

"What about copies of Bob's work upstairs?"

"It's all there, in a little safe in the closet. Bob gave me the combination."

"Do you think anybody might have been in that bedroom?"

"Just Trixie," Huey replied. "And she isn't much interested in that sort of thing."

"Does Trixie know anyone who is interested in things like data records?"

Huey shrugged. "I don't know."

Stone's phone rang and he looked at the caller. "It's Dino, excuse me." He left the table, went into the living room, and answered it.

"Hey," Dino said. "I just finished work. You want some dinner?"

"Come to my house," Stone said. "Sol Fink and Huey Horowitz are here, there's plenty left."

"I'm already nearly there," Dino said, then hung up.

Stone went back to the table. "Dino's going to join us," he said.

"I saw him at lunch today at that club, across the dining room," Huey said.

"He's there often." Stone called down for Helene to bring another place setting and some hot bread.

Dino used his own key and bustled in. Stone made the introductions and poured Dino a scotch.

"I saw you at lunch," Dino said to Huey, "with Charley Fox."

"That's right."

"Dino," Stone said, "can you send somebody from your safe squad over? We've had a yegg in the house."

"But he didn't get it open," Sol said, before Dino could speak.

"When?" Dino asked.

"A few days, maybe a week. He screwed up the Excelsior, and we had to get Sol in to open it."

"Tomorrow morning do?"

"That'll be fine."

"A pro isn't going to have left any prints," Dino said.

"Maybe he left something—anything—that might be of use."

Dino's dinner arrived, and he dug in. "Huey, are you considering investing with Charley Fox?" he asked.

"I am," Huey replied.

"You won't regret it," Dino said.

"That's what I hear. Can anybody recommend an architect?" Huey asked.

Nobody spoke for a moment, then Sol did. "Fella at the home has a great-grandson just got certified," he said. "He's been doing his apprenticeship at a big-time firm uptown, but now he's opening up on his own."

"I'd love to meet him," Huey said.

"Get you the number tomorrow."

Huey gave him his card. "I'm easy to reach."

"I'll look into an Excelsior for you, too."

"Thank you, Mr. Fink."

"Sol. You want to make me feel old?"

Huey laughed. "Thank you, Sol."

• • •

THE FOLLOWING MORNING a detective arrived with a small satchel and introduced himself to Stone. "I'm Joe Carney," he said. "I hear you've had a visit."

"Come with me," Stone said and led him into the storage room. Carney let out a low whistle. "An Excelsior. Jesus, Mary, and Joseph. Only the second one I've ever seen."

"I hear they're rare," Stone said.

"Don't tell me your yegg got into *that* without nitro."

"He did not. He just got the mechanism locked up by entering the wrong combination twice."

"How do you know that?" Carney asked.

"I had an expert in."

"Who the hell is an expert in Excelsiors?"

"A very old man who used to help build them in his youth."

"I'd like to meet him."

"Maybe," Stone said, "we'll see."

Carney had a good look at the safe and dusted for prints. "A woman's been here," he said.

"My secretary, Joan. You met her on the way in."

"Also, a man." He examined Stone's left index finger. "That was you."

"Nobody else?"

"Pros don't leave prints." Carney sniffed the air. "You smoke?"

"No. Nobody here does."

"Where's the nearest outside door?" the cop asked.

"Follow me," Stone said and led him out of the storeroom, through his small gym and the kitchen, to the back door.

Carney opened it and stepped out onto the patio. He looked

around, then climbed two steps into the common garden and stopped. He reached into an inside pocket and produced an evidence bag, then came up with a pair of tweezers.

Stone watched as he bent over, picked up a cigarette butt, and dropped it into the bag. "Maybe he wasn't as careful as I thought," Carney said.

52

It was late afternoon when Stone got a call from Detective Carney.

"We got a DNA hit on the cigarette butt," he said.

"Who's the guy?" Stone asked.

"It isn't a guy," Carney replied.

"A woman?"

"Yep. Her name is Ruth O'Donnell. We wouldn't have got a hit at all, if she hadn't had an altercation with a cop at a party when she was a teenager—that got her DNA on record. She doesn't have an arrest record, though. She's been clean since the party thing."

"Have you ever known a yegg who was female?" Stone asked.

"Once, when I was a rookie. The lady picked up some skills from her boyfriend, but she wasn't a threat to safe making."

"Do you have an address for Ms. O'Donnell?"

"Nope. I remember a yegg named Barry O'Donnell, who was real good, but he's been dead for four or five years."

"Did he have a daughter?"

"No kids at all. A confirmed bachelor, Barry was."

"So what's your next move?"

"I don't have one," Carney said. "I spoke to my supervisor about it, and he pointed out that, even if we found her, we don't have a case, since we found the cigarette butt outside your house. She could say she was just looking at the flowers."

"She'd need a key to get into the gardens from the street."

"If she can open a safe, she can open a garden gate," Carney said. "At least there's no harm done. Want some advice?"

"Sure."

"Arm your security system *every* night."

"Thanks, I'm sometimes lax about that." He thanked the man again and hung up.

HUEY HOROWITZ was standing in his new loft, talking to the architect Sol Fink had recommended. He liked the man and his ideas. His phone rang, and he answered. "This is Huey."

"Good evening, this is Sol Fink," the caller said.

"Hello, Sol. I'm standing here talking to Will Mather, the architect you recommended. We seem to be of like mind."

"Glad to hear it," Sol said. "While he's there, you better have him take a look at the floors."

"The floors? Why?"

"Because I found you an Excelsior, and it weighs six hundred pounds."

"That's great news, Sol. I'll mention it to Will."

"Fella wants five grand for the safe. A new one would cost ten times that, if it were available. Fella says it's in fine condition and working order. I remember the safe from when I used to service it."

"Tell him I'll give him a check on delivery," Huey said.

"He wants cash, and you'll have to hire a mover to pick it up and get it down to you. I'll e-mail you the owner's name and number."

"Thanks, Sol," Huey said.

Sol hung up.

"Will," Huey said, "we've got to find a spot that will support a six-hundred-pound safe."

They walked around the rooms, then Will stopped. "I can build you a closet right over there that will hold your safe, if you'll give me the dimensions. It's in a corner, so the floor will hold it."

Huey's iPhone made a chiming noise, and he looked at the screen. "Holy shit," he said. "Will, do you have a car?"

"No," Will said, "I came on my motorcycle."

"Great. Can you give me a lift uptown?"

"Sure."

Huey ran for the street.

Stone was finishing up for the day when Huey burst into his office. "They're moving money!" he yelled and ran for the elevator, with Stone close behind.

Huey opened the bedroom door and sat himself down before the monitors. "Look at that," he said, pointing to a graph on one of the screens. "They're wiring funds every eight to twelve minutes, and the sums are all just under a quarter of a million dollars. I guess that's the level that might trigger alarms at the central bank."

"What are you going to do about it?" Stone asked.

"I might be able to interrupt what they're doing," Huey said, "but then they'd know they've been hacked. I think it's better to wait until they stop, then download their software to our computer."

"When will that be?" Stone asked.

"Probably at whatever closing time is, wherever the central bank is operating from. We'll just have to wait. These transfers are going all over the world, to dozens of banks."

Stone got out his phone and called Jamie Cox.

"We still on for dinner?" she asked.

"Sure we are, but I have news."

"I love news."

"The semi-supercomputer has come to life and is transferring funds to accounts all over the world."

"Then we've got the bastards!"

"Not yet we haven't. We have to wait until they stop for the day, so Huey can download their software without getting caught at it."

Huey looked over his shoulder. "We might get caught at it anyway," he said. "We don't know what protections might be in their software."

"I heard that," Jamie said. "I'd better go tell Jeremy and Scott."

"Okay, but don't bring them over here," Stone said. "We could be waiting for hours, and I don't want them clogging up my house unnecessarily."

"All right. I'll tell them to wait for our call, but I'll be there in an hour; I have to finish a piece."

"We're in the third-floor bedroom," Stone said, then hung up. He sat down on the bed and waited. "It's five o'clock on the east coast of North America," he said, checking his watch.

"If the bank is in Switzerland, it'll be midnight there soon, and that could be closing time."

"Let's see," Stone said.

They had been waiting for another half hour when the door

opened, and Trixie came in. She threw some things onto the bed and ran for the bathroom, closing the door behind her.

Stone leaned in close to Huey. "Huey, is Trixie your girlfriend's given name?"

"No, it's Ruth. Ruth O'Donnell," Huey replied, "but only her mother calls her Ruth. She's been Trixie forever."

"Don't let her know what we're doing," Stone said, "and get rid of her if you can think of a way without tipping her off."

Huey turned and looked at Stone. "What's going on?"

"Trust me," Stone said.

53

Huey's eyes were fixed on the screen, but he seemed to be thinking. Trixie was still in the bathroom. "What's going on?" he whispered to Stone.

"Trixie is the yegg," Stone replied.

"What?"

"And she's working for the opposition."

"That's crazy."

"Did you give her a key to the house?"

"I loaned her mine."

"Get it back, and get rid of her."

Trixie came out of the bathroom and headed for the bed.

"Hold it, babe," Huey said, looking up from his monitor.

"Is something happening?" she asked.

"No, I'm just running tests on some software I wrote for a client. I could be at this all night, so you might as well go home."

"You're trying to get rid of me?" she asked.

"I *am* getting rid of you, but reluctantly. I'll call you tomorrow."

"*Well,*" she said, "if that's what you want."

"And I need my key back," Huey said. "I may have to deliver the disks to my client tonight."

She fumbled in her bag, came up with a bunch of keys, and

tossed them to him. "There you go," she said. She went back into the bathroom and slammed the door.

"Quite a lot of keys she carries," Stone said, extracting his own from the key ring.

"She says they're for self-defense," Huey said.

Trixie came out of the john, grabbed her purse, and stomped out of the room. They heard the elevator door open.

"Now," Huey said, "tell me what that was all about."

"An NYPD detective, a safe specialist, came in today and inspected the case. Does Trixie smoke?"

"Yes, and it drives me crazy."

"The detective smelled smoke. He went out the back door and found a butt, and sent it in for DNA testing. Ruth O'Donnell's name popped up. Does she have a relative named Barry O'Donnell?"

"Her uncle, father's brother. He died in prison a few years ago."

"Not before teaching her something about safes. She wasn't good enough at it to open the Excelsior, though."

"That's good to know because Sol found me one. It's being delivered tomorrow. What's Trixie's connection to the Thomases?"

"I don't know," Stone said. "Maybe she picks up a few bucks safecracking on the side."

"Well, she won't be back, I can promise you that. I'm glad she hasn't seen my new loft, either. Sol found me an architect, and he's already at work on plans for the remodel."

"What's that?" Stone asked, pointing at the computer. The images had stopped moving.

"They're done," Huey said, typing furiously.

"Are you copying their software?"

"No, I'm trying to reverse their transfers before they shut down. There," he said, "that's a day's work undone. Now I'll copy the software." He went back to typing. Finally he sat back. "There."

"Won't they miss it?" Stone asked.

"I didn't steal it, just copied it. It's still on their computer, but I've made a couple of changes that will make it work erratically."

"Won't they notice?"

"Sure, they'll notice, but they won't know why it's happening. They'll think it's a bug in their code. They will notice that the transfers didn't go through. When they try to move the money again, it won't be there. That'll drive them crazy."

"They're going to know it's you, Huey."

"How?"

"Trixie will tell them what you've been doing."

"I've never explained it to her," Huey replied.

"Can you get her on the phone?" Stone asked.

"If she picks up," Huey said.

"Then do it. I want to talk to her."

Huey pressed a speed-dial button, waited for her to answer, then handed Stone the phone.

"Trixie?"

"Who's this?"

"It's Stone Barrington. I want you to know that the police know you tried to open my safe last night."

"I don't know what you're talking about."

"They found your DNA. I guess Uncle Barry didn't teach you about that."

"You're nuts."

"If you tell anybody anything about my house or about Huey or me, I can have you in jail the same day."

"You don't have anything on me."

"We have your DNA, and that's all we need. By the time the courts get through with you, you'll be broke from the lawyers' fees and very likely in prison."

"You can't do that to me."

"You've already done it to yourself, and I want some answers from you right now."

"What answers?"

"Who hired you to open the Excelsior?"

"Nobody."

"You think they're going to get you out of the hole you're in? Do you trust them that much?"

Long silence.

"A man named Damien. I don't know his first name."

"How did he get your name?"

"From a friend of Uncle Barry's."

"Have you done any work for Damien before?"

"No."

"Then tell him you failed to open the safe, which is the case."

"I've already told him that."

"What did you tell him about Huey?"

"Huey? Why would I tell them about him?"

"I'm just asking, and I want the truth."

"His name never came up."

"See that it doesn't. Now, you'll be all right if you keep your mouth shut and stop breaking into people's houses. Do you understand?"

"Yes."

Huey leaned into the phone. "And I won't be calling you again," he said. He took the phone from Stone and ended the call. "You think that'll work?"

"Probably."

"Who's this guy Damien?"

"He's a relative of the Thomases, works for them. Have you heard the name before?"

"No."

"Then you'd best forget it. If you hear it again, from *anybody*, I want to know about it."

"Sure, Stone."

Jamie walked into the room. "What's going on?"

Stone brought her up to date.

54

Stone and Huey sat in Stone's office with Jamie, Jeremy, and Scott from the *Times*, who had brought a lawyer with them.

"Bruce is from our legal department," Jeremy said. "His specialty is digital."

"Okay," Stone said. "Huey, tell everybody where we are."

Huey talked them through what he had done with his software, then sat back, expecting approval.

"Wait a minute," Bruce said, "did you say you caused the withdrawals they made from the central bank to be returned?"

"That's right," Huey said. "They transferred more than forty million dollars to their own accounts, and my alterations to their software caused them to be returned."

"Then the *Times* can't run the story," Bruce said.

"Why the hell not?" Jamie demanded.

"Because we have no evidence of what they did. Huey wiped it out—with the best of motives, of course—but the evidence is no longer there."

"Huey," Scott said, "did you copy all the transactions?"

"Yes, but Bruce is right, I'm afraid," Huey said ruefully. "I wiped out our evidence."

"But they can do it all again, can't they?"

"It's going to be a lot harder for them because of some alterations I made in their code."

"Then how are we going to get publishable evidence of what they've done?"

"I'll have to catch them making a new batch of transfers, which they'll do, as soon as they learn they have zero balances in the receiving accounts. But their process is going to be very slow."

"How much are they transferring at a time?"

"Just under a quarter of a million dollars per account. I think that's because the central bank has alarms that go off when somebody transfers more than that amount."

"And how have you made the transfers more difficult to accomplish?"

"They'll take a lot longer, perhaps as much as an hour, even two hours per transfer, instead of a few minutes."

"Bruce," Stone said, "how should we handle this?"

"I think we'd better get an expert from the Treasury Department in here to watch this happen on Huey's computers, and see if they can find enough evidence for a charge."

"Maybe somebody from the NSA, too," Stone suggested.

"I'm sorry I screwed this up, guys," Huey said. "I was just trying to stop them from stealing, and I wasn't thinking ahead."

"If we can get quotes from Treasury and the NSA as to what they're doing," Jeremy said, "then we can run our story, which will alert the central bank and blow them out of the water. Isn't that what we want to accomplish?"

"I'll need to see how far the Treasury and the NSA are willing to go in their public statements," Bruce said. "The NSA, for one, isn't known for that. Shall I make some calls?"

"You'd better let me do that," Jeremy said. "I can probably get high-ranking officials on the phone more easily."

"I'm acquainted with the secretary of state," Stone said. "She might help."

"No," Scott said, shaking his head. "She's a victim in all this, and if we bring her into it we're dabbling in politics. I'd rather the first she hears of it to be when she reads it in the *Times*."

"You have a point," Stone said.

"All right," Jeremy said, "let's get this moving and meet back here tomorrow morning."

The meeting broke up, leaving only Huey and Jamie there.

"This is good for my book," Jamie said. "It's good plotting to have a setback, then recover from it."

"You're writing a book about this?" Huey asked.

"Yes."

"Am I in it?"

"Of course, unless you don't want your name mentioned."

"I want my name mentioned," Huey said, "but only if we're successful."

Jamie and Stone laughed.

"You should be in public relations, Huey," Stone said.

Huey's phone rang. "Yes, Will?" He covered the phone. "Am I done here? I need to meet my architect at my loft, downtown."

"Sure, go ahead," Stone said.

"Will, I'll be there in half an hour." He hung up and left.

"Huey has a loft downtown?" Jamie asked.

"He does."

"How little I know about him," she said.

. . .

TRIXIE MADE HER WAY through a darkened restaurant in Chelsea, picked out a table, and ordered a drink.

Five minutes later Damien joined her. "What's going on?" he asked.

"I fucked up," she replied, taking a swig of her drink.

"How did you do that?"

"I couldn't open the safe, and it locked itself. And I somehow left DNA behind, and the cops discovered it."

"Have they identified you?"

"Apparently so. Barrington knew it was me."

"So we have none of the contents of the safe, and the cops are onto you. Have you told anybody anything?"

"No, nothing," she lied.

He kicked her shin sharply under the table. "Tell me the truth."

"Jesus, that hurt," she said, rubbing her leg.

"It's going to hurt a lot more, if you don't tell me everything."

"All right, Barrington knows your name."

"You told him?"

"He was threatening to have me jailed. I can't go to jail, it would ruin my career with the magazines."

"Not to mention your career as a safecracker."

"That safe is a monster," she said. "I've never seen anything like it."

"Did they get it open?"

"Apparently, but I don't know how."

"Trixie, you're on thin ice here. Tell me what you know."

"I guess they must have some sort of an expert who knows the safe and how it operates, but I have no idea who."

"Get Huey to tell you."

"Huey isn't speaking to me."

"You're becoming less and less useful, Trixie."

She dug into her purse and came up with a thick envelope. "Here's your ten thousand," she said. "I didn't earn it."

"No," Damien said, "you didn't." He pocketed the money and left her sitting there. On the way out, he told the waiter to take her another drink. He handed the man a hundred. "Make it a double, and tell her it's on the house." Outside, in the car, he said to the two men in the front seat, "She's in there, and she'll be coming out eventually," he said. "She should not survive the experience. I'll get a cab." He got out of the car and walked quickly away.

55

An hour after Damien had left, Trixie sat, staring into her empty glass. A waiter passed, and she grabbed at his coat-tail. "Check, please."

"You're all paid up, sweetheart," the man said. "Can I get you a cab?"

"No, no, I'm fine." She got unsteadily to her feet and moved toward the front door.

"Good night," the waiter said.

"Yeah, thanks," Trixie replied. She made it to the street and found that it was raining heavily. "I'll never find a cab in this," she said aloud to herself. She stood under the restaurant awning and looked down the street. A cab sat by the curb, its rooftop light on. She stepped into the street and waved a hand. "Taxi!!!" she screamed.

The cab switched on its blinker, signaling a stop, and moved toward her. Trixie stood with one hand still up, the other clutching her bag. She stepped slightly back, out of its way, looking down to see that she didn't trip over the curb.

She heard the engine of the cab rev and looked up just in time to see it swerve toward her.

. . .

STONE AND JAMIE were having a drink in his study and watching the local evening news. A "Breaking News" banner filled the screen.

"This just in," the anchor said. "A young woman has been killed in a hit-and-run incident just a few minutes ago in Chelsea. We had a camera in the neighborhood on another story, and he managed to shoot the aftermath." A knot of people stood in the street, gathered around a lump on the pavement, as two cops herded them back to the sidewalk. An ambulance siren could be heard approaching. "We have a reporter on the scene, now, and we'll give you more news as we get it."

"Poor girl," Jamie said.

"It's a filthy night out there," Stone said, "and Fred is off tonight. Why don't we dine here instead of braving the storm?"

"I'm all for staying dry," Jamie said.

Stone called Helene and told her of their change of plans. When he hung up the phone, he glanced at the TV. A woman in a trench coat stood in the street under a golf umbrella. "We've just heard that the victim of this hit-and-run was one Ruth O'Donnell, a photographer whose work appears in *Vanity Fair* and other magazines under the name 'Trixie.' She died in an ambulance on the way to Bellevue Hospital. The police have found an abandoned taxi with a smashed fender a couple of blocks away. The vehicle had been reported stolen."

STONE AND JAMIE stared at the screen. "That was no accident," he said.

"It doesn't seem so," Jamie agreed.

Stone picked up his phone and called Huey's cell.

"This is Huey."

"It's Stone. Have you been watching TV?" he asked.

"No, I'm still at the loft with the architect. There's no TV here."

"Bad news, I'm afraid: Trixie has been the victim of a hit-and-run in Chelsea. She died on the way to the hospital. She was run down by a taxi that had been reported stolen."

"Oh, shit," Huey said.

"I agree. It doesn't look like an accident."

"I don't believe it."

"I think it would be a good idea if you stayed here tonight," Stone said. "Don't go home. I'll get Fred to pick you up. What's your address?"

Huey gave it to him.

"Do you know any of her family?" Stone asked.

"I met her mother once, for about a minute. I don't have her number."

"Leave it to the police, then." He tried Fred's number.

"Yes, sir?" Fred answered.

"Where are you?" Stone asked.

"In a cab on the way home."

"When you get here, please take the car downtown and pick up Huey Horowitz." He gave Fred the address.

"On my way," Fred said. "Should take me half an hour, forty-five minutes in this weather."

"Good." Stone hung up and called Huey. "Fred will pick you up as soon as he can get there. We'll wait dinner for you here."

"Thank you, Stone. Can I invite my architect? He's on a motorcycle, and he shouldn't be driving it in this weather."

"Of course." Stone hung up and gave the news to Helene. Stone called Dino.

"Bacchetti."

"It's Stone. Have you seen the TV reports about a hit-and-run in Chelsea?"

"Yeah, I'm home, the TV's on."

"The girl was Huey's girlfriend."

"No kidding?"

"She was our yegg. She was working for that guy Damien, who's a member of the Thomas family," Stone said.

"I already knew it wasn't an accident," Dino said. "Let me find out what's going on with the investigation, and I'll get back to you."

"Okay. You want dinner here with us?"

"No, Viv is trying out a new cook as we speak. I'm the guinea pig."

DINO CALLED BACK ten minutes later. "What you've heard on the news is all correct. What they don't know yet is that the girl was having a drink with a guy at the restaurant where it happened, and she was wasted. He left an hour before she did."

"Anything on the identity of the guy?"

"Mid-thirties, fairly tall, dark hair, business suit. People are on their way to have a chat with Damien."

"I'd like to hear about that chat."

"Sure." Dino hung up.

NO ONE HAD MUCH to say at dinner. Stone tried to get them talking. "Will, what do you think of Huey's loft?"

"I think that, by the time I'm finished with it, it'll be the best loft south of Houston Street, and I'm being modest."

"How long?"

"If I can get the builder I want, maybe six months. There's a lot to do."

Huey just stared into his plate, pushing his food around.

Dino called back. "At the time of the hit-and-run, Damien was having dinner at a restaurant on the East Side, in the eighties. His date backs his story. So does the headwaiter there."

"It would be interesting to know who owns the restaurant," Stone said.

"We're checking." Dino hung up.

56

They were on after-dinner drinks when Jamie got a call. She listened for a minute, then said, "I'm on it." She hung up. "You're all going to have to excuse me," she said. "That was my editor. We're going with the piece on the Thomas computer activity. I've got to get back to my office. Stone, I may be there very late."

"Right." He called Fred to deliver her to the *Times* office.

"Can he drop me at my apartment?" Will asked.

"Of course," Stone replied.

Huey stood up. "I'm bushed. I'm going to turn in upstairs."

Stone was alone. He called Dino.

"Bacchetti."

"Anything new?"

"Nothing. Oh, the cook turned out well. Viv hired her and her assistant."

"Great, you'll be gaining weight soon."

"Not going to happen."

"I have some news," Stone said. "The *Times* is going with the Thomas story. They're going to rip the scab off the whole thing."

"That's going to be fun," Dino said.

"I think it would be a good idea if you called the D.A., the FBI, and the U.S. Attorney and gave them a heads-up. They're going to be besieged by the press as soon as the *Times* hits the street."

"Where's Huey?"

"Upstairs, asleep."

"They're going to want to talk to him."

"Tell them to call me for access."

"Okay. Did you figure out what the Thomases were doing with their computer installation?"

"I forgot to bring you up to date." He ran it all down for Dino.

"Does Holly know about this?"

"No, the *Times* people want her to learn about it from reading their paper. That way, they won't be accused of colluding with her to get Hank."

"Do you think the story is going to really get Hank?"

"He may not end up in prison. He'll play dumb and blame his computer people. But I don't think he's going to be the next President of the United States."

"That's good enough for me," Dino said. "I'm going to bed, good night." They both hung up.

Stone decided to finish his cognac before going upstairs. Then his phone rang, or rather, Bob Cantor's did. He answered.

"Hey, there."

"Hey, yourself."

"How's it going on the computer front?"

Stone gave him a complete update.

"They're going to get away with it," Bob said.

"Why do you say that?"

"What Huey doesn't seem to understand is that they're probably already onto him—or onto *somebody*. You don't invest that much in equipment and people without planting adequate safeguards in your hardware and software. They'll know they've been hacked; they just won't know why, until the *Times* hits the street."

"Huey's safe. He's upstairs, sleeping with your computers."

"That's good. You should keep him there."

"Are you ready to tell me where you are?" Stone asked.

"Not yet."

"What are your plans? Are you just going to walk away from everything?"

"I don't think I'll have to do that once the story comes out. The Thomases will be under too much scrutiny to mess with me."

"They've already messed with Huey. They murdered his girlfriend earlier this evening, ran her down in the street with a stolen cab."

"Oh, shit."

"That's what we're all saying. Turns out, she was messing with the Excelsior—she comes from a family of yeggs."

"She didn't get into it, did she?"

"No, but her attempts made it lock up. We had to get Sol Fink over to fix it."

"Is Sol okay?"

"He's great. He just goes on and on."

"I'll go by and check on him, take him to dinner."

"You're slipping, Bob."

"What?"

"Now I know you haven't gotten any farther than Brooklyn."

"You're right, I'm slipping. I'll call you after I read the *Times* piece."

"You do that, and watch yourself."

"I intend to," Bob said, and hung up.

STONE WAS IN BED after midnight, but still awake, when Jamie called.

"I finished my part of the piece," she said. "We start on the front page, above the fold, then move to a double-page spread inside, and a whole page of Tommassini ancestors. There'll be a big editorial, too. I've arranged for circulation to hand-deliver copies to H. Thomas & Son. They should get them around four AM."

"Sounds great. Do you need a bed for the night?"

"I'm already in a cab," she said. "I'll let myself in."

LATER, AFTER THEY had exhausted themselves with each other, they lay in bed panting.

"I'm trying to think ahead," Jamie said.

"Is that so hard?"

"Well, I know tomorrow will be chaotic, but what about after that?"

"First, you finish your book. If you want to do it in England, I'll arrange our flight."

"Let me think about that for a day or two."

"Have you told your agent about the book?"

"Not yet."

"You'd better get that out of the way. Tell him to start with the *New Yorker*, maybe a three-part series."

"It's a her, and I'll tell her that. I'll e-mail her the early chapters, too."

"Don't use e-mail. Put it on a thumb drive and have it hand-delivered. She can print it at her end."

"Tell me about the house in England," she said.

"House, stables, a few cottages, a private airstrip, dates back to World War II. An hour and a half's drive to London, faster on the train."

"Sounds good," she said. She laid her head on his chest and dozed off.

57

Jack Thomas was awakened by a sound he always dreaded: the dedicated red telephone to his father's house. The terrible thing about the phone was that it didn't ring, pause, and ring again: it rang continuously, until it was answered. Old Henry didn't like to be kept waiting.

"Yes, Poppa?" Jack said, taking deep breaths to calm himself.

"I take it you haven't seen the *Times*," Henry said.

Jack looked at the bedside clock. "It's a quarter past four AM," he said. "Why would I be reading the newspaper at this hour? Come to think of it, why would you?"

"Old people don't sleep," Henry said. "Go look on your doorstep."

"Why? What's in the *Times*?"

"Everybody," Henry replied. "All of us. Call me when you've read it." He hung up.

Jack got into a silk robe and his slippers and went downstairs to the front door. The paper was there, and he saw his name on the front page before he even picked it up.

JACK READ THE ARTICLE fast, and with growing horror. Photographs of his family—some of them mug shots—stared back at him from an entire page of the newspaper.

The red telephone began ringing again. Jack snatched it off its cradle. "I read it," he said. "Most of it, anyway. The horrible thing about it is it's all true."

"Not a fucking word of it is true," Henry said. "Well, not much of it. I've already called the PR people. We're meeting in my office in half an hour, and we'll decide what's true and what's not. Get your ass in gear, boy."

Jack hated being called "boy" by his father. He started to say goodbye, but Henry had already hung up. Jack ran for the shower.

THERE WERE FOUR PR people, one man and three women, and the man was not in charge. They had brought a stack of the *Times* and pages were scattered around the big office.

The eldest of the women, one Marge Spooner, spoke up. "Gentlemen, this is appalling."

"Listen to me, you stupid cow," Henry said. "We don't pay you what we pay you for that kind of advice."

She didn't flinch. "Then give me some basis on which to deny this," she said, holding up the front page.

"We obviously can't deny any of it," Jack said. "Our story has to be that it's ancient history, that none of us living now ever even met any of these people." He shook the page of photographs for emphasis.

"Now," Marge said, "that's something we can work with. Henry, is there anybody on that page that you actually remember?"

"My grandfather is on it," Henry said, glowering. "I remember him."

"What do you remember about him?"

"I remember that he would come home from work—could be

290

any hour of the day or night—and tell me that he had just murdered somebody, and how he had done it. A straight razor was his favorite weapon. He enjoyed watching them bleed to death."

"Well," Marge said, "I don't think I can do much with that story. You'd best start forgetting it now: you were just a child, your grandfather didn't confide in you, you hardly ever saw him. Did he have any legitimate occupation?"

"He owned a bar on the Bowery," Henry said. "He ran a numbers operation and a sports book in a back room and a poker game and a roulette wheel in another. There was a whorehouse upstairs."

"Jesus Christ," Marge said weakly.

"Don't you take God's name in vain in my presence!" Henry shouted.

"Marge," Jack said, "Poppa is very good at forgetting what he doesn't want to know. He'll do just fine."

"What about you, Jack? Did you actually know any of these people?"

"Not a one of them," Jack said calmly. "I tell people my grandfather was a Bible salesman, and my grandmother worked in the office of the archdiocese."

"Now *that* I can use," Marge said.

THE PR PEOPLE had left the office to go and write their press releases and type up a list of questions likely to be asked. Jack was left alone with his father and, somewhat to his suprise, Rance Damien, who had been sitting in a corner chair the whole time, his face obscured by a newspaper.

"The girl yegg is taken care of," Damien said.

"Thanks, Rance," Jack said acidly, "I watch TV. Christ, what a mess!"

"She's gone, and nobody cares," Damien said. "That's what I call neat and clean."

"Are there any other messes we should know about?" Jack asked. "Let's get them out of the way now."

"There are one or two waiting to happen," Damien said. "There's the Barrington guy: he's at the root of all of this."

"And what would be the purpose of killing him?"

Damien shrugged. "Am I the only one in this family who likes *revenge*? Revenge does all sorts of things for you. It shuts up people who were thinking about talking. It scares the shit out of people— suddenly, they can't even remember their names."

"This is not a Warner Bros. movie, Rance," Jack said, "and Al Capone is dead."

"God rest his soul," Damien said. "Then there's a computer whiz, who somehow got into our equipment downstairs. He managed to reverse nearly fifty million dollars in transfers yesterday."

"But the program removes all traces of itself, right?"

"We lost *fifty fucking million dollars!*" Damien said. "Somebody has to pay for that!"

"You're a goddamned throwback," Jack muttered.

Henry came to life again. "Sometimes we need a throwback, boy," he said.

Jack wheeled on his father. "If you ever again refer to me as *boy*, I'm going to wheel you out on that terrace and dump you into New York Harbor."

"You're not going to do anything, unless I tell you to . . . *boy!*"

Jack was white and speechless with rage.

"Go back to your office," Henry said, "and wait for my call. Oh, something you can do: call Hank and tell him to come down with a sudden and complete attack of amnesia."

Jack got up and left, but the thought of Henry alone with Rance Damien gave him the willies.

58

Henry was left alone in his office with Rance Damien.

"Henry," Damien said, "is Jack going to be a problem?"

"I've been wondering about that myself," Henry replied. "For some time."

"How can I help?" Damien asked. He needed the old man to tell him directly.

"What do you suggest?" Henry replied.

"Henry, what do you *want*?" Damien asked.

"I want Jack to be at peace," Henry replied.

"If that's what you want, you're going to have to explain to me what it means."

"It means no more strife, no more indecision, no more waffling about how we're going to handle things."

"That sounds like custodial treatment," Damien said, "with daily injections of Thorazine."

"I don't think Jack would like that," Henry said. "He just needs a good rest—a long one."

"You're going to have to say it, Henry. I have to know what you want to happen."

"Sometimes I worry that, in situations like this, the stress might become too much for Jack. I worry that he might take his own life."

"Is that what you want, Henry? For Jack to take his own life?"

"At times like this, I fear for Jack," Henry said.

"Do you, really?"

"I do. I know that he keeps a loaded pistol in the top, right-hand drawer of his desk. Now why would he do that, unless he was considering using it? He's in no danger in his office."

"Tell me, Henry, if Jack were no longer on the scene, who would assume his duties in the company?"

"Well, Rance, we've been bringing you along for some time, now. Do you feel that you could step in and handle all that Jack handles?"

"I think I could handle what Jack handles better than Jack handles it."

"I like self-confidence in a young man," Henry said. "Jack has always lacked confidence in himself. I certainly feel that if Jack could not continue, his duties should be assumed by a younger man. How old are you now, Rance?"

"Thirty-one."

"And how many departments of this company have you worked in?"

"All of them," Damien replied. "Every single one. And I've taken on our digital operations, something Jack has never known the first thing about."

"I've admired the way you handled that, Rance," Henry said. "At least, until this . . . *unpleasantness* occurred."

"Things will be running smoothly in that regard before the day is out," Damien said.

"Have I your personal assurance of that, Rance?"

"You have my solemn word. On my mother's life."

"How about your own life, Rance?" Henry asked. "Will you pledge on that?"

"Certainly," Damien replied, after only a short pause.

"Where are the PR people working this morning?" Henry asked.

"In the conference room, just down the hall."

"Why don't you look in on Jack and see how he's doing?"

"I'd be happy to do that, Henry," Damien said. "Are you concerned that he might end his life this morning?"

Henry inspected his nails. "I don't think Jack could make it through the news conference we're holding at noon. He couldn't hold it together to do what has to be done."

"Would you like me to conduct the press conference?" Damien asked.

"I think it's best that I do that myself," Henry said. "Why don't you look in on Jack and see if you can . . . soothe his nerves?"

"I'd be glad to do that, Henry."

Henry looked at his watch. "It's a quarter to six," he said. "I'd like to meet with the PR people again at seven o'clock. Do you think you can deal with Jack's problem by then? Staff people start to wander in around that time."

"Yes, I can do that."

"Good. Come and see me at seven o'clock, and we'll go talk with the PR people about what I'll be saying at the press conference."

"I think that's a good plan," Damien said, getting to his feet. "I'm meeting with our computer people at eight."

Henry nodded. "Good."

Rance left the office. He looked into the conference room. "Yes?" Marge Spooner said.

"Henry would like to meet with us all at seven o'clock," Damien said.

"Of course."

Damien closed the door, then walked around the office area and checked that all the desks were empty. Then he walked down the spiral staircase to the floor below where Jack's offices were. It was similarly deserted. He went into his own office and took a pair of latex gloves from his desk and put them on, pulling them up over his sleeves, then he went to his coat closet and removed a dry-cleaning bag from a suit, made a hole at the top and slipped it over his head. Only then did he walk to Jack's office door, and open it.

Jack was sitting at his desk, the newspapers spread out before him, his head in his hands. He was sobbing softly. Damien walked across the room toward him. Jack seemed unaware of his presence. Damien walked at a normal pace to Jack's desk and silently opened the top, right-hand drawer. The pistol, a Beretta .380, lay on top of some papers. Damien picked it up and slid the slide back an inch. There was a round in the chamber. He flicked off the safety, then picked up a sheet from the *Times* and held it close to Jack's head. He pressed the gun barrel to within an inch of Jack's temple and fired a single round.

Jack fell sideways onto the floor. Damien dropped the pistol near him, then he stepped back, removed the gloves and the dry-cleaner's bag and wrapped them together with the *Times* sheet. He carefully inspected his clothing and face to be sure they contained no splatter, then he walked back to his office, closed the door behind him, and burned the bloody parcel in his fireplace, making sure there was no trace of it left.

He walked to his office door and opened it. Jack's secretary stood at her desk, removing her coat. "Good morning, Janet," he said.

"Good morning, Mr. Damien," she replied.

"Did you hear a noise just now?"

"No, I just got off the elevator."

"I heard something a minute ago. Will you please look in on Jack and tell him we have a meeting upstairs with his father at seven o'clock?"

"Certainly, Mr. Damien."

Damien walked to his desk and stood there, until he heard the woman scream.

59

Bob Cantor drove slowly past his house in his van and inspected it as closely as he could. The second time around the block he opened his garage door with the remote, had a look inside, then continued. The third time around he opened the garage, drove in, and closed the door behind him.

He rolled down the truck's windows and sat in the driver's seat with the engine off, listening. Having heard nothing, he got out of the van, tapped in his security code, went to the house's electrical system and checked it thoroughly, resetting each circuit breaker.

Then he entered his basement workshop from the garage and found it in wild disarray. Power tools were overturned, hand tools scattered everywhere, and drawers full of screws and connectors had been strewn around the floor. On his desk, a message had been spray-painted: GET OUT OF NEW YORK. YOU WON'T BE TOLD AGAIN.

THE POLICE ARRIVED at the H. Thomas building and taped off the top two floors. Intercession by Rance Damien got the PR people in the conference room left alone, once they had been questioned. They wouldn't allow Rance upstairs to see the old man.

Rance welcomed two detectives into his office, seated them on comfortable chairs and offered them coffee, which they accepted with alacrity.

"Gentlemen, how can I help you do your job?"

"Please tell us everything you did from waking up this morning until now."

"I was awakened shortly after four AM by a phone call from Henry Thomas, our chairman, and asked to come to the office immediately to discuss a story in the *New York Times*. When I arrived, Henry Thomas was there with the public relations team you just met in the conference room. Jack Thomas, Henry's son and our president and CEO, joined us almost immediately.

"I remained in Henry's office while he discussed with the PR people what he would say at a noon press conference. Jack went downstairs to his office."

"Why?" a detective asked.

"Henry didn't need him until later."

"What was Jack Thomas's frame of mind at the meeting?"

"He was very upset, even distraught, about the content of the *Times* article, even more so than Henry, who was calm and collected. Jack contributed almost nothing to the meeting. I think that must have been why Henry dismissed him."

"Did Henry dismiss him angrily?"

"I would say coldly," Damien replied.

"And did he return to his office?"

"I believe he did. Half an hour later the PR people went downstairs to the conference room to confer with each other, and Henry asked me to return to his office at seven, to prepare for the press conference."

"What happened after you returned to your office?"

"I read the rest of the *Times* story, then I heard a loud noise. My first thought was that someone had slammed a door, but it occurred to me that I was the only person on the floor, except Jack. I got up and went to my door just as Janet, Jack's secretary, got off the elevator. I asked her if she had heard the noise, but she said she had been on the elevator.

"I went back to my desk, and as I sat down I heard Janet scream. I hurried into Jack's office, where she had discovered him on the floor behind his desk. I checked for a pulse and found none, so I called 911 and reported the death and asked for the police and an ambulance."

"Mr. Damien," a detective said, "when you poured our coffee I noticed what appears to be a spot of blood on your cuff."

Damien examined his cuffs and found the spot on the left one. "That must have happened when I checked his neck for a pulse."

The detective nodded. "What did you do next?"

"I went upstairs to Henry's office and told him what had happened."

"How did Mr. Thomas react?"

"He said something to the effect that he had been worried about Jack."

"He had anticipated his son's suicide?"

"He didn't say that. Just that he had been worried about him."

"What did you do then?"

"I poured him a glass of water and sat down with him until your people started to arrive."

"Mr. Damien, did you share Mr. Thomas's concerns about Jack?"

"I thought Jack had been somewhat overwrought for some time, and the *Times* story appeared to shock him to his core."

"What did he say about it?"

"He looked at the page with all the photographs of deceased family members, then said he didn't remember a single one of them. I think he may have said he was a small child when the last of them died."

"Did Henry Thomas remember any of them?"

"He said there was a photograph of his grandfather in the paper, but that he had few memories of him."

"Was your family aware of the criminality of some of those people?"

"There had been rumors, I suppose, but nobody in my immediate family seemed to be acquainted with any criminality. Certainly, the story was a big surprise to me."

"Mr. Damien, have you received any sort of a promotion as a result of Jack's death?"

"No. Henry asked me to act for Jack until the board can convene and appoint a successor."

"Act how?"

"Just to handle anything that came up that Jack would normally have handled."

"Did he ask you to conduct the scheduled press conference?"

"No, he just asked me to be there. He said he would conduct it himself."

"Did the PR people come up with something for him to say?"

"Henry doesn't need that sort of advice. He's perfectly capable of handling such an event. They had given him some notes, but he threw them away in disgust. He does not like it when people try to manipulate him."

"Were the PR people trying to manipulate him?"

"I meant people in general. Anyone who knows him knows enough to be careful about what they suggest to him."

"Including yourself?"

"Certainly. I am always very deferential to him."

"How, exactly, are you related to the Thomases?"

"My mother was a cousin of theirs, but Henry treated me like close family and was always complimentary of my work."

"What is your work here, Mr. Damien?"

"I have worked in every department of the firm at one time or another. I suppose it was sort of an informal training program. Currently, I'm in charge of digital services, a department that I established." Damien looked at his watch. "Gentlemen, I must ask you to excuse me. I have to be with Henry now. You may watch the press conference on my television, if you wish." He picked up the remote and switched it to CNBC, then got out of there.

SEETHING WITH ANGER, Bob Cantor went back to his shop and spent most of the day cleaning the rooms and restoring everything to its proper place. By late afternoon, he was still very angry.

60

Stone, Jamie, Jeremy, and Scott were gathered in Stone's office for the noontime press conference. To Stone's surprise, Hank Thomas greeted the press.

"Good morning," he said to the gathered media. "My grandfather, Henry Thomas, the chairman of H. Thomas & Son, scheduled this press conference for the purpose of addressing the scandalous and reckless story about my family in this morning's edition of the *New York Times,* so I will turn the proceedings over to him. After he has made his statement he will not entertain questions. At that time, I will have further announcements to make." He turned toward Henry. "Poppa?"

Henry Thomas was pushed forward in a wheelchair by a uniformed nurse, and he faced the camera without a script or notes.

"I beg to differ with my grandson," Henry said. "This is not a good morning. I awoke to find a slanderous article in the *Times,* which was about members of my family who are long dead. In fact, I am the only living member of my family who can remember any of them when they were alive.

"One of the photographs is of my maternal grandfather, whom I hardly knew. I was a small child when he was around and a teenager when he died, so I can offer nothing of him. Every one of my family members whose photograph is in the *Times* would now, if still alive, be more than a hundred years old.

"Who among us can answer for his long-dead ancestors? And yet, I and my living family are expected to do so.

"I have no personal knowledge of whether or not any of the many allegations by the *Times* are true, and I do not plan to spend my remaining days substantiating or denying them. H. Thomas & Son is an excellent and properly run business with a sterling reputation in the financial world and with thousands of clients here at home and around the world. I say to them now: your confidence in us has not been misplaced. We are, as ever, at your disposal."

He nodded to the nurse, and she wheeled him off camera.

Hank Thomas came on again. "I have two announcements to make, and I will not take any questions on either of them. Early this morning, after reading the *Times* piece, my father, John Thomas—known as Jack—returned to his office and took his own life." He paused to wait for the gasps and exclamations to stop. "He had, for some weeks, been of unsettled mind, and the allegations in this morning's *Times* apparently drove him over the edge. He will be missed in these halls.

"Second, I have decided to discontinue my candidacy for President of the United States, and to return to H. Thomas & Son, where I spent my youth, to try and fill the void left by the death of my father. I ask those who have placed their confidence in me for their understanding and patience. To the extent possible, my campaign will refund all the donations made by my supporters in amounts both large and small. We will live to fight another day. Thank you."

The broadcast was immediately transferred to a television studio, where a panel of financial and political pundits opined on the meaning of what had been said. Stone turned off the television.

"Well," said Jeremy Green. "No mention was made of the attempt to loot the world banking system."

"Dino tells me the FBI will lead the investigation into our allegations," Stone said. "I expect you'll all be hearing from them tomorrow."

"Jeremy, Scott," Jamie Cox said. "You'll need to replace me on the story. I'm either resigning or taking a leave of absence—up to you which—in order to write a book about all this. I will present the manuscript to you in due course for comment, and, if necessary, corrections."

Jeremy spoke up. "Scott and I had anticipated this, so please take a leave of absence—as long as you like—and we wish you well with your book." He looked around the room. "Where is Huey Horowitz?"

Stone spoke up. "He's in Connecticut, helping to make funeral arrangements for his girlfriend, Trixie, who was murdered yesterday."

"I assume the police are investigating," Jeremy said.

"Yes, they are, and I hear they have some leads."

"Good. I'll write Huey a note of condolence."

"Stone," Scott said. "Have you heard anything of Bob Cantor?"

"I have," Stone said. "He will be returning to the city shortly, and he will resume his work."

"Good," Jeremy said. "Please express our gratitude to him for his work on this project. It wouldn't have happened without him."

"I'll do so as soon as I see him," Stone said.

• • •

Bob Cantor got out of his van in the parking garage of the Thomas building, wearing his copy-machine technician's clothes and mustache and carrying his toolbox. He made his way upstairs to the reception desk, which was unmanned. People up and down the halls were watching some sort of press event on televisions.

Bob plodded down the hallway, past the large room where the computer staff worked, to the room where the copying machine lived, let himself in, and partially disassembled the unit, so as to make it appear that he was working on it. He then went next door to where the stacks of computers hummed quietly.

He removed the two upper trays of his toolbox and removed an object the size of an ordinary brick, but with wires protruding from it. He chose one of the PCs and slid it from its shelf, then he replaced it with the object and began to connect it to some of the wires that ran along the wall. Finally, he attached a small box with an antenna, and connected that, as well, then he pushed his work against the wall and reinserted the PC into its slot, concealing the fact that he had been there.

He replaced the shelves in his toolbox, reassembled the copying machine, and printed out a test sheet, then he let himself out of the room and walked back down the hallway to the front desk, where the young woman he knew was now sitting.

"Your machine checks out very nicely," he said. "See you next month."

The young woman who had a large bite of sandwich in her mouth, simply gave him a wave, and he left.

He got back into his van and drove home. There he removed the business name from the van, took off his coveralls, and walked everything to his backyard, where he turned on a gas firepit. Everything went into the flames. He walked into the kitchen, opened a beer, then went and sat in a lawn chair until nothing recognizable was left in the firepit. He collected the ashes, placed them in a trash bag and added it to his garbage, which would be collected the following morning.

Finally, he went back to his workshop, switched on his computer, and entered a secret website with a very long and complicated password. He typed in an instruction, received a confirmation, then switched off his computer.

RANCE DAMIEN ENTERED the computer room shortly after the press conference, and everyone stood up. "We're very sorry for what's occurred," a supervisor said on behalf of everyone.

"Thank you all," Damien said. "Steve, you and Marty stay with me for a few minutes. The company will be closed until Monday morning, you are all excused until that time."

Everyone began shuffling from the room.

"Now," Damien said, taking a seat at a computer. "We're going to rerun the program from before and make those transfers again, plus, all the other transfers we had planned. By the time we leave here tonight, you guys will have earned a handsome bonus for your work. When the FBI arrives tomorrow morning, there will be no trace of what we have done, and we will be a billion dollars richer."

Damien logged on to a website, then used his password to enter system operations. He inserted a thumb drive into his computer and downloaded the software his people had written, entered another password and a command, then sat back to watch the computer work. His two coders stood behind him looking over his shoulders at the screen.

A moment later, they were lifted off their feet and slammed into a wall, followed by a storm of monitors and keyboards, and by a wall of flame that consumed everything before it.

STONE AND JAMIE were driven to Teterboro Airport by Fred, where Stone's Citation Latitude and its two pilots awaited. The customs car arrived and cleared them, and Stone got into the cockpit and started the engines.

Twenty minutes later Stone pushed forward the throttles, and the airplane rolled down Runway One, then lifted off into the evening sky.

Stone flew the airplane until they had left American airspace, then turned over the controls to Faith, his chief pilot, and joined Jamie in the rear of the airplane for dinner, before their refueling stop in St. John's, Newfoundland.

On the transatlantic crossing, Stone would spell the two pilots in turn, then they would set down the aircraft on Stone's airstrip in the south of England at midmorning the following day, where the forecast was for cool and sunny.

AFTER DINNER, Stone switched on the satellite television and tuned in to CNN. A few minutes later, they were watching a huge fire burning in downtown New York.

"The fire was contained to a first-floor computer room," a reporter on the scene was saying. "The building had been emptied and closed for the remainder of the week after the death of Jack Thomas, president and CEO of H. Thomas & Son, so there are no reported casualties, except for three persons in the computer room, one of whom died of his injuries. Their names have not been released, pending notification of their families.

"A source in the FBI ventured an opinion that the explosion and blaze might have been set deliberately to cover illegal wire transfers, which the *Times* have alleged took place."

Stone turned to Jamie. "Looks like Bob Cantor is back in town," he said.

AUTHOR'S NOTE

I am happy to hear from readers, but you should know that if you write to me in care of my publisher, three to six months will pass before I receive your letter, and when it finally arrives it will be one among many, and I will not be able to reply.

However, if you have access to the Internet, you may visit my website at www.stuartwoods.com, where there is a button for sending me e-mail. So far, I have been able to reply to all of my e-mail, and I will continue to try to do so.

If you send me an e-mail and do not receive a reply, it is probably because you are among an alarming number of people who have entered their e-mail address incorrectly in their mail software. I have many of my replies returned as undeliverable.

Remember: e-mail, reply; snail mail, no reply.

When you e-mail, please do not send attachments, as I *never* open these. They can take twenty minutes to download, and they often contain viruses.

Please do not place me on your mailing lists for funny stories, prayers, political causes, charitable fund-raising, petitions, or sentimental claptrap. I get enough of that from people I already know. Generally speaking, when I get e-mail addressed to a large number of people, I immediately delete it without reading it.

Please do not send me your ideas for a book, as I have a policy of writing only what I myself invent. If you send me story ideas, I will immediately delete them without reading them. If you have a good idea for a book, write it yourself, but I will not be able to advise you on how to get it published. Buy a copy of *Writer's Market* at any bookstore; that will tell you how.

Anyone with a request concerning events or appearances may e-mail it to me or send it to: Publicity Department, Penguin Random House LLC, 1745 Broadway, New York, New York 10019.

Those ambitious folk who wish to buy film, dramatic, or television rights to my books should contact Matthew Snyder, Creative Artists Agency, 9830 Wilshire Boulevard, Beverly Hills, California 98212–1825.

Those who wish to make offers for rights of a literary nature should contact Anne Sibbald, Janklow & Nesbit, 445 Park Avenue, New York, New York 10022. (Note: This is not an invitation for you to send her your manuscript or to solicit her to be your agent.)

If you want to know if I will be signing books in your city, please visit my website, www.stuartwoods.com, where the tour schedule will be published a month or so in advance. If you wish me to do a book signing in your locality, ask your favorite bookseller to contact his Penguin representative or the Penguin publicity department with the request.

If you find typographical or editorial errors in my book and feel an irresistible urge to tell someone, please write to Sara Minnich at Penguin's address above. Do not e-mail your discoveries to me, as I will already have learned about them from others.

A list of my published works appears in the front of this book and on my website. All the novels are still in print in paperback and can be found at or ordered from any bookstore. If you wish to obtain hardcover copies of earlier novels or of the two nonfiction books, a good used-book store or one of the online bookstores can help you find them. Otherwise, you will have to go to a great many garage sales.